T0105887

By the Same Author

Showcase

Alison Glen

Trunk Show

A Charlotte Sams Mystery

SIMON & SCHUSTER
New York London Toronto Sydney Tokyo Singapore

SIMON & SCHUSTER
Rockfeller Center
1230 Avenue of the Americas
New York, New York 10020

This book is a work of fiction. Names, characters, places and incidents are either
products of the author's imagination or are used fictitiously. Any resemblance to
actual events or locales or persons, living or dead, is entirely coincidental.

Copyright © 1995 by Cheryl Meredith Lowry and Louise Vetter

All rights reserved,
including the right of reproduction
in whole or in part in any form whatsoever.

SIMON & SCHUSTER and colophon are registered trademarks of
Simon & Schuster Inc.

Designed by Hyun Joo Kim

Manufactured in the United States of America

1 3 5 7 9 10 8 6 4 2

Library of Congress Cataloging-in-Publication Data

Glen, Alison.
Trunk show: a Charlotte Sams mystery/Alison Glen.
p.   cm.
1. Women journalists—Ohio—Columbus—Fiction. 2. Columbus (Ohio)—
Fiction. I. Title.
PS3557.L4418T78 1995
813'.54—dc20
94-34288
CIP

ISBN: 978-1-4767-9997-1

*Thank you to Sandra Kerka and
John E. Murphy III, D.O.,
who are not responsible for any errors.*

Prologue

Most summer nights at the Columbus Zoo are dark and quiet, with few lights and even fewer staff. Even so, security workers enter every building except the reptile house at some point during their shift—just to make sure all is well. (All they want to know about the snakes and lizards is that their door is locked.)

On this night, the security workers' inspection of building interiors revealed nothing unusual. They could not know that whatever action would take place at the zoo that night would be thirty feet up—on the roof of the pachyderm building.

That's where, shortly before midnight, the elephant keeper was startled by the response to a little speech he had just made. The response was loud, threatening, over the top. Obviously, his remarks had been far more enraging than he had expected. Maybe his timing *had* been a little off, he thought.

He rose with slow and deliberate movements in hopes that his apparent calm would be contagious. He didn't want any more surprises. Slowly he leaned over to pick up several items they had with them and prepared to leave. But he never had a chance to straighten up. He was shoved violently from the side, which caused him to lurch over the edge of the roof, one hand scrambling helplessly to pull himself back. There wasn't even enough time for him to cry out before he hit the rock-hard dirt surface of the yard below.

He died on impact. Otherwise, he would have been among the first to note the irony of dying in the yard of the most dangerous animals in the zoo—but by human hands.

Chapter 1

Very early the next morning, the woman that zoo staff called Cheetah Rita spotted Jerry Brobst's body as she walked past the African elephant yard on her way to the cheetahs. Jerry's khaki uniform blended so perfectly with the ground on which he lay that even her sharp eyes would have missed him had her attention not been caught by the two elephants who had stationed themselves at his head and feet as though they were standing watch over his body.

With her heart pounding in her ears, Cheetah Rita set down the scarred vinyl briefcase and camp stool she always used at the zoo and leaned over the railing for as close a look as possible at Brobst. In her haste, she nearly fell into the yard herself. He didn't seem to be moving at all, and it was with mixed feelings that she considered that he might well be dead.

She hadn't actually wanted him to *die*, she realized, although such a wish had escaped her lips on more than one occasion. He looks dead, he looks dead, she thought over and over. But then she reasoned, if he was really dead, the most constant impediment to her research had been removed. Both she and the elephants would be better off without Jerry Brobst, to say nothing of her beloved cheetahs.

She sternly told herself to calm down. She would have to tell someone about Brobst. Once his body was removed, the elephants could go back to the business of being elephants instead of acting like gigantic gray guard dogs. Cheetah Rita hated dogs.

Who to tell? She had no desire to delay her work with the cheetahs by hiking all the way to the administration building, from which that cowboy zoo director and his silly young assistant pretended to run things. On second thought, it might be worth a few moments' delay to get to see them thrown into a proper frenzy at what Brobst's death could do to the zoo's image as a family-oriented park.

Firmly, she decided not to indulge herself by observing anything but cheetahs and immediately gathered up her brief-case and stool. She would mention Brobst's body to the first staff member she passed and then get on about her business.

This being early morning on a Monday in July, the first staff member she came across was one of the clean-up crew frantically trying to undo the damage done by a horde of summer weekend visitors before the next batch of visitors arrived at 10:00 A.M. He was concentrating so hard on blowing paper trash into a pile with a leaf-blower that he didn't seem to notice tall, thin Cheetah Rita, clad in a camouflage jump-suit, standing silently in his path. When he looked up, her presence startled him and he let out a cry, unconsciously raising the nozzle of the blower as though it was the barrel of a gun.

She laughed at the "gun" pointed at her, and the grounds-keeper looked embarrassed.

"Go on, you old thing. Get outta here," he said brusquely, resuming his blowing and keeping a wary eye on Cheetah Rita.

"There's a keeper lying in the elephants' yard" was all she said before shuffling on down the path in rubber boots whose metal fasteners jingled merrily in contrast to the grim news she had just delivered. The groundskeeper didn't know whether to take her seriously or not, but he went to investigate.

When Cheetah Rita looked back, she saw him speaking into his walkie-talkie up by the elephant yard, and already she could see golf carts driven by staff members streaming in that direction from all parts of the zoo. It was a dramatic tableau—colorful carts moving across the green lawns from all directions and converging on the elephant yard.

Occasional animal deaths, of course, were inevitable at the Columbus Zoo. But the death of a human was something altogether different. How like Brobst to call attention to himself even in death, she thought.

She knew it wouldn't be long until the whole place would be swarming with outsiders. Among them would be that nosy woman writer who had been hanging around all summer. Cheetah Rita had considered her annoying but harmless, but now she knew better. In fact, she wouldn't mind seeing the writer, too, face down in the dirt early some morning at the zoo.

Chapter 2

Freelance writer Charlotte Sams pushed determinedly on the gas pedal and sent her old red LeBaron convertible racing along Powell Road as fast as she dared. Afraid she was going to be late for today's first appointment at the zoo, she had the top down less because of the perfect summer weather and more because the rush of the wind made her feel like she was getting somewhere faster.

She barely looked at the countryside she was passing, having marveled during previous trips to the zoo at how this area northwest of Columbus had exploded with upscale housing developments. Recently she had read about a house in the area that had a reproduction of some of the Sistine Chapel artwork on its dining room ceiling. God creating Adam. That was a bit much, she thought.

She preferred the days when going to the zoo meant going out in the country. Now one only seemed to slide from suburb to suburb.

Today Charlotte was to interview Stephanie Kimmel, assistant to zoo director Bob Stitcher, and, later, elephant keeper Jerry Brobst. The interviews were for the series of zoo-related articles she had been working on all summer for *Ohio Magazine.*

Stephanie went by the nickname "Stevie," which was about the only thing casual about her. In Charlotte's opinion, Stevie worked overtime at being Ms. Perfection. And in particular, Ms. Punctuality. She would not be amused at Charlotte's immediate lack thereof.

Charlotte had no excuse for being late today—not even a good explanation, and certainly not one that she would share with Ms. Kimmel. The truth was that she had merely taken too long at breakfast with her husband and fourteen-year-old son.

Now she was going to be late for an interview with a woman in her mid-twenties who all summer long had made the fortyish Charlotte feel over the hill and, at the same time, like a school child in need of correcting.

Resolutely clutching the convertible's steering wheel, she ran the Village of Powell's single red traffic light and before long caught sight of the zoo's water tower on the road up ahead. The water tower, a metal ovoid atop a slender fifty-foot stalk, looked like it could be the doorknob to hell. Today it reminded her that the exit to the zoo's parking lot emptied out onto Powell Road opposite the tower.

Why not save some time by driving down the exit lane rather than driving all the way around to the entrance? She shouldn't meet any oncoming cars at 7:45 in the morning: zoo employees would already be on the job, and the zoo wouldn't be open to the public for more than an hour. It would be some time before anyone was entering, let alone exiting.

Slowing down as she approached the tower, she turned the wrong way down the one-way, single-lane exit. Confidently, she rounded a bend among the trees but then nearly collided with a Columbus police car coming the other way. She veered to the right, off the pavement. In her side mirror she saw that the police car had stopped and figured she'd better, too.

The officer, who looked too young to have graduated from the police academy, walked back to Charlotte's car with one thumb hooked in his wide black Garrison belt.

"May I see your driver's license, ma'am?"

She fished it out of her purse and handed it over without saying a word.

The officer alternately looked at her license and stared at her for a few moments, as though trying to match the real short-blond-haired, gray-eyed Charlotte with the anemic version in her license photo. Apparently satisfied, he took her license with him back to the cruiser and got inside.

Conscious of the minutes ticking away, Charlotte drummed her fingers on the steering wheel and absently recalled that Boston police cruisers were called "black-and-whites" in the Spenser novels she loved to read. Nothing so traditional would do for Columbus, where the ungainly-looking Chevy Caprices that served as cruisers were all-white except for their red and blue numbers and insignia.

She wondered whether the officer in *this* cruiser even had jurisdiction over this strip of pavement. The Columbus Zoo belonged to the city as well as Franklin County, all right, but it was located in Delaware County to the north.

When the officer returned her license a few moments later, he asked what brought her to the zoo so early that morning. She explained, relieved that he had not handed her a ticket.

"Well, I'm afraid you'll have to postpone your interviews this morning, ma'am," he said. "There's been a little trouble at the zoo, and they don't need any outsiders there right now."

From his tone, Charlotte was afraid that at any moment he was going to call her "Little Lady."

"What kind of trouble?" she asked.

"I suggest you come back when the zoo is open to the public," he said, ignoring her question. "They're going to open on time. Come back then."

She hated being patronized on a good day, let alone on one like today was shaping up to be.

"You don't understand," she said. "They're expecting me. It's my *job* to be there."

"Yes, and I know all about your freedoms of the press and all that. But I don't see you wearing any press ID, so just turn your vehicle around and get along."

"I'm a freelancer," Charlotte said. "I *never* have press ID, because I'm not attached to any one news organization."

The officer was unmoved, some might even say uninterested. He merely crossed his arms in front of him and rocked back on his heels a little.

Charlotte reached for her tote bag. She was startled to see the officer uncross his arms and move his right hand slightly back toward his pistol. Perhaps he thought the Little Lady could be armed and dangerous. She liked the idea, but quickly told him she was just getting more ID.

"Zoo ID," she said, handing him a card identifying her as a temporary zoo employee through the summer. The ever-competent Stevie Kimmel had given Charlotte the card when she had first started working on her series, hoping it might provide her greater accessibility to the zoo at all hours. But Charlotte had never needed to use it and had nearly forgotten it.

"So I'm not an outsider after all," she said to the officer.

He studied the card, frowning. Handing it back to Charlotte without a word, he stepped away from her car and waved her on toward the zoo. She immediately pulled the car back onto the road, her mind already turning to the question of what "little trouble" had occurred at Columbus's world-famous zoo.

Perhaps, she thought with amusement, director Bob Stitcher had gotten tired of just yelling at the coordinator of volunteers and had finally clobbered him. The two of them were generally at loggerheads on any given day. Of course, that could probably be said of Stitcher and the entire rest of the world. She never could decide whether his personality was really as abrasive as it appeared or whether he simply suffered by comparison with the zoo's charming and charismatic former director, Jack Hanna.

Her amusement vanished when she pulled into the parking lot. The five police cars parked next to the admission gate indicated something serious had occurred. She began to worry about the zoo staffers she had come to know. She had been there enough to genuinely appreciate the danger they worked with daily. After all, the place was full of wild animals.

Hurrying over to the gate, she noticed a van from WCMH-TV also parked near the gate. Even though her assignment had nothing to do with whatever had happened here today, she truly regretted that other members of the press had beaten her to a news scene.

When stopped at the gate by another police officer, she wasted no time in showing him her temporary zoo employee card and got right in. Up ahead, past the administration and education buildings and the cluster of wooden kiosks that sold film and souvenirs, Charlotte could see several zoo employees talking in small groups.

Then she spotted Bob Stitcher, with Stevie at his side. Stitcher was always easy to identify. In his mid-forties, he was very tall and very thin, with lots of unruly dark hair that he sometimes corralled under a big gray Stetson. Upon coming to Columbus, he had made it plain that he had no intention of perpetuating the "Jungle Jack" safari uniform worn by Jack Hanna. Instead, he had his own uniform: Western-cut pants and shirts, a string tie with turquoise slide, and elaborately tooled leather cowboy boots.

Charlotte had trouble believing that such an outfit would have played well even at a Western zoo—say, in Tulsa, where he had worked last. Regardless, it was a disaster in central Ohio.

The Stetson was nowhere to be seen today. Stitcher and Stevie were surrounded by a reporter and camera crew from WCMH and a reporter and photographer Charlotte knew from the *Columbus Dispatch*. The group seemed to be making very slow progress toward the administration building.

Before reaching Stitcher's group, she stopped at a cluster of employees to ask Maria Pickard, the zoo's animal dietician, what had happened. As always, the short, dark-haired woman was wearing a white lab coat.

"Oh, Charlotte!" she said, turning away from her coworkers and grabbing Charlotte's arm. "They found Jerry Brobst dead this morning!"

"Dead? Here?"

"That's right."

"But I have an interview with him this morning," Charlotte said, too shocked to realize how stupid that sounded.

"It's just too horrible," Maria moaned.

Jerry Brobst dead? Charlotte wondered how bad things had to get before the police officer who had stopped her would upgrade his assessment from "a little trouble."

She recalled the irrepressible Jerry, who she always thought looked like Tom Selleck. She had last talked with him a few days ago, to set up today's interview.

She asked Maria what she thought was the obvious question: "Did Koko get him?"

Koko was a bull elephant who threw anything he could get his trunk on at keepers and zoo visitors. He had thrown more than one keeper against his enclosure wall.

"It couldn't have been Koko. Jerry was found in the *African* elephants' yard, and Koko's Asian," Maria said. "Oh, look." She pointed to the pachyderm house about a hundred yards northeast of where they were standing.

Charlotte could see two uniformed police officers on the roof of the pachyderm building, a rough-finished concrete structure that was designed to look like a pile of boulders. Around the building's perimeter were separate yards for Asian elephants, African elephants, rhinos, warthogs, and tapirs. Enormous doors connected the enclosures for each kind of animal inside the building with its designated yard outside. The yards were separated from one another by low cement walls and from zoo visitors by a dry moat.

"I don't think they'd be looking up there for evidence against the elephants," Charlotte said.

Maria seemed to shiver, despite the sunshine and her lab coat. "You're probably right," she said. She managed a weak smile, told Charlotte good-bye, and then walked away with little of her usual brisk purposefulness.

Now Charlotte could hear Stitcher's loud voice saying, "No, buddy, you got that wrong. I don't have to tell you *anything!*" By the time she reached them, he had turned to Stevie and said, just as belligerently, "You handle this." Then he stomped off to the administration building. Charlotte noticed that two men in suits who had been standing by the door of the building entered immediately after Stitcher did, as though they had been waiting for him.

She and the other news people rearranged themselves around Stevie, who noticed Charlotte and nodded a greeting. So did the *Dispatch* reporter and photographer. Then they turned their attention back to Stevie, who was to be interviewed on camera by WCMH's handsome and crisply professional Ned Ellison.

Stevie, Charlotte noticed, was dressed for the occasion. She wore a raspberry-colored summer wool suit with pearl necklace and earrings. Her expensive-looking shoes wouldn't be much good for walking over some of the zoo's rough terrain, but they would look just fine on the six o'clock news.

How like Stevie to be prepared for an impromptu media event, Charlotte thought, glancing down at her own much more informal blue shirtwaist dress and canvas espadrilles.

Prepared she might be, but Stevie's voice quivered as she responded to Ellison's question about what happened that morning. "There's been a tragic accident here at the zoo," Stevie said, with the videocamera rolling. "A keeper was found dead early this morning. We can't release his name until we are able to notify his next of kin, so I'm afraid there's not much more I can say at this point."

"Was he an elephant keeper?"

"I can't say."

"Where was his body found?"

"I'm sorry, but I can't release that information yet."

"Well, we can see police officers in one of the elephant yards. Was his body found there?"

"I just can't comment on that."

"Will the animal that killed him be destroyed?"

"We don't know yet what killed him. The police haven't had time to determine the cause of death."

"Are you saying the keeper could have been killed by someone other than an elephant—by a human, for instance?" Ned asked.

"I'm saying we don't know yet."

"How long had the keeper worked at the zoo?" Ned probed.

Stevie was beginning to look like she wanted out of this grilling, Charlotte thought.

"We'll be glad to share whatever information we have about that as soon as his family has been notified," Stevie said. "I'm sure Director Stitcher is trying to reach them right now. And, of course, all of us here feel terrible about his death."

"Maybe you can just tell us whether any of the animals at the zoo has ever killed anyone before."

"I'm afraid not."

"Who found the body?"

Stevie ignored this question and very deliberately stared right at the camera. Smiling and using her best hostess tones, she said, "We're opening on time today, just as usual. I hope that everybody who planned to come out to the zoo will do so, and we'll get past this terrible tragedy."

Then she turned to Ned and said that was all she had time for. Nodding at everybody else in the group, Stevie headed for the administration building. She stepped lightly along in her expensive shoes and never strayed from the paved path.

Chapter **3**

Ned and his camera crew left right away, but Charlotte had a chance to talk with Chris James, the young *Dispatch* reporter. Unfortunately, he didn't seem to know anything more than she did about Jerry's death. Not as much, actually. She did not let on that she knew the body discovered was Jerry Brobst's, but wasn't exactly sure why. Habit, maybe. After all, there was no chance that she'd "scoop" the *Dispatch* with a story on the identity of the victim. Once Stitcher reached Jerry's next of kin, his identity would be public long before Charlotte could get anything into print.

"None of these zoo people will talk to me," the reporter complained.

"I heard Stitcher yell at you," Charlotte said, sympathetically.

"It's not just him. It's all of them. To hear them tell it, nobody knows nothing. Nobody has a thing to say."

"Well, the zoo *is* a kind of small city unto itself up here," she suggested.

"Unto itself? When did you get religion, Charlotte?"

"I just meant that the zoo is isolated by its self-sufficiency. It has all the services of a city: there's a security force, a water department, clean-up, a hospital—for the animals, anyway. The concessions provide food for the humans and the commissary provides it for the animals. The garbage gets picked up, and Stitcher and his staff act as the government. I think all that self-sufficiency contributes to the staff feeling that they are their own dominion. It seems to take them a while to warm up to people like us."

"People who don't talk to the animals, you mean?"

"I've had to work hard all summer to get people to talk with me," Charlotte said. "I think it's just that so many of them have worked here for so long that anybody else seems like an outsider."

"I think they've just spent too long communing with nature," James said. "It's been a long time since I've had to work so hard to pry quotes out of people at an accident scene. Makes my job a lot harder."

Charlotte commiserated for a moment. Then James left to join the photographer and drive back downtown to the *Dispatch* building.

Figuring that Stevie probably would be tied up with the police or Stitcher for a while, Charlotte walked over to the pachyderm building to see what she could learn about Jerry's death. Maybe she could talk with Barbara Champion, head pachyderm keeper and Jerry's boss.

On the way, she had time to recall what she herself knew about Jerry. She hadn't known him well, but it was impossible not to become at least acquainted with someone so outgoing in a community as small as the zoo. He was—had been—one of the most interesting people there.

It didn't hurt that he was handsome, of course: over six feet tall, with dark brown hair and a moustache, intelligent-looking brown eyes, and a muscular body. She figured he had been around thirty years old.

Jerry's personality had been the real draw, Charlotte thought. He was playful. He laughed a lot and was always doing silly things, like juggling scrub brushes or singing slightly off-color songs. He continually made jokes and puns and played with language. On the few occasions they had spent time together, Charlotte was willing to play his straight man, and that had obviously pleased him.

There was a daredevil aspect to Jerry's personality, too. She had heard that Stitcher had nearly fired him in the spring for walking the top edge of the cheetah yard. The only thing that had saved him (from being fired, anyway) was that he had walked the cheetah fence after the zoo had closed instead of in front of visitors.

When nobody else was around, Charlotte herself had seen him do tricks with the elephants that looked more appropriate for a circus than a zoo: tricks of the dangerous, person's-head-inside-the-animal's-mouth variety. Now that she thought about it, it was easy to think that Jerry's death had been caused by some stunt he was pulling on top of the pachyderm building—but only if there was someone there to watch him.

When Charlotte arrived at the pachyderm building, the two police officers were still on the roof, close to the edge over the African elephants' yard. Two more were in the yard beneath them, squatting on the ground packed hard by elephant feet, their eyes roaming over the cracks in the surface of the ground.

She thought the police officers in the yard were brave to be in there, even without the elephants. What a horrifying (and probably lethal) experience it would be to look up and see a six-ton gray behemoth running at you at full speed through a door that everybody was certain had been locked.

Several years earlier, a tiger had seriously mauled a volunteer who was cleaning its cage while she thought the tiger was locked in a holding cage. As a result of that accident, volunteers were no longer allowed to work close to the animals, even under the supervision of a keeper.

A police officer stopped Charlotte at the south door of the pachyderm building, but she bluffed her way through with the zoo ID and her insistence that she must have a word with Barbara Champion.

Once inside, it took a few moments for her eyes to adjust to the dim lighting. Finally, she could see elephants, rhinos, warthogs, and tapirs in the enclosures that lined two sides of the building. She could smell and hear them, too.

She had never been in the building while all the animals were in their enclosures at the same time. It was incredibly noisy, perhaps because every surface—the concrete floor and walls, the steel-beamed ceiling—was hard and flat, incapable of absorbing sound. She wondered whether this morning's change in routine, by keeping all the animals in the building while the police were outside in the yard, would make the animals nervous. The racket of animal snorts and keeper shouts and work noises was making *her* nervous.

She could see Barbara cleaning the Asian elephants' enclosure on the right and walked over. Standing at the low railing designed to keep the public a few feet from the two-inch steel bars of the enclosure, she called out a greeting. Barbara nodded as she pushed a broomful of dirty straw and elephant waste toward a two-wheeled cart near the interior door of the enclosure. Koko and Indy eyed Charlotte suspiciously from the far side.

When the floor was swept clean, Barbara uncoiled a dark green hose from the corner and hosed the area down with warm water. Indy and Koko kept sticking their trunks into the water and stepping back from advancing puddles.

Finally, Barbara came over to Charlotte's side of the enclosure, smiled, and said in her usual no-nonsense manner, "I suppose you want to talk about Brobst."

She was a sturdy five feet nine inches tall and had long dark hair that she had pulled up and through the back vent in a baseball cap. Like the other keepers, she wore khaki pants and a shirt that said Columbus Zoo on the front pocket.

"Well, yes," Charlotte said. "It's terrible, isn't it?"

"Awful." The noise in the building went up a notch as two keepers tried to catch a warthog. Charlotte recalled Barbara telling her that keepers in the pachyderm house worked their way up to keeping elephants: first they worked with wart hogs, then tapirs, next rhinos, and, finally, with the elephants. Everybody loved the warthogs, she said. But few could handle the elephants.

Now, at Barbara's suggestion, Charlotte stepped across the low railing and up to the bars so they wouldn't have to shout.

"I was supposed to interview Jerry today," Charlotte said.

"I know."

"Who found his body?"

"Cheetah Rita," Barbara said, rubbing the side of Koko's face. "Know who I mean?"

"Sure." Charlotte had seen the zoo's cheetah groupie but had never talked with her. "Did she find him out in the Africans' yard?"

"Yep. Up next to the building." Barbara paused a moment, while Koko used the tip of his trunk to investigate the palm of her hand. Indy lumbered over to join the fun.

"Have you heard what killed him?"

"No, but nobody better accuse my Africans, that's all I've got to say."

Koko pulled back at the harsh tone in Barbara's voice. She spoke soothingly and calmed him down, but Indy took off for a far corner.

"Were the elephants inside when his body was found?"

"No, I had let them out earlier this morning," Barbara said. "Like usual." Then she blew into Koko's trunk as though she was blowing into a handheld microphone.

She looked pretty silly, even though Charlotte knew that trunk blowing produced one of the elephants' favorite sensations. Evidently, the way to an elephant's heart was through his trunk.

"I guess you couldn't see Jerry lying out there," Charlotte said.

"Of course not." She frowned. "What'd you think? That I saw Brobst's body and left him lying in the dirt?"

"No, no. Nothing like that," Charlotte said apologetically. Koko blew some water through his trunk at Charlotte, and Barbara moved herself and Koko further from the bars.

Koko shook his head from side to side and walked over to join Indy across the enclosure.

Barbara looked after him. "Well," she said, "I'm going to see if I can get these guys outside. We're behind schedule enough already. Hand me that ankus right inside the bars there."

Without thinking, Charlotte bent and reached through the bars to pick up the short wood-and-metal club keepers use to control elephants. She held it out to Barbara, who moved forward to take the other end just as Koko trumpeted and flapped his enormous ears. Charlotte looked up to see the bull elephant charging at them from the right. She gasped, feeling like she was watching a freight train bearing down on her as she and Barbara stood immobilized with the ankus between them in their outstretched hands. Koko barreled between them, grabbing the ankus with his trunk and nimbly avoiding crashing into the bars.

In the process, he knocked Barbara backwards and wrenched Charlotte's left arm against a bar. She yelled out in pain and surprise, which evidently upset the elephant even more. It was several minutes before Barbara could calm him down again.

Meanwhile, Charlotte sat on the floor, gingerly feeling over her arm to figure out whether it was broken and testing whether her shoulder was still in place. She didn't know whether to be angry at Barbara and Koko, or simply thankful that her arm was still attached to her body.

"Oh, I'm so sorry!" Barbara said, finally rushing over to Charlotte. "Are you all right?"

"I'm okay. Nothing's broken, just pretty sore." Charlotte could already see a line of bruises forming. "Have you ever seen him do anything like that before?"

"Well, he *is* pretty unpredictable. It's all my fault, really. I never should have asked you to put your hand in the enclosure." Barbara looked properly contrite. "That was truly stupid of me. Careless and dumb. Are you sure you're okay?"

"I think so."

"Let me help you to your car. Or can I call someone to pick you up?"

"No, thanks. First Jerry dies here and now Koko nearly takes my arm off. I may stick around the zoo for a while today, but I'm staying clear of this building."

Charlotte slowly walked to the office the zoo had provided her for the summer, carrying both her purse and tote on her good arm. The little room was tacked onto the side of a wooden building that housed lawn mowers and snow blowers in the area where North American animals were exhibited. Reached by three rickety steps outside the building, it had apparently been used by groundskeepers to keep machinery maintenance records before computerization.

There was an old splintered desk, a comfortable wooden desk chair, bulletin boards with maintenance schedules from five years ago still pinned to them, and a bare lightbulb hanging from a cord in the ceiling. However, it had served Charlotte well as a place to leave her material between interviews and where she could type up her notes on her laptop computer.

The ruggedness of the office was easier to bear since she knew how spartan the staff offices were in the administration building. Nobody—except maybe the animals—was housed in luxury at the zoo. Also, there literally was no other office space Stevie could have arranged for her—except for a tiny corner in the reptile house, which Charlotte had turned down flat. There was absolutely no chance that she would agree to spend the summer in a building with snakes.

The office was already very warm when she unlocked the door and turned on the light. Since there was not even a window (let alone air-conditioning), she left the door open. She put her purse and tote on the desk and took a diet pop out of the tote. Then she collapsed into the big old desk chair and propped her feet up on the battered desk.

After a few more minutes to recover from the incident with Koko, she picked up her notebook and set off for the administration building, determined to get as much information as possible about Jerry's death. The *Dispatch* reporter and the TV people would be hard to beat for the breaking news, but she had the advantage for the feature stories because she already knew so many people at the zoo.

Maybe she could do an extra article for *Ohio Magazine* on how safe zoos actually are and how a zoo reacts to a crisis. What would the zoo do if a dangerous animal actually got out of its enclosure? Was there a visitor evacuation plan? Did other people also do dumb things like put their hands inside animal enclosures? Maybe she could sell such an article to other markets—even *Smithsonian*, if she could get some good pictures.

Safety at the zoo did not seem to be a concern of the visitors flooding the front gates. To Charlotte, it looked like a bigger crowd than usual for a Monday morning. Maybe the news of an employee's death had added an extra thrill to the day's outing.

As it happened, she appeared at the doorway to Stevie's office at about the time her interview with Jerry would have taken place. Seven-foot-tall acoustical partitions provided the walls for most of the offices in the crowded administration building. She tapped on a partition frame at the edge of Stevie's space, off in the corner, and went in without waiting to be invited.

As usual, there was nothing on the desk except the telephone, the calendar blotter pad, and a single rosebud in a crystal vase.

"Oh, hello, Charlotte," Stevie said. "You must be here for our interview, I know, but I'm afraid this morning's tragedy has me preoccupied."

"I already know it was Jerry's body that was found in the Africans' enclosure this morning, Stevie. What happened to him?"

"Now, you know Mr. Stitcher makes all the official announcements about the zoo. He gets very upset if anyone else presumes to speak for our organization."

"I thought you did okay this morning."

"Why, thank you." Charlotte was sure that was a smug smile trying to break through on Stevie's mouth.

"Would you help me put together some personal information about Jerry?"

"Why do you need that?" Stevie asked suspiciously.

"Well, once you release his name, everyone will want to know something about him, including how long he worked here and whether he was a good elephant keeper. I can do a story on that."

"I'm afraid I didn't know him well enough to help you."

"You could just loan me his personnel file for a while," Charlotte said. When she saw Stevie's eyebrows shoot up, she amended, "Or you could look in his file yourself and tell me the information."

"I think not. At least not today. Our personnel files are in Mr. Stitcher's office, and I'm not going to interrupt him."

"Suit yourself," Charlotte said mildly, although she knew that before long Stitcher would ask Stevie to prepare a press release with the kind of information she was asking for now. But then it would be made available to all members of the press, and Charlotte would have lost her advantage. She decided to try another tack.

"I heard that Cheetah Rita found his body," she said.

But Stevie ignored Charlotte's remark, opened the top drawer of her desk, and took out a manila folder. "I have a whole folder of news clippings on the zoo that I can share with you," she said, obviously turning the interview to its originally intended focus.

All of which I could have gotten from the library, Charlotte thought. Stevie usually did better than this.

"You'll see that most of our publicity started with the birth of the first gorilla born in captivity. That was Colo, born here in 1956. Of course, that was years before I was born. Do *you* remember all the hoopla about Colo's birth, Charlotte?"

Score one for Stevie. "Barely. I was pretty young myself then."

Stevie smiled. "There are all kinds of interesting tidbits of information in here," she said, indicating the folder. "For instance, Amanda Blake—Miss Kitty on 'Gunsmoke,' you know—helped with our cheetah breeding program. There's nothing about Cheetah Rita, though, thank goodness. We've been able to keep the media uninformed about her."

Then, as though the thought had just struck her, Stevie said urgently, "You're not going to put anything in your series about Cheetah Rita, are you? It makes the zoo look so bad when odd creatures like that hang about."

Obviously, Stevie was so divorced from the animals that she had no idea just how odd some of the zoo's creatures could be, Charlotte thought. Including Bob Stitcher, although she had never thought Stevie was as devoted to Stitcher as her "employee of the week" patter would lead one to believe. Unwilling to promise not to write about a good human interest character like Cheetah Rita, Charlotte just mumbled something about being interested in the entire zoo community and accepted the file folder.

Unexpectedly, Stevie asked to put off her in-depth interview for a week and Charlotte gave in gracefully. Stevie had been helpful in running interference for her and introducing her to other zoo staff members when Stitcher had brushed her off with curt refusals. He wouldn't even let Charlotte interview him. Consequently, she didn't want to push her luck with Stevie at the moment.

And besides, even if Stevie wasn't willing to talk right now, some other people at the zoo might be. There's nothing like bad news to get people talking.

Chapter **4**

By late afternoon, lots of zoo staffers had been willing to talk with Charlotte about Jerry, but none of them seemed to know anything about his death. She had been unable to locate the one person who should be able to tell her *something:* Cheetah Rita.

A groundskeeper told her Cheetah Rita had been very casual when she told him about Jerry's body.

"She just kind of mentioned that Jerry was lying up there," he said. "Quiet like. Might as well have been talking about some litter left by a zoo visitor."

Charlotte had some idea how odd a character Cheetah Rita was, having been told that she had showed up every day for two years, in good weather and bad, to observe the cheetahs. Former zoo director Jack Hanna, always one to appreciate the unconventional, thought she added an interesting note to the zoo and left her alone. However, Bob Stitcher had tried to get rid of her when he took over.

Unfortunately for him, she carried her zoo membership card, and evicting her every day had proved to be too much trouble. Besides, no one could figure out how she got into the zoo, even when it was closed to the public. She came early and stayed late.

But today no one had seen Cheetah Rita since early morning. The strange woman could still be somewhere on the zoo's four hundred acres, but Charlotte couldn't find her and was tired of looking. Her left arm ached, and it felt like she had been at work for a long, long time. It was time to go home.

Forty-five minutes later and a few blocks from home, she swung her car into the crowded parking lot of the Olympic Swim and Racquet Club, thinking she might be in time to offer her son a ride home.

Membership for Tyler in a private swim club—even a modest one like Olympic—did not exactly fit with Charlotte's egalitarian instincts. But Olympic was inexpensive and she had never heard of it turning down anyone seeking membership. And, not unimportant to two working parents of a teenager, it was the only swimming pool within easy walking or bike-riding distance of the Sams' home.

Ty was standing in a thicket of friends clustered around the bicycle rack. When he saw Charlotte, he asked his friend Andrew if he wanted a ride home, too, and both boys moved toward the car. Before Charlotte could protest the maneuver, they hoisted themselves into the back seat of the convertible without opening the door. She felt like a chauffeur as she drove down the street to Andrew's house.

As soon as his friend got out of the car, Ty scrambled into the front seat and asked if she had been working at the zoo.

"I heard they found a body up there," he said.

"And you wondered if it was your mother?"

"Not really," he said, grinning. "You know how Dad is always saying that only the good die young."

She thought about that one for a moment, then said, "At least it's nice to know you think I'm still young."

"Well, everything is relative, Mom."

"So. How'd you hear about the body?"

"Tanya Loar had a radio. But I never heard who it was or how they died."

She filled him in with the little she knew. Then, as they pulled into their driveway, she asked if he had stayed off the highest diving platform at Olympic.

"Yes, like always," he said in an exasperated tone. "But just because *you're* afraid of heights shouldn't mean *I* can't go off the high dive."

The diving platform in question was ten meters high, making it over thirty feet tall and, in Charlotte's opinion, a height from which no one could possibly dive or jump safely. In fact, the owner of the pool did not allow swimmers in general to use that platform. Only members of Olympic's diving team and the Ohio State University diving team, who also practiced there, could use it. Ty was one of the former, whom Charlotte would like to see live at least long enough to become one of the latter.

"Just indulge me on this, okay?" she asked.

"I've said I would."

Once inside the house, he went upstairs to his room to phone a friend, and Charlotte, who would have appreciated some company, was left to bemoan the fact that she saw less and less of her son.

She changed into old cutoff jeans and a T-shirt and went out in the backyard to read in a wooden lawn chair. Before long, the family's cat jumped up and settled into her lap, and for the thousandth time Charlotte marveled at how closely the cat in her lap resembled his ferocious cousins in the zoo. It was disconcerting to watch her pet go through the same instinctive motions of stretching and washing that she had seen a four-hundred-pound tiger doing behind bars earlier in the day.

Walt came home from work and found her out back. He leaned over and kissed her, saying, "You know, I've heard of women who meet their husbands at the front door wrapped in cellophane with a drink in their hand."

"I've heard of those women, too," Charlotte said. "But they're all short-timers, Walt. Flashes in the pan of life."

He smiled and sank down in a nearby lawn chair.

"Hard day, huh?"

"It's just more busy-season aggravation," he said. Walt's company rented and sold mobile platforms used on construction sites to lift workers to various heights up to sixty feet. Summer was the company's busiest time of year because that's when most construction took place in Ohio, and Walt looked tired.

Sympathetically, Charlotte reached out to take his hand.

"Those are interesting bruises you've got there on your arm," he said. "Been wrestling alligators at the zoo again, Charlotte?"

She laughed, got up, and pulled him to his feet. "Let me tell you about my day," she said and began with Koko's charge as they walked toward the kitchen door.

She continued her tale as Walt sat at the counter and she poured them some wine and started dinner. She was a spasmodic cook, just throwing a dinner together one night and then fixing something new and complicated the next—whatever fit her mood. Tonight what fit was chicken stir-fry, with its therapeutic chopping.

Walt cautioned her to be more careful at the zoo even before she got to the part about Jerry's death. Eventually, she flipped on the nine-inch-screen television on the counter so they could see the local news.

Before long, reporter Ned Ellison was telling Columbus that elephant keeper Jerry Brobst's body had been found in the elephant yard at the zoo. His report used several video portions of Stevie's interview under his narration, but none of the audio portion since she had said little that was useful once Jerry's identity could be revealed.

He also had Columbus homicide detective Jefferson Barnes on tape. Barnes, a large middle-aged African-American man with a small moustache, looked dourly into the camera and said, "We don't know the cause of death yet.

However, Mr. Brobst had a broken neck, which he most probably sustained when he landed after being pushed from the roof. There was evidence of a struggle on the roof."

"My God, Walt, Jerry was killed!"

"That's what the man said. Kind of puts the zoo in a different light, doesn't it?"

"You mean that maybe they've got the wrong creatures in the cages?"

"Just don't take any chances up there, Charlotte. You've already been hurt—"

"So I got some bumps and bruises," she said, suddenly willing to dismiss her injuries because Walt's tone sounded so damn parental. "An occupational hazard, that's all."

Before he could reply, the phone rang in the Sams' kitchen.

"Given that we just saw Barnes, that should be Lou," she said, and Walt picked up his wine and went into the living room.

It was Lou Toreson, Charlotte's longtime friend and a retired psychologist who specialized in research on career development. "Did you see your favorite homicide detective on Channel Four?" she asked without greeting.

"Yes, I was watching. In fact, I was at the zoo shortly after they found the body. I watched Ned do that interview with Stevie Kimmel."

"That's nice. But wasn't it good to see Barnes after all this time?"

"Sure. Just like old times—another body, another Barnes." Charlotte was referring to the time when she and Lou had become acquainted with Barnes after a relative of Charlotte's had been found dead outside a local art exhibit, and she and Lou had been helpful in solving the mystery of his death.

"It's been a long time since I've seen him interviewed on TV or quoted in the paper. I thought he might have left the police force," Lou said.

"Well, it looks like he's back."

"Did you know the keeper who was killed?"

"A little. In fact, I was to interview him this morning. He

was funny and smart and talked a lot. Drove a white Corvette."

"So he was killed right before you were to interview him?"

"Right. But . . ."

"What were you planning to talk about?"

"I know what you're driving at, Lou. I can hear it in your voice, but I don't buy it. Jerry could not have been killed to prevent our interview. We were just going to talk about how they train the elephants at the zoo, the plight of elephants as an endangered species . . . stuff like that."

"For someone who reads as many mystery novels as you do, you have a singular lack of imagination about these things," Lou said.

"What things?"

"Things like the possibility of people being murdered right before they spill their guts to some reporter."

" 'Spill their guts'? What are *you* reading these days?"

"Never mind. But I'd bet Detective Barnes will be anxious to talk with you, once he finds out about the interview with Jerry that you didn't get to have. And now," she added ominously, "never will have."

"Are you trying to make me feel somehow responsible for his death?"

"Of course not. I'm trying to get you to be careful while you're working at the zoo."

"Maybe you and Walt could get together on this."

"So he's been after you, too?"

"Look. This is silly," Charlotte said, exasperated. "Jerry's death—"

"His *murder*, Charlotte."

"All right. His murder and the fact that it happened right before I was to interview him are merely coincidental. We were going to talk about elephant training, for heaven's sake. Nobody cares enough about elephant training to *kill* over it."

"That's what *you* were planning to talk about. But we'll never know what the keeper had on his mind, will we?"

"I don't believe this whole conversation. Are you bored these days, Lou? Not consulting enough, maybe? Because I think you should have better things to do than to embroider elaborate schemes like this out of thin air. Schemes that involve me, anyway."

"What are friends for, Charlotte?" Lou said sweetly. Then, her voice turning more serious, she said, "I wasn't kidding about you being careful at the zoo. Sometimes you don't pay attention to what's going on around you when you're concentrating on your stories."

"Ha!"

"I'm serious. You've already told me that some of the zoo staff doesn't like outsiders."

"They seem to appreciate the over one million visitors who show up every year."

"I'm not talking about visitors. Visitors are different: they ooh and aah over both the staff and the animals. But you keep asking pesky questions." Lou paused a moment. "I don't think a person can be too careful around wild creatures."

"You know Jerry wasn't killed by one of the zoo animals."

"Those are not the ones I had in mind," Lou said.

Long after dinner, when Walt and Charlotte were reading in bed and a thunderstorm companionably beat against the bedroom window, she told him that Lou had suggested the police would want to talk with her about Jerry's murder.

"Do you think they will?" she asked.

"They'll have their hands full for a while, just talking to the zoo staff."

An especially loud clap of thunder seemed to rattle the window. Walt put down his book and asked, "Do the police even know you were going to interview Brobst?"

"Not that I know of."

"Someone will probably mention it to them, though."

"Probably."

"Well, I bet they'll get around to you eventually. Maybe sooner if they think you can provide some special information." He paused. "Can you?"

"What an odd question." The lamp dimmed from the storm and then came back up.

"Well, can you?"

"Such as . . . ?"

"I don't know. Did you set up the interview with Brobst or did he ask to talk with you?"

"It was kind of a combination, actually. I was watching him put Gert through her paces last Friday—Gert's an African elephant—and I told him I'd like to talk with him sometime about why a zoo goes to the trouble of training its elephants and exactly how you go about it. Jerry immediately suggested Monday morning."

"Do most people respond like that? Are they so eager to be interviewed?"

"Depends. But Jerry was a big show-off. Maybe he just wanted some attention."

"I like attention, too," Walt said, reaching over and turning off the light.

[faint bleed-through text, illegible]

Chapter 5

Charlotte's arrival at the zoo the next morning was considerably different from her last: no tardiness, no speeding, no entering the exit, no bodies. But all of her questions about Jerry's murder remained.

This time she came in the "front door," where the zoo was spread across both sides of Scioto River Road, with O'Shaughnessy Reservoir serving as its western border. She was in good spirits. Her left arm had ceased its throbbing and last night's thunderstorm had cleared out the humidity so that it was a positive pleasure to breathe.

Last night's TV news and the morning paper had made no mention of who discovered Jerry's body, so, evidently, Stevie had been successful at keeping Cheetah Rita from the prying eyes of the press. The prying eyes of *other* members of the press, thought Charlotte, as she resumed her search. She looked first at the cheetah enclosure on the west side of the zoo but didn't see her.

When she reached the polar bear exhibit, the keeper was

putting out dog food for the big female. Oreo cookies were what Charlotte and her family used to feed the polar bears on regular zoo visits when Tyler was young. At that time, the zoo didn't have enough staff to catch visitors who were feeding the animals. Besides, it didn't seem so bad then to feed the bears food that was good enough to eat yourself.

The enormous polar bears stood upright on their hind legs and begged for the Oreos, and the cookie tossing always drew a crowd. Tyler had loved being able to make the bears perform by waving a cookie over his head and then sailing it toward a mouth that neatly snared it in midair.

Today she wished she had brought Oreos for the bear keeper, who was known to have as big a sweet tooth as his charges. He was a short, fifty-year-old African-American who had worked at the zoo since leaving his family farm twenty-five years before. Today he immediately launched into a story of when the female polar bear got halfway out of her enclosure one visitor-filled Sunday afternoon.

"She's got guts, I'll say that for her," he said appreciatively. He had had to get the rifle kept for just such emergencies with the dangerous animals, he told her, "although it would have broken my heart to have had to kill her."

Since the conversation was already on death, it was easy for Charlotte to slip smoothly into a question about Jerry's demise. "Who do you think pushed him off that roof?" she asked.

"Well, nobody from the zoo, that's obvious," he said disdainfully. "Do we look like a bunch of killers, Charlotte?"

"It only takes one person," she responded, and the keeper, apparently insulted, said he didn't have any more time to talk and walked off. She saw him shake his head as she called after him, "Have you seen Cheetah Rita today?"

Next she walked over to Maria Pickard's schizophrenic office near the administration building. Spotless stainless-steel tables and cabinets occupied one room of her office—the food lab portion. But in the cluttered room next door, old wooden office furniture and a computer sat among stacks of professional journals. Opened reference books layered one over the other carpeted the desk top. The computer monitor was plastered with yellow Post-it notes stuck around its perimeter, making its amber screen look like the center of some oddly glowing sunflower.

Maria stood at a cabinet in the food lab, reading the labels on a package of vitamins. After greeting Charlotte, she nodded at the vitamins and said, "We've got an overweight orang that arrived yesterday, and I've got to increase his vitamins while we lower his calories." She chuckled. "He's a real porker."

As zoo dietician, Maria was responsible for working up the diets being fed to all the animals. Keepers actually mixed the food, following color-coded menus posted inside buildings scattered around the zoo grounds. But it was Maria who devised the menus.

"I guess you heard that Jerry was *murdered*," she said to Charlotte.

"Right. Do the police have any suspects?"

"I don't know."

Trying to avoid offending Maria as she had the bear keeper, Charlotte said, "Do you suppose somebody who doesn't work at the zoo could have killed him?"

Maria looked surprised at the question. "Honestly, Charlotte, I don't know what you're thinking. Of course it was somebody from outside the zoo."

"But how would they have gotten in after the zoo closed?"

"Jerry could have let them in himself. Or they could have come in with everybody else and then hung around inside the zoo after hours. Remember that young couple from Ohio State who got locked in the reptile house and had to spend the whole night there?"

"Who could forget that? But doesn't Cheetah Rita skip in and out whenever she wants to?"

"That's what I hear. And don't you think it's funny that it was she who found Jerry's body?"

"Seems logical to me. Isn't she always lurking about somewhere on the grounds at all hours?"

"But she also didn't like Jerry, and then to have found his body, well . . ."

"What do you mean she didn't like him?"

"I guess it's really more fair to say they didn't like *each other*. They quarreled all the time."

"Why would a keeper argue with a harmless old lady?"

"Well, Cheetah Rita can be pretty obnoxious, you know. Especially because she just won't give in. And she's devoted to the animals. Unfortunately, she thinks she's the only one who knows anything about taking care of them."

"No wonder she's so popular with the keepers," Charlotte said. "I had no idea that she actually talked that much."

"Only when she's angry, it seems. She doesn't have much to say otherwise, just keeps up that rather forbidding presence over by the cheetah yard."

"How did Jerry and she even come into contact? With the elephants and cheetahs housed on different sides of the zoo, I mean."

Maria looked surprised and then said, "Oh, of course, you wouldn't know that. You've been around here so much, Charlotte, I forget sometimes that you don't actually work for the zoo." She gave Charlotte's arm a collegial pat. "Only female cheetahs are in the yard that the public sees. The males are in another one, not far from the pachyderm house but beyond the wolves and a big thicket of trees. I'm sure visitors don't even know they're there. But that's where Cheetah Rita spends most of her time."

That explains where she's been since finding Jerry's body, Charlotte thought, and why I haven't been able to find her. She couldn't help feeling a little stupid about not knowing about the male cheetah yard. After all, as Maria described it, it couldn't be far from her zoo office. She asked Maria what Jerry and Cheetah Rita argued about.

"His care of the elephants, mostly. She specializes in cheetahs, but she's been known to pay attention to other animals as well. And she drove Jerry crazy."

"Crazy is what I've heard people call her."

"With some justification, let me tell you. She gives me the creeps. And she brought out the worst in Jerry."

"What do you mean?"

"It was like they had a real personality conflict or something. Instant sparks whenever they were around each other. With him she was less eccentric and more—well, kind of schoolmarmish, you know? I've even heard her call Jerry 'Young man!' "

"I can imagine how that went over."

"In response to her schoolmarm routine, he was like a naughty kid, acting out. Not really bad, but *annoying*. You know, the kind of rotten little kid who would steal something off the teacher's desk or put something gross on her chair so she would sit on it. That type of thing. He just sort of toyed with her, and Cheetah Rita was enraged by it, of course."

Before she left, Charlotte said she was glad Maria thought it would have been easy for someone who didn't work at the zoo to have gotten in to kill Jerry.

"The thing of it is, though," Maria said, looking thoughtful, "the zoo was Jerry's whole life and it's hard to think he had much to do with people who weren't involved here."

Chapter **8**

A few minutes later, Charlotte set off to find the male cheetah yard and, she hoped, Cheetah Rita. Maria had said the yard was beyond the North American section, past the wolves and behind some trees. When she got to that section, Charlotte was glad there were no visitors to witness her excursion, and that the wolves, sleeping near their shelter, seemed oblivious to her.

Accustomed to poking her nose in unexpected places because of her job, she nonetheless felt uncomfortable as she stepped off the paved path, climbed over a low pole fence, and entered a densely wooded area south of the wolves. Maybe it was because she subliminally expected Koko to come charging out of the trees, she thought.

Or maybe it was just because she felt so isolated once she was over the fence. Looking back now, she couldn't even see the space where she knew the pavement wound among the North American exhibits. A strip of towering trees blocked her view—and what would have been the view of anyone looking for her. No wonder the zoo had been able to so successfully hide the male cheetah yard from visitors, she thought.

In a moment, the trees thinned out and she came upon a small meadow containing the cheetah yard: a fenced quarter-acre of grass and small trees, with seven or eight flat-roofed doghouses and a narrow fenced run attached to each. The male cheetahs were apparently kept in individual runs instead of allowed to run free in a single yard like the females. Charlotte assumed that the males would fight if they were kept together.

The whole meadow seemed to shimmer in the bright sunlight. Beside the fence, up by the gate, sat Cheetah Rita, dressed in camo fatigues despite the heat. As Charlotte got closer, she could see that her dirty socks had lost their cling and had collected around her ankles above misshapen canvas shoes. She looked to be about sixty years old, with eyeglasses and dull brown hair that looked like it could have used a good brushing—maybe a good washing.

Greeting Cheetah Rita as she approached, Charlotte positioned herself near the odd-looking woman, who paid no attention to her but remained seated on her camp stool, staring out into the yard and occasionally making a notation in a thick three-ring binder notebook in her lap.

Charlotte didn't exactly know how to start talking with Cheetah Rita. She desperately wanted to learn what Cheetah Rita knew about Jerry's death but worried that if she didn't ask the questions just so, she might refuse to talk with her, maybe even run away.

She started by casually introducing herself but got no response.

Trying again, she gazed into the yard and said, "How many are out there?"

No response.

Anxious to demonstrate that she took observing the cheetahs as seriously as Cheetah Rita did, Charlotte scanned the grass until she was able to pick out four cats lying in their runs. Then she said, "Do you see that one lying by the far tree?"

Still no response.

She decided to try flattery. "These big cats are so beautiful," she said.

Cheetah Rita turned a fierce glare on her. "They are not big cats," she said, the irises in her yellow-brown eyes seeming to narrow as she stared at Charlotte through horn-rimmed spectacles.

"They look pretty big to me."

Cheetah Rita snorted in disgust and continued to study the cheetahs.

"Why aren't they big cats?"

Without turning from her observations, Cheetah Rita said, "They can't roar."

"Only big cats can roar?" Charlotte asked. "That's what distinguishes big cats from other cats?" It was so simple as to be charming.

When Cheetah Rita did not respond, she asked, "Then what kind of noise *do* they make?"

"They growl, snarl, purr, and chirp. The chirping is mostly to call young ones to dinner after a kill." She laughed hard and slapped her knee. Charlotte could only guess that the thought of a kill cracked Cheetah Rita up.

"How else are they different from the big cats?"

The older woman's face took on a dreamy expression as she recounted as though by rote: "Cheetahs cannot retract their claws. The big cats can. And their bodies are different. Cheetahs' bodies are built for speed, not power. Their shoulders are high and their heads are small. Their legs are long and thin. They don't have canine teeth, either, like the big cats do. And like dogs do."

Having finished her little speech, she looked at Charlotte and said, "I despise people like you."

Startled, Charlotte wanted to say she wasn't too crazy about Cheetah Rita, either. Instead, she said, "You don't even know me."

"I've been watching you all summer. You don't belong here. You're not an animal lover. You're just looking for amusing information to feed the people who read your articles. You do it for the money."

"But my articles will interest people in the zoo, and then they'll be more likely to support the zoo. Is that so bad?"

"Yes. Animals are better off without money from people who think they are entertainment."

Neither of them said anything for a moment. Then Cheetah Rita said, "They would eat you if they could get to you, you know." She nodded toward the cheetahs and smiled, making it clear whose side she'd be on in any dispute Charlotte had with the cats.

"You, too," said Charlotte. Then, trying to lighten things up, she said, "That's nothing. My husband says that our tabby *house* cat would eat us if he could."

"He's right."

"Then you understand why Walt prefers dogs."

"*No* one of any breeding prefers dogs," Cheetah Rita said seriously, becoming more animated. "Dogs are the vermin of the animal world, outside knocking at the door to the cat kingdom."

Charlotte stared at the other woman, searching her face for some hint of humor. There was none.

"Right," Charlotte managed. "The kingdom of cats. Exactly how I feel." She was glad nobody else was there to hear this loony conversation.

"My cats will triumph when they all learn to work together," Cheetah Rita said.

"My thoughts to a tee," said Charlotte, wondering why she had ever thought she could learn anything useful about Jerry's death from Cheetah Rita. Still . . .

"Speaking of working together, maybe you can help me. Maybe you could tell me how you came to find Jerry Brobst's body in the elephant yard," she said.

Cheetah Rita made a strangled sound. "After what you did?" she finally said.

Charlotte's jaw dropped. "What I did?"

Cheetah Rita ignored her and returned her attention to the cheetahs.

It occurred to Charlotte that maybe Cheetah Rita thought she had killed Jerry. On the other hand, if Maria was right, killing Jerry would not be something Cheetah Rita would hold against her.

She tried again to find out exactly what the strange woman had meant, and this time Cheetah Rita wasted no time in getting to the point.

"You stole my notebook!" she burst out. "You stole my research and you're a writer. So now you'll write it up for the journals and take all the credit for my work!"

"Your notebook is right there in your hands," Charlotte said gently, perhaps even patronizingly.

Without warning, Cheetah Rita swung the notebook toward her so violently that she nearly spun herself off her camp stool. "Not this one, you fool!" she shouted. "You know which one. The one I've been using for two years!"

After dodging the notebook, Charlotte managed to say, "Why would I? I write newspaper and magazine articles. I wouldn't even know how to write a research article or what journals would be interested in publishing it."

Nothing she said seemed to do any good. Cheetah Rita had her pegged as a notebook thief and that was that. After a few minutes of fruitless denials, Charlotte turned and started walking back toward the North American section. Behind her she heard a loud hiss. She turned to look, and since there were no cheetahs close by, decided that the catlike noise had to have come from Cheetah Rita herself—particularly since she had it on good authority that hissing was not among the noises cheetahs make.

Later that morning, Charlotte wandered over to the Gorilla Villa, the screened room filled with climbing toys and swings for the apes. She was surprised to find Maria standing

outside the room, gloomily watching a family group of gorillas at play inside. Before Charlotte could tell Maria about her
encounter with Cheetah Rita, Maria launched into her own
complaint.

"It's that stupid Stitcher again," she said. "He's making all
zoo employees who go to Jerry's funeral use vacation time
for it."

"You have to use some of your vacation time to go to the
funeral of a coworker?" Charlotte was appalled.

"Yes. It would only be a couple hours, but he says that
since we're on the public payroll, he can't just not count
those hours. And you know how little vacation time most of
us get."

"That does seem unnecessarily strict. Why can't he let
people make up the time by working extra hours?"

"Because he doesn't have the human compassion God
gave those gorillas," Maria said, waving her arm toward the
hairy family group on the climbing toys.

"Well, you couldn't all go at once, anyway, could you?
Not without closing the zoo."

"Right. But Stitcher had his little lackey—"

"Stevie?"

"Yes. He had her put up a list of all employees with a
place for us to check off whether we're going to the funeral
home Wednesday night or the funeral Thursday. Now, I ask
you: doesn't this sound like elementary school?"

"A bit controlling, anyway."

"There's more. Once we've all signed up, if it looks like
too many of us will be leaving the zoo to attend the funeral,
Stevie is supposed to talk us into going to the funeral home
the night before—when it will be no skin off the zoo's nose.
But I don't think she'll have to talk with many folks: most of
us get only a week's vacation a year, and few of us will be able
to use any of it for poor Jerry's funeral."

"I didn't know that funeral arrangements had been made
yet."

"Yes. We heard that the police released his body today.

You know, I just can't imagine who could have been angry enough at Jerry to push him off the roof."

"Any idea why he would have been up there in the first place?"

"None. I'm really going to miss him."

Charlotte nodded sympathetically. "Do they know what time he was killed?"

"Between ten and midnight Sunday night, the police said."

"Long after the zoo closed," Charlotte mused.

"Anyway, it looks like there will be a full house at the funeral home tomorrow night."

"Will it be so much worse to go there than the funeral?"

Maria was quiet for a while, and Charlotte was afraid that she had offended her.

"Probably not," Maria finally said, as though she hated to admit it. "Why should I think that somehow we're doing more for Jerry by going to the funeral rather than the funeral home? But it's the principle! Stitcher does this sort of thing all the time, Charlotte. We could have figured it out ourselves: who was going to go where and who would have to staff the zoo to make sure we had all the bases covered. But instead he mucks about in our affairs and treats us like children. It's infuriating."

"Was Hanna like that?"

"No way."

Charlotte met Lou for lunch at the Riverview, south of the zoo on Riverside Drive. By the time she arrived, her friend had already been seated and looked relaxed as she smoothed her salt-and-pepper hair back into its Dutch-boy cut. They both took a long time to look at the menu, and Charlotte still had time to recount the entire Cheetah Rita episode before a harried-looking manager came to take their order. He apologized for the slow service.

"We've been short a waitress for two days now," he said.

"If Naomi doesn't get herself in here tomorrow, she's history. Now what can I get you, ladies?"

Charlotte winced at the "ladies" and figured the manager had categorized them as "ladies who lunch." They might as well play it that way, she thought, and launched into a long-winded story about Naomi being Lou's sister's name, too, and wasn't that an unusual name these days?

The impatient manager bolted away as soon as he got them to tell him their order.

"I thought you said Cheetah Rita missed you with her notebook," Lou said.

"I did. Why?"

"Well, all that blather about my sister made me wonder if she had hit you on the head."

"Naomi *is* your sister's name."

"Of course, but why would you want to share that with the man taking our lunch order?"

"I was just angry because he called us 'ladies.' I thought I'd see how he liked it if we conformed to his stereotype of women who make a career out of lunching."

"Well, I don't think he was an enthralled audience for your little story. Unlike me, of course." Lou chuckled. "I've never known you to be so interested in my family."

Charlotte looked chagrined. "Oh, I guess that *was* a little odd. I'm probably getting eccentric like some of these characters I'm around at the zoo every day. I've told you about Cheetah Rita. And then there's Cowboy Bob Stitcher and his assistant, the pristine Stevie Kimmel. And *someone* up there is likely to have murdered Jerry Brobst." After a moment, she said, thoughtfully, "Maybe I could do with more contact with certifiably regular folks."

"Let me know when you find any."

"I'm serious. I've been hanging around the zoo so much this summer that people are beginning to think I'm employed there."

"You're losing perspective, you say?"

"Seems like it. Hey, Lou, why don't you come back to the

zoo with me after lunch? The only thing I have planned is a tram ride that covers the entire zoo grounds. To help me see things the way a visitor would. And if you're along, that would be even better—you'll supply a fresh set of eyes and ears."

Lou agreed to go, and about forty-five minutes later they boarded the tram with a few other passengers, mostly couples with small children.

It was when they were on the undeveloped northwest side of the zoo that something caught Charlotte's eye west of the tram path.

"Look! There!" she told a startled Lou.

"Where? Is an animal loose?"

"No, no. There, near that fallen tree," Charlotte said, starting to point and then thinking better of it as she attracted the attention of another passenger.

Although Lou never caught sight of them, Charlotte was certain she had seen marijuana plants waving in the breezy sunlight.

"How can you be so sure it's marijuana?" Lou said, craning her neck to look back as the tram sped them away.

"Well, after all, I did write that story on Meigs County's favorite cash crop last year. For *Southeast Ohio Life*, remember? So I've seen more than my share of pot in the ground."

"Maybe you should hire yourself out like one of those drug-sniffing dogs at the airport," Lou said dryly.

"You're just jealous because you didn't see it."

Lou allowed as how that might be true.

"What possible reason—other than the obvious—could someone have for growing marijuana at the zoo?" Charlotte wondered.

"Why rule out that somebody is growing their own?"

"Because I know the zoo grows all kinds of surprising stuff for the animals."

"You're suggesting the zoo has some kind of pot-eating animal to feed?"

"It's just a thought."

"Think again," Lou suggested.

"Well, then, what if there were some drug connection with Jerry Brobst's death?"

"Now, *that's* more like it."

"You weren't kidding when you agreed to help me get a fresh perspective on the zoo, were you?"

Chapter 7

The next morning, Wednesday, Charlotte came puffing into the Sams' kitchen while Walt was still eating breakfast. He looked up from the sports pages, but before he had a chance to say anything, she croaked, "It's as sticky as molasses out there. It's like taffy. It's . . ."

"Metaphor and simile," said Walt, who occasionally liked to remind Charlotte that he had majored in English before moving to the business world. He smiled. "And just a touch of hyperbole. Not bad for 7:45 in the morning."

She collapsed onto one of the high-backed wooden chairs that surrounded a round oak table, saying, "*You* ought to try walking in this humidity. I'm so sweaty I can hardly stand myself."

Congenitally opposed to exercise in any form, Walt responded mildly, "It's been nice in here."

She refused to be drawn into one of their discussions on the value of exercising. No matter how much they talked,

Walt would not even concede the possibility that regular exercise could be good for him. Charlotte, on the other hand, was convinced that her morning walk was the only thing that stood between her and an early death.

Just sitting still in the air-conditioning felt wonderful, but eventually she stood up, saying, "A shower is the next step."

"The *Dispatch* has a story about Brobst on page one of the Metro section," Walt said. "There's no byline," he added, knowing that was something she'd be interested in.

Sitting back down, Charlotte began pawing through the newspaper he had spread out on the table. When she found the article, she quickly scanned it. "Nothing new. Just a rehash of what we already know," she said. "Channel Four said it better last night."

"It's been two days now since Brobst's body was found. I think your buddy Barnes had better be catching his murderer soon or he never will."

Charlotte hooted at the thought of Barnes being her buddy, but Walt misinterpreted which of his comments she had reacted to.

"I was serious, " he said, getting up to leave for work. "I've read several times that if the police haven't caught a murderer within the first forty-eight hours after the crime, they never get him."

After he had left, Charlotte showered, dressed for the weather in a loose-fitting sage green tunic and pants, and woke Tyler. Over breakfast they discussed his upcoming diving meet and the fact that after diving practice today, he and Andrew planned to ride the city's bike path that ran along the Olentangy River from downtown to the outerbelt.

She suggested that for two guys who prided themselves on not really being jocks, they seemed to do a lot of physical activity. Ty seemed genuinely surprised to learn she thought a fifteen-mile bicycle ride was acutely physical, and she marveled once again at the energy level of fourteen-year-old males.

• • •

After breakfast she drove the ten minutes to her Clintonville office, on the second floor of a four-story building. She listened to messages on her phone tape; wrote a note to her part-time assistant, Claudia Pepperdine; and reviewed the marijuana article she wrote last year.

Then she headed for the zoo. On the way, she contemplated what information about Jerry's murder she had gathered for an article: exactly nothing. The only person who might have some real information—Cheetah Rita—had turned out to be more than a little strange *and* to hate Charlotte for imagined transgressions. She would have liked to have been there when Detective Barnes interviewed Cheetah Rita. It would have been fun to watch Barnes's reaction to any mention of the kingdom of the cats.

What would be his reaction to the marijuana? Maybe he already knew about it. Who could have planted it? It didn't look like much. Definitely not enough for commercial success. But could it have anything to do with Jerry's murder?

Charlotte had come of age as a journalist during the Watergate scandal, and Deep Throat's advice to Woodward and Bernstein to "follow the money" had always stood her in good stead, too. Unfortunately, she didn't know much about money connected to the zoo. There had never been a hint of monetary scandal there, and the public kept voting more and more tax money to support it. The 275 acres purchased for the zoo in 1989 had made it the third-largest municipal zoo in North America, behind Toronto and Miami. Could there be something wrong with that deal?

Maybe it was time to consider Jerry's own money. For instance, was it odd that he could afford a Corvette? Maybe keepers were paid more than she thought.

Once she parked at the zoo, Charlotte walked toward the undeveloped northwestern section and the marijuana plants she had seen yesterday. About ten minutes later, she heard a hand-operated saw and saw a groundskeeper cutting up the fallen maple tree she had seen yesterday from the tram. From her vantage point today, it was easy to see that it was the tree's falling that had exposed the marijuana plants to the view of tram riders.

"Hi," she said to the groundskeeper. "Good thing that tree didn't fall on any of the fences around here, or we might be wondering where all the animals went."

He acknowledged her only with a curt nod. He was a puny-looking figure to be wielding the long saw, but Charlotte saw the muscles in his upper arm flex as he swung the saw further over the tree trunk.

"Are you using the handsaw because a power saw would disturb the animals too much?" Charlotte asked.

No response from the groundskeeper. He was as good at ignoring her as Cheetah Rita had been yesterday.

She tried again. "I'm Charlotte Sams. I'm writing a series on the zoo for *Ohio Magazine*. I've talked with several groundskeepers, but I don't think we've met yet."

"No, we haven't met," he said, sounding surly. He paused to wipe the sweat off his face and wispy, straw-colored beard with his shirtsleeve. Since he wasn't wearing a safety helmet or even a hat, she could see that his no-color hair was quite thin on top. Perhaps to compensate for this, what was left of his hair was pulled into a ratty-looking ponytail that hung six inches down his back.

Charlotte persisted. "I see you took the trouble to move those vines out of the way before you started cutting up the tree. It's interesting that the vines are now covering up the marijuana plants that I spotted yesterday."

"Lady, you don't know what you're talking about."

"I was just curious about the plants. I wrote a magazine story about the crop in southeastern Ohio about a year ago. For *Southeast Ohio Life*."

"Never heard of it."

"It's just a small Ohio magazine. I didn't catch your name, by the way."

"Hogan. John Hogan," he said, lifting the saw as though to make it a barrier between them. She noted that his fingernails had been bitten to the quick, and there appeared to be nicotine stains on the fingers of his right hand.

"Do you sell this stuff?" Charlotte asked, nodding toward the marijuana plants.

"What are you, lady? Some kind of do-gooder?"

"Not me. I'm not going to spoil anything for you. I was just curious, that's all. I wanted to see how somebody could explain a marijuana farm at the Columbus Zoo."

" 'Cause if you *were* some kind of concerned citizen, I'd have to ask you to mind your own business."

Charlotte didn't like this obnoxious little man at all. "Actually," she said, gesturing with her arm back toward the more developed areas of the zoo to the west and south, "it all *is* my business. For the rest of this summer, the zoo is my 'beat.' "

"Then I think it's time for you to 'beat' it outta here," Hogan said, catching Charlotte by surprise at his wordplay— she wouldn't have thought him capable of it. She laughed, said again that his secret was safe with her, and walked off toward the rest of the zoo with a clear conscience. The insignificant-looking Hogan didn't seem like a major dope dealer to her.

Charlotte stayed later than usual at the zoo that day because she planned to stop at the funeral home on her way home. When it was time to leave, she trudged through the zoo's gravel parking lot, knowing that hers, like all the cars she passed, must be covered with dust an inch thick. But she soon found out that wasn't all that was wrong with her car.

The convertible top had been slashed in two dozen places, with particular emphasis on the area over the driver's seat. She couldn't escape the message.

Hogan had apparently felt it necessary to let her know what could happen to her if she changed her mind about exposing his marijuana, she thought. If only he knew how little she was interested in him or his plants!

Furious, she walked to a security person in a nearby kiosk

whose job seemed to be to watch traffic in the lot. She described the condition of her car. He said he had been there
most of the day but hadn't seen anybody messing with any of
the cars. Then he pointed out that the zoo's admission tickets
stated that the zoo was not responsible for lost, stolen, or
damaged property.

"Well, somebody's responsible!" she stormed and walked
back to her car. She quickly unlatched the top above the
windshield and pushed the button that folded the top down
behind the back seat. Then she roared out of the parking lot.
Even though it was folded down, the top's condition could be
detected in the little strips of furled canvas that blew in the
wind as she drove.

Maria's prediction was right: there was a full house at the funeral home when Charlotte joined others who had come to pay their respects to Jerry Brobst and his family. Unable to find space in the funeral home's lot, she had to park on the street, which was probably just as well, given how bad her car looked.

As was true with many funeral homes in central Ohio, this one had obviously been a large family mansion in its earlier days. She entered and was directed to the viewing room by a well-combed, somber man with a dark suit and respectfully lowered eyes. She stood by the door for a moment and surveyed the scene. There were about thirty people in the room, with an elderly couple and a man who looked like a younger version of Jerry standing near the closed casket at the far end. Charlotte assumed they were Jerry's parents and his brother. Someone had said he had a younger brother.

She recognized most of the other people as zoo staffers

but wondered why the room looked so festive. It took a moment for her to figure out that it was the clothing people were wearing. She was used to seeing the staff in their khaki or olive drab zoo uniforms, but now most of them were all dressed up. Unlike Charlotte, many had apparently gone home from work to change clothes before coming to the funeral home.

It was also obvious that many more women than men were present. She wondered whether it was because most of Jerry's friends had been women or because women were expected to take care of the social amenities in a situation like this.

She entered and, nodding to those she recognized, walked slowly to the casket. Maria Pickard, for once without her white lab coat, met her on the way. She walked with Charlotte and made the introductions. Charlotte shook hands with Jerry's family, murmured sympathetic remarks, and turned back toward the center of the room and the zoo staffers.

Maria seemed more subdued than usual, but was still ready to chat. She mentioned that Jerry's parents farmed near Marysville, a small town northwest of Columbus. The family had selected this funeral home near the zoo, instead of one in their hometown, in order to make it easier for Jerry's zoo colleagues to attend.

Jerry's brother, Bruce, was a mechanic in Marysville. "And a very good one, too," Maria said. "He was the only mechanic that Jerry trusted to work on his car."

Charlotte's investigative ear perked up immediately. "Jerry's Corvette? Do you know whether he bought it new?"

"Brand-new, fully loaded. I asked him if he had won the lottery, but he just laughed and said that the loan was as big as a mortgage on a house."

"I suppose, since he was single, he didn't mind having a mortgage on his car."

"Well, he was certainly single."

"What happened to the car after he died?" Charlotte asked.

"I assume the family has it. At least it was moved from the zoo parking lot sometime yesterday. Wouldn't Jerry's estate have to pay it off?"

"I think that's how it works. Talking about cars, you should hear what happened to mine today. I—"

"I'm sorry, Charlotte," Maria said, putting a hand on Charlotte's arm. "I can see something getting started with the commissary staff. I better go over and talk with them before they start quarreling about the new shipments. You know how those guys are."

She sped away, leaving Charlotte feeling somewhat at loose ends. All around her she could hear soft voices and an occasional sniffle or outright sob. One of the most consistent snifflers was a woman she did not recognize, seated in a chair against the wall. She looked very much alone, so Charlotte walked over to sit in the seat next to her.

She looked about thirty years old and was wearing a gray short-sleeved dress with black pumps and purse. She held onto wadded-up tissues in both hands, which she occasionally used to dab at her eyes. This had the effect of smearing what was left of her eye makeup.

Charlotte introduced herself and mentioned her zoo articles. "That's how I met Jerry. But I don't believe you and I have met."

"I'm Deborah Mancini," the young woman said. "Sorry to be on such a crying jag here . . ."

"You don't have to apologize," Charlotte said soothingly. "Jerry's death must have been a terrible blow to you."

"It was just so unexpected."

"My husband has a habit of saying, 'Only the good die young.'"

The young woman smiled ruefully. "Doesn't apply in this case. Jerry wasn't always good. But he was always there for me, you know?"

Charlotte found herself liking Deborah. It was somehow refreshing to have someone not immediately deifying the deceased.

"I don't know how you all do things here . . ."

"Here?" said Charlotte, thinking they didn't exactly live in Outer Mongolia.

"I mean, will there be a wake after the funeral tomorrow?" Deborah asked.

"Oh, you must not be from around here. I just assumed that you worked at the zoo with Jerry."

"Not this one. Tulsa City Zoo. I'm here just for Jerry's funeral."

"That's a long way to come."

"Right. But I felt so bad when I heard he died, I just had to be here." The tears started again and she dabbed at them.

"What sort of work do you do?" Charlotte asked, hoping to distract her.

"I'm an elephant keeper. Like Jerry. We met when we worked on a couple of National Zoo Association committees together."

Glad that her attempts at distraction seemed to be working, Charlotte said, "I've never been to Tulsa, but . . ."

"Did you say you're a reporter?" Deborah interrupted, all of a sudden looking intently at Charlotte.

Charlotte nodded.

"I know Jerry was anxious to talk with a reporter. About something that was going on at the zoo."

Charlotte demanded, "What's going on?"

But Deborah shook her head and sniffed hard. "He wouldn't say. Just that someone ought to know."

Charlotte didn't know how to feel about Deborah's revelation, certain only that she did not want to have had anything, however inadvertent, to do with Jerry's death. She could clearly hear Lou's voice in her mind, saying, "I told you so."

A large part of her wanted to ignore that Deborah's statement might indicate Jerry was killed so he couldn't tell Charlotte something during their scheduled interview. However, with a strong sense that she was casting the die, she asked, "Did you come with anyone, Deborah?"

"No. I don't know anyone here."

"Have you eaten dinner?"

"No, and I haven't found a motel yet either."

"Well, when you're ready to leave, why don't you and I go have something to eat at a restaurant down the street." Thinking about her tattered car, she added, "It's within walking distance. While we're there, I can draw you a map that shows where some local motels are."

"That's very nice of you. Thank you."

They sat in silence for a few moments, tears and conversation both having stopped. A man greeted Charlotte and sat in the empty chair next to her. She recognized the longtime manager of the zoo's souvenir shop.

"A nice turnout for Jerry, don't you think?" she said to him.

"And all nicely engineered," he said with surprising vehemence.

"You mean Stitcher's sign-up sheets?"

"Right. Wouldn't you think the son of a bitch could lay off for once and not have to direct our every move?"

"I guess you don't like him, either."

"Hah!"

"I've noticed he doesn't seem to have a very big fan club," Charlotte said. "But wouldn't you have been here anyway? Or at the funeral? For Jerry?"

"Maybe," he allowed. "I just don't like somebody monitoring my every move."

He looked toward the door, turned his mouth down, and nodded his head in that direction, saying, "Look at him now. The way he felt about Brobst, I don't know how he has the gall to show up here."

Bob Stitcher, with Stevie in tow, had just entered the room. Nodding to several staffers as he passed, he started immediately for the casket and Jerry's family.

Charlotte wanted to ask the manager to explain what he meant about Stitcher's feelings about Jerry, but Deborah seemed to have come to life with some urgency, dry-eyed and ready to leave.

"Can we go now, Charlotte?" she said. "I feel a little light-headed—probably from not eating."

So Charlotte said good-bye to the shop manager, waved to Maria and some other staffers, and left the room with Deborah.

As they went out the front door, they met Detective Jefferson Barnes and a uniformed officer coming up the steps. Barnes was bigger and better-looking than she remembered and was wearing an expensive slubbed silk sports coat. The effect was imposing.

"Well," the detective growled. "Ms., uh, Sams, isn't it?"

"Yes, that's right, Detective Barnes. Charlotte Sams."

"Imagine seeing you here."

Deborah was looking from Charlotte to Barnes and back again, and Charlotte didn't know whether she should introduce her. Somehow it didn't seem exactly like your usual social situation, and, in an effort to cover up her awkwardness, she explained to Barnes, "I've been writing articles about the zoo."

"So I've heard. Maybe we should talk."

"All right."

"Tomorrow morning, at the zoo administration building. Eleven o'clock."

"Okay."

Then, as though Charlotte had been purposefully keeping him from his sworn duty, Barnes said with some impatience, "Now, if you'll excuse me, I'd like to pay my respects to the family."

He and the other officer swept past them, but Barnes paused before going in the door and said over his shoulder, "Don't do anything stupid like last time, Ms. Sams."

She was too startled to reply.

"Wow. Who was that?" Deborah asked.

"Makes quite an impression, doesn't he?"

"What did he mean about not doing anything stupid?"

"I don't have a clue," Charlotte lied, steering Deborah down the street toward the restaurant.

Chapter **9**

By the following morning, Charlotte's life seemed considerably darker and more complicated. There was the matter of her lacerated car top, for instance, and a husband who took the slashes on the driver's side very seriously.

Going out to examine the car as it sat in the sunny driveway before work, Walt gave out a long, low whistle as he caught sight of the top. Silently he carried out his inspection, walking around the car, with his shoulders hunched and both hands in his pants pockets. Then he demanded, "Promise me you'll report this when you talk with Barnes today."

"Sure, but by that time I will have already talked with Hogan myself and—"

"Great, Charlotte. That's just great," he said, stomping around the car. "Why can't you just let the police talk to the son of a bitch?"

"Because they aren't going to be able to do anything about my top. Nobody, including me, saw Hogan cut it—"

"Stab it," Walt interrupted. "He stabbed it, Charlotte."

"All right, but nobody saw him stab it. So it's just going to be my word—my suspicion, really—against his word."

"But you can tell Barnes about Hogan's marijuana and he'll understand why he wanted to frighten you into keeping quiet and—"

"Sure, but Hogan has probably gotten rid of the plants by this time, and then the existence of the marijuana will just be my word against his, too."

"Just make sure you tell Barnes all about Hogan. Then stay away from him."

Taking a deep breath, Charlotte said, "Stop telling me what to do, Walt."

"I'm allowed to tell my wife what to do when I'm trying to keep her from getting hurt," he said. "It's even in the Feminist Husband's Handbook."

Charlotte would have smiled at his words, but his serious facial expression stopped her.

He hurried on. "What if Hogan had slashed you instead of your car?"

"But he didn't, did he?" Charlotte said, vaguely aware that the two of them sounded like they were pint-sized combatants on the playground. "Hogan obviously doesn't want to hurt me or he already would have. This top is just a scare tactic, Walt. At this point, I just want to have the satisfaction of yelling at him. That's more than the police will be able to do about my top, I'm sure."

"You're as crazy as he is" was Walt's frustrated assessment, and he got in his own car to drive to work. Apparently he forgot that he always kissed Charlotte good-bye.

Ruefully watching him drive down the street, she knew Walt only wanted to protect her. *Just imagine how he'd carry on if he knew that Jerry may have been killed so I couldn't interview him,* she thought.

She had put off sharing Deborah's information with Walt when she came home last night, and then this morning, the time just hadn't seemed right. Now she went back into the house, thinking that maybe after she got used to the idea herself, she'd manage to slip it into a conversation as though it was something they had discussed early on and he had just forgotten. Of course, unless Walt had a lobotomy before then, there probably wasn't much chance of pulling that off.

Charlotte hated the thought that she might have been even unwittingly involved in Jerry's death. What an odd occupational hazard journalists had, she thought: *other* people could get killed because of *your* occupation. It made you think you owed them something for having gotten them into this trouble. Made you feel responsible, even though it was they who had picked you out. All of which was slightly irrational, she knew, but there it was.

And another thing: She couldn't help but wonder whether Jerry's killer would have been willing to kill her as well as Jerry, if it had been necessary—if Jerry had been able to evade the killer earlier and had shared his information with Charlotte.

She couldn't very well confess this to Walt, but by this time she was actually glad she had Hogan to blame for her car's damage. The puny groundskeeper and his vandalism were a lot less worrisome than whoever pushed Jerry off the pachyderm building.

Tyler was sleeping in this morning, so Charlotte left early and arrived at her Clintonville office by 8:15, expecting to find a pot of hot coffee waiting and her assistant, Claudia Pepperdine, already at work. But Claudia was not there, and it took Charlotte a moment to remember why: she had asked her assistant to spend the morning checking to see whether some potential story ideas had already been covered in central Ohio publications.

She made the coffee herself and then spent the next half-hour arranging to have her car top replaced. Still smarting from Walt's opinion about her ability to take care of herself, she was unwilling to ask him to pick her up at the repair shop once she delivered her car. So she agreed to pay an exorbitant fee in order to get a shop "loaner" car for the day while the repair was being completed. The loaner sounded like a beauty.

At 9:15 she figured it was late enough to phone Lou. She filled her in about running into Detective Barnes at the funeral home, conveniently skipping Deborah's revelation in order to avoid hearing Lou say "I told you so" about the potential motive for Jerry's murder. Lou, however, was not shy about pointing out that, of course, it was she who had predicted Barnes would want to talk with Charlotte.

"Well, yes," Charlotte said, "but you can gloat later. At the moment, I'm after some occupational information."

Having specialized in the field of career development before her early retirement, Lou had often provided information about specific occupations for Charlotte's articles.

"Ask away," Lou said expansively.

"Okay. Do you know how much zookeepers make?"

"No, I'd have to look it up. But why don't you just ask that Stevie Kimmel how much Jerry Brobst made? That's what you really want to know, isn't it?"

"Right. But Stevie would know there's no reason I need to know his salary for a story and I don't want her to know that I'm interested for any other reason. She probably wouldn't tell me, anyway."

"Who else could you ask to get the information for you? Where do they keep the personnel records, anyway?"

"They're in Stitcher's office. And he's even more unlikely than Stevie to tell me."

"I was thinking more along the lines of secretaries you could talk into helping you."

"Why would a secretary be willing to look up confidential information for me?"

"Well, if Stitcher is as obnoxious as you say, his secretary is bound to be seeking ways to take revenge against him on any given day. And not too many people up there can like Stevie, either."

"I think everybody's too afraid of losing their jobs to take action against either Stevie or Stitcher."

"Well, it was just a thought," Lou said. "Why *are* you interested in Jerry's salary, by the way?"

"It has to do with his car. Remember, I told you he drove a sports car—a Corvette? I'm thinking that that's a pretty expensive car to have on a keeper's salary. But that's just a guess until I find out how much keepers make and how much a car like his costs. I don't have a clue about the car price. Walt and I have not exactly been in the market for a Corvette, you know."

"The Saturday *Dispatch*," Lou said.

"Huh?"

"That's the day all the car ads are in the classified section. You can get an idea of Corvette prices from any Saturday paper."

"Oh, right. Listen, Lou, I've got to go if I'm going to be on time for my meeting with Barnes."

"I wonder if he remembers me."

"Barnes? Oh, he must," Charlotte said. "I have the feeling the two of us made quite an impression on him."

She dropped her car off at the repair shop and then drove the loaner to the zoo. As she had expected, the vehicle she was paying through the nose for was a real clunker: dented from one end to the other and in need of a new muffler. Worst of all, it seemed to consist of the parts from at least two separate cars. Its front and rear ends were white and the middle section was black. The car actually looked like a saddle shoe, she thought, but driving it was still better than asking Walt for a ride right now.

Once at the zoo she had time only to run over to the site of Hogan's marijuana plantation before she was due to meet with Barnes. As she had predicted, Hogan had moved the plants. He'd been quite thorough: there was not a stalk of illegal flora in sight.

As she turned back toward the developed area, Hogan's voice rang out from behind a tree, "We don't generally allow visitors back here, ma'am. I'm afraid you'll have to leave."

Startled, she managed to shout, "I want a word with you, you dumb-ass!" and walked over to him. She was relieved to see that today he did not seem to have a saw or other piece of equipment nearby. Did his supervisor know how much time he spent not working? she wondered.

"I know it was you who cut my convertible top, so you're going to have to pay to have it fixed," she said.

Hogan looked surprised.

"You slashed my convertible top," she repeated. "To make me afraid to tell anyone about your marijuana."

"Lady, I don't know what you're talking about. I've never seen you before in my life. How would I know what you drive?"

"Don't give me that. I wasn't going to tell anyone about your pot. Not because I was afraid, but because I was *uninterested.* Got that? You are *boring*, Hogan, boring. *No* one would want to read about you." She had the sense that maybe she was getting a little carried away here but pressed on. "But now you've got my attention, and I'm telling the police everything I know about you."

He gave her a patronizing look. "Which can't be much, can it, considerin' we never met." He turned to walk away but stopped and said as an afterthought, "You know, there's another crazy woman here at the zoo. Spends a lot of time with the cheetahs. Maybe the two of you could hang out together."

She could hear him laughing as he walked down the tram path. If there had been anything handy, she would have thrown it at him.

She steamed on over to the administration building to meet Barnes. A secretary told her that Barnes was using the director's office, Bob Stitcher being away from the zoo for the day. Barnes was seated behind Stitcher's desk when she came in. Dressed in a white shirt, yellow tie, and navy blue suit, he seemed to fill the whole office. He stood to greet her but barely smiled.

Probably against regulations, she thought.

"Ms. Sams," he said, stretching his arm across the desk to shake hands. "I appreciate your coming."

"I'm more than happy to," she said, settling into the guest chair at the side of the desk. "Especially since I have a crime to report."

He looked at her, dumbfounded, and then said, "Unless it has some bearing on the Brobst case, please call downtown to report it." He pushed his business card across the desk to her. "This is the main number at headquarters."

Charlotte said, "Why would I want to do that, when I have a perfectly good police detective right in front of me?"

"A homicide detective, Ms. Sams. Is it a murder you want to report?"

"I only wish. I'm mad enough to kill him, that's for sure."

"In that case, I'll have to encourage you to make your report downtown," Barnes said, clearly anxious to focus on the murder that had already taken place. "Now, tell me about these articles you've been writing about the zoo."

Allowing herself to be distracted from the charges she wanted to levy against Hogan, Charlotte described her series for *Ohio Magazine* and suggested that Barnes become a subscriber. "I would think someone in your position would need as much information about the state and community as he could get," she said.

He didn't comment on her suggestion but asked when she had started working on the series and how much time she was spending at the zoo. She told him. He asked whether she had been at the zoo last Sunday, the day before Jerry's body had been found. She had not, so he didn't get to ask the follow-up questions that she imagined he had ready.

She had some questions of her own, including "Do you have any suspects in the case?"

"You know I can't divulge that kind of information to the public, Ms. Sams. Or to you reporters."

"But, having known Jerry as I did, I'm not exactly 'the public.'"

"A lot of people knew Brobst. You're exactly who this policy was made for."

"I'm just concerned because I've read that if the police

don't identify a killer within the first forty-eight hours of a case," she said, quoting Walt, "they're not likely to ever find out who did it. And you're well past that deadline, Detective Barnes."

"We're well aware of the timeline on this case. Now, tell me how well you knew the deceased."

Charlotte explained what she knew about Jerry, including Deborah Mancini's information that apparently Jerry had wanted to talk with a reporter about something more exciting than elephant training.

Barnes took an occasional note, but, in Charlotte's opinion, did not express sufficient interest in her and Deborah's suspicions.

"I thought that bit of information would be particularly helpful to you," she finally said.

"Well, we'll be glad to give this Ms. Mancini a call to check it out, but I'm afraid it's a pretty common story."

"Are you saying you think Deborah is lying?" Charlotte bristled.

"No, of course not. But in my line of work, everyone I hear about seems to be anxious to spill their guts to a reporter."

"Now, where have I heard that phrase before?"

"I beg your pardon?"

"Sorry. I just got distracted. How come we reporters don't know about all these folks who are so anxious to tell us important things?"

"Because there's nothing really for them to tell you. It's just everyone's gut reaction: 'I'll get back at so-and-so by going public with what I know.' Not that they really know anything incriminating. And certainly nothing worth getting killed over." Barnes looked a little weary. "I've come to believe that it's the dream of every disgruntled employee, for instance, to get to rat on their employer. A symptom of their frustration, I guess."

"But then why did you want to talk with me?"

"I'm more interested in the talks Mr. Brobst *had* with you

than the one he was prevented from having," Barnes said. "Did he tell you something, anything, that could help? Not necessarily something of a whistle-blowing nature in a formal interview, but maybe something when you were just chatting." Barnes gave her a moment to think and then prompted, "Maybe he seemed upset. Or maybe he mentioned someone who was giving him trouble?"

"No, nothing like that. Jerry seemed pretty well liked, it seemed to me. It's only been since he died that I've found a person who *didn't* like him."

"Just stumble across this person, did you, Ms. Sams?"

Charlotte smiled innocently. "Just doing my job," she said. When Barnes scowled but didn't say anything, she took the opportunity to mention Cheetah Rita by name.

"You must have talked with her, because she found Jerry's body."

"You're apparently pretty good at your job, Ms. Sams."

"I've been curious about your reaction to the notion of the kingdom of the cats," she said, and saw Barnes fully smile for once. "An interesting concept, don't you think?"

"I'm a dog lover, myself."

"Well, don't tell Cheetah Rita." Charlotte paused to consider whether she should tell Barnes about Cheetah Rita's irrational belief that Charlotte had stolen her notebook, but decided not to. It seemed stupid to tell the police that someone—anyone—considered her a thief.

Instead, she said, "Now I'd like to tell you about John Hogan, who is the perpetrator of my crime—the one you're insisting I report downtown." And before he could stop her, she quickly told the tale of Hogan's marijuana plants and of her slashed car top.

"Marijuana growing at the zoo," Barnes said.

"Yes. I saw it myself."

"And you're confident that marijuana was what you were looking at?"

"Completely. But, of course, by now he's moved the plants."

"Well, then let's go take a look at your car."

"We can't," she was forced to say. "It's being repaired."
Luckily, this admission did not have to include the fact she
was currently driving a saddle shoe around town.

"Then we can't really verify that any vandalism was done
to your car, can we?" Barnes said. "Assuming we wanted to,
that is."

"Well, you could talk with the manager of the repair
shop. He could verify that my top was slashed."

"But it would have been much better to see the evidence."

"I guess I really didn't think about it being evidence,"
Charlotte said. "I was just so angry and wanted to get it fixed
as soon as possible. And then my husband was so unreason-
able that . . ."

"Your husband must have the patience of Job, Ms. Sams,
if you don't mind my saying so."

"My husband's state of mind is really none of your business," Charlotte snapped.

Barnes seemed taken aback by her tone and said he had
no more questions for her. That was fine with Charlotte, who
had decided she was fresh out of answers.

Chapter 10

A few hours later, Charlotte was sitting in the hot little shed she was using as an office at the zoo, organizing notes from interviews on her laptop computer and, she told herself, staying out of mischief. Earlier in the afternoon she had been sorely tempted to sneak into Stitcher's office and steal a look at Jerry Brobst's personnel files once Barnes seemed to have cleared out of there.

She understood that it was simple frustration that had made her even consider such poor journalistic form, not to mention illegal derring-do. But it was frightening to realize that it was only the knowledge that Stevie could have caught her red-handed that had brought her to her senses before the actual attempt.

She was surprised when Lou appeared at her open door.

"Hi," she said, having no idea why Lou had dropped in on her. Then, "Oh, no—we weren't supposed to meet someplace for lunch, were we?"

"Of course not. I was just bored with my work and needed a break. I thought I'd come hear what Barnes had to say this morning."

"Nothing very interesting, I'm afraid." Since there was no place for Lou to sit in her office, Charlotte suggested they sit on the steps to the shed. It was cooler out there anyway. Then she filled Lou in on the details of her talk with Barnes.

"Well, you disappoint me," Lou said a short time later. "This is not much more interesting than things back at my house."

"Such is the life of a freelance journalist," Charlotte said philosophically. "I had the chance to be a little more adventuresome this morning, but the moment passed."

Immediately the germ of an idea began to form in her mind, despite her earlier fits of conscience.

"Why are you looking at me like that?" Lou demanded.

"This is your lucky day, Lou Toreson. You have definitely come to the right place for excitement, something to appeal to your higher self."

"Spare me, Charlotte. What are you planning, with that evil look in your eye?"

"You can help me get Jerry's personnel files."

"Oh, right. Have a little breaking and entering in mind?"

"I'll do the entering once you've gotten Stevie out of the way. It'll be easy."

"You're nuts!"

"There you go, using those professional psychologist terms on me again."

"You know I couldn't get Stevie out of the way—the woman doesn't even know me."

"That's the beauty of it. She'd have no reason to suspect you. You'll just appear to be a regular zoo visitor, feeling important to be the one delivering a message from the director to his assistant."

Lou didn't say anything, so Charlotte pressed on.

"You could tell her that Stitcher wanted her to join him on the other side of the zoo, maybe at the female cheetah yard."

By this time Charlotte had left the steps and, in her excitement, was pacing around on the ground in front of the shed. "You could imply that it had something to do with Cheetah Rita—Stevie is obsessed with Cheetah Rita's inappropriateness and the necessity of keeping her a deep, dark secret—"

"I thought you said Stitcher was away from the zoo today," Lou said with a "gotcha" edge to her voice.

"He is, but he could have come back. Who says he has to check in at his office as soon as he's back on the zoo grounds? Stevie does whatever Stitcher asks and she'd never be able to risk ignoring what could be a legitimate request from him. And while you've got her on the other side of the zoo, I'll grab Jerry's file."

"Forget it, Charlotte," Lou said, standing up. "I came up here looking for something interesting, maybe even something exciting. But definitely nothing criminal."

"Okay, I won't take the file. I'll just look at it real quick and put it right back."

"Oh, well, that makes all the difference," Lou said sarcastically. "You know I'm always happy to contribute to your excellent articles, but I don't think even a Pulitzer Prize–winning story would be worth my taking these kinds of risks."

Charlotte knew she had to do something fast to persuade her friend to help. Reluctantly, she made her decision. "Sit down, Lou. There's something I haven't told you," she began dramatically.

Then she shared the knowledge that Jerry might have been killed because of information he wanted to tell Charlotte—just as Lou had suggested when his body had been found. She was plainly after more than a good story: she wanted to to be absolved of any responsibility for Jerry's death, and finding his killer would make her feel like she had done her best to make up for her inadvertent part in his murder. Surely that was worth a little danger.

After hearing Charlotte out, Lou agreed to decoy Stevie even before she said "I told you so."

• • •

Lou entered the administration building while Charlotte stayed back out of sight. Panting a little as though she was out of breath, she asked Stevie's and Stitcher's secretary if Stevie was in.

"Why, yes. She's in her office. May I help you?"

"I have a message I'm supposed to give to her. Could you show me where she is?"

The secretary obligingly got up from her desk and pointed the way to Stevie's cubicle.

Lou tapped on the partition and entered quickly as Stevie looked up from the papers on her desk.

"Mr. Stitcher sent me to get you," Lou blurted out. "He wants you over at the cheetah yard right away."

"Mr. Stitcher isn't at the zoo this afternoon. And who might you be?"

"Big guy in a cowboy outfit?" Lou said. "Used to giving orders? He wants you over at the cheetah enclosure right away."

"Then why didn't he call this building on his walkie-talkie? I would have gotten the message."

This was one question Lou and Charlotte had not anticipated. Lou did the best she could. "He told me he left it in the car," she said, and then added, "There's an elderly woman with the cheetahs who's acting a little odd . . ." She let her voice trail off.

Stevie looked alarmed and then put the papers in a side drawer of the desk. "All right," she said.

"I'm going in the same direction," Lou said companionably. Stevie frowned at her and walked quickly out of her office and out of the building, with Lou tagging far behind.

From her vantage point, Charlotte watched as Stevie climbed into a golf cart parked beside the administration building and drove off, obviously with no intention of taking Lou with her. However, she hadn't gone but a few yards before she stopped the cart and leaned out to ask Lou, "*Which* cheetah enclosure?"

To Charlotte's delight, Lou hurried up and took a seat in the cart before answering. She must have said the female cheetah yard on the west side of the zoo because Stevie drove off in that direction while Charlotte walked into the administration building.

To the secretary, she said, "Is Detective Barnes still here? I think I left a notebook in Mr. Stitcher's office while I was talking to the detective this morning."

"He's gone out," the secretary said. "You can go on in and look for it yourself, if you like." Then she went back to her keyboard. Clearly, she had had enough interruptions in her work for the moment.

"Thank you," said Charlotte, unaware that the secretary hadn't bothered to mention that Barnes would be back soon to finish going through the personnel files he had been examining.

Moving as quickly as she dared, Charlotte went down the aisle past Stevie's office and on into Stitcher's. She quickly perused the labels on the filing cabinets, hoping that the zoo hadn't completely computerized their personnel records. No, here was a four-drawer cabinet with "Personnel" on the label. A locked cabinet. No, the lock was open. Curious, but maybe her luck was changing. She quickly opened the top drawer (A-G on the label) and flipped to the B's. No folder for Jerry Brobst.

Damn, she thought. This is probably just for current employees. But they're being awfully efficient to have pulled Jerry's folder already. She looked around the office and noticed the pile of folders on Stitcher's desk—folders that had not been there a few hours earlier when Barnes had interviewed her.

She moved to the desk and checked the top folder. Definitely a personnel file. Coolly flipping through the folders, she found Jerry Brobst's file and scanned it quickly. There. The salary information she needed, plus Jerry's job description, a reprimand for walking the cheetah fence, and something she didn't expect: a reprimand for fighting with John Hogan. Hogan again! What could the fight have been about?

Voices interrupted her concentration before she could read the details and she gasped.

"She asked to look for her notebook," said the exasperated secretary. "She said she left it in there this morning."

"I see." It was the deep voice of Detective Barnes. "I'll be here for another hour or so. Please don't let anyone else back into the office."

Charlotte whipped a notebook out of her purse and walked out of Stitcher's office toward the voices. "Oh, hello again," she said innocently to Barnes and "Thanks, I found it," to the secretary. Without pausing, she walked directly out of the building and back to her office.

Lou showed up with an enormous grin on her face a half-hour later. "I spent at least ten minutes apologizing," she said. "The cowboy director just wasn't there when we got to the cheetah yard, so we walked around a bit but never did find him. You look as though you had some success."

"Eighteen thousand a year," Charlotte said. "That's how much money Jerry made. Not much to finance a sports car."

Lou agreed and suggested that Jerry might have been in the dope business with Hogan.

"I've been thinking about that myself. But the crop wasn't big enough to involve many people for anything other than personal use. You couldn't make much selling it, I mean. Maybe Jerry was just a customer of Hogan's."

"Even so," Lou said, "just think about all the newspaper stories you've read about violence that occurs when drug deals go sour."

"But it was only a fist fight. It's not like Jerry and Hogan blew each other away with AK-47s."

On her way home, Charlotte returned the loaner to the repair shop, only to find that the work was not yet completed on her own car. She argued with the shop manager until he agreed to let her keep the loaner at no extra charge until her car would be finished (or so he promised) the next day. Driving

away, she couldn't believe she had actually fought for the right
to prolong her experience with that ridiculous-looking car.

A stop at her Clintonville office brought more bad news
in the form of a note from her assistant, who had spent the
day checking to see whether central Ohio publications had
covered some topics Charlotte wanted to write about:

Charlotte—

I think you should forget the architecture topics.
Just last year, *Ohio Historical Magazine* did a feature
on the local houses people ordered from the Sears
Roebuck catalog—including the apartment buildings. (You were right. A lot of them are in Clintonville.) However, if you think of another angle
and need them, I can get copies of the Sears catalog pages very easily. Too bad you can't get a house
from Sears today. I hate my landlord. The elephant keeper from the zoo called to say you can
watch her do their feet on Monday. But skip the
camera or you'll scare them. See you next week.

Claudia

Charlotte sighed. Even though, as a freelancer, she often
got to pick her own topics, sometimes it seemed as though
everyone else was picking the same thing. Finally she left for
home.

Walt loved the loaner.

Frank Snow

Chapter **11**

The audiotape Charlotte chose to listen to on her walk the next morning was music rather than one of her usual mysteries. Chopin to soothe the savage breast. It seemed to do the trick—midway through her walk, she felt loose and lyrical, humming along to the music as she sort of sashayed her way down the sidewalk on East North Broadway. (Chopin did not exactly make for a power-walk step.)

As the music reached a particularly melodic section, a small child's sing-song voice said, "You better stop asking all those questions at the zoo-ooo!"

It was a stunning interruption, one that stopped Charlotte in her tracks. She tore the earphones out of her ears as though they were burning, punched the stop button on the recorder, and spun around to see if a child was in sight. She simply could not believe that the child's voice had come to her from the tape.

When it was clear that she was alone on the sidewalk, she

rewound the tape a bit, gingerly put the earphones back on, and pushed the play button.

A childish treble repeated the admonition to stop asking questions at the zoo. But this time Charlotte left the tape on long enough to complete the message. ". . . Or something bad will happen to you!" the child finished with a flourish. Then the Chopin picked up again.

Charlotte was dumbfounded. How did that child's voice get on the tape she bought at the music store? She thought all such tapes could not be recorded-over. Who had put it there? She couldn't recognize the child's voice—couldn't even tell if it was a boy or girl, although she thought the child sounded like a preschooler. Who had been willing to use a child this way? What bad things did someone have in mind for her? How dare they threaten her! And most important: who were they?

She walked home by the quickest route, looking over her shoulder most of the way. If somebody could tamper with an audio tape she had been carrying around in her tote bag for a few days, they obviously could tamper with her, too.

On the way she tried desperately to figure out who had had access to her tape long enough to record that voice. Would Hogan be smart enough to pull off this tape trick? she wondered. She couldn't recall seeing him anywhere close to her zoo office the day before. Unfortunately, she couldn't be sure that she had kept her zoo office door locked yesterday, although she usually was very careful to do so. It was just that once Lou had agreed to help with Jerry's file, she may have gotten a little careless in all the excitement. How ironic it would be if in her haste to steal information from Stitcher's office she had left her own belongings at risk.

When she got back home, Tyler was spreading out his camping gear in the backyard. Walt had left for work before her walk, but since Ty was the one in charge of electronics in the Sams household, he was the one she wanted to talk with anyway.

"I thought I'd better check out my stuff before I have to

use it next week," he explained when she came into the back-yard.

"Good idea." There didn't seem to be any point in making a fourteen-year-old worry about his mother, so she decided not to mention the threatening tape. But it might be difficult to find out what she needed to know without telling him why. She hoped he would be so involved with the camping gear that he wouldn't think to inquire. In the absence of a real plan, she just forged ahead.

"Ty, do you know whether it would be possible for me to tape over an audiotape I bought at the music store?"

"You mean tape over the music that's already been laid down there?"

"Yes."

"To record your own stuff over it?"

"Right."

"No problem," he said, starting to pump up an air mattress. "There are two little square holes in the edge of the cassette. All you have to do is to put a piece of tape or something over those holes."

"I don't follow you."

"It's just like on a videocassette. You know those videos Dad made of me when I was little? After he recorded one, he would break the plastic flaps off the back edge of the cassette so we wouldn't be able to record something over it."

"But this—"

"Is the opposite, I know. You *want* to record over something. That's why you put the tape over where that flap would have been on a new blank tape."

He squeezed the air mattress and looked critically at it, trying to judge whether there were leaks. After a moment, Charlotte said, "That's all there is to it?"

"Yep. I keep telling you guys that all this electronics stuff is not as complex as you think."

"Then why can't I set the clock on our VCR?"

"Well, *some* things are complicated . . ."

She left him counting tent pegs.

• • •

An hour later, Charlotte was speeding along a highway northwest of Columbus in her own car, determined to take hold of her situation. First, her car had been vandalized and now she had received the threatening taped message. It required effort, but she was working hard to avoid feeling victimized. Taking action, she thought, would help her feel in control again.

The first thing on her agenda had been to get back her own car. Next was what she hoped would be an enlightening conversation with Jerry's brother, Bruce. Maybe he could explain why Jerry and John Hogan had fought.

Since the funeral had been only yesterday, she wasn't sure that Bruce would be back to work yet. If he wasn't, she hoped that he lived somewhere other than the family farm so that she could avoid talking with his and Jerry's parents. Somehow it seemed in less bad taste to talk with the brother of a murdered person than with the murdered person's parents.

The trip to Marysville was uneventful, taking only about forty-five minutes. When she entered town, she started pulling into gas stations as she came to them and asked for Bruce Brobst and whether anyone knew where he worked. At the third station, a young man of Japanese descent told her that Bruce worked at his own garage two streets over. She thanked him and drove west.

In a few moments, she spotted a large sign ("Brobst Mechanics") over the door to a garage, whose three bays were filled with cars in various stages of repair. But Bruce, it turned out, was working on a car on the pavement surrounding the building. When she approached him and he raised his head from under the hood, she could see again his strong resemblance to Jerry. He looked about twenty-five years old.

Charlotte introduced herself, said that she was sorry his brother was dead, and explained that she had come to find out whether he knew why Jerry had wanted to talk to a reporter.

Bruce looked at her suspiciously. "Weren't you at the funeral home?"

"Yes. Wednesday night."

"You weren't at the funeral yesterday."

"That's right. I had to work."

"Well, I've got to work right now," he said. With that, he stuck his head back under the car's hood, disconnected a hose, and straightened up. Wiping the greasy fingers of his right hand on the rag hanging out of his hip pocket, he walked rapidly toward the garage.

Charlotte waited by the car until he came back with a new hose and started putting it on. Then she said, "Maybe Jerry was planning to tell me something about the person who ended up killing him."

"No shit," Bruce said, straightening up and closing the hood. "But the cops know all about you and Jerry, and they haven't turned up his killer yet, have they?"

"Not that I know of," Charlotte admitted, encouraged that he had started talking. "But I had hoped that you could tell me why Jerry had a fight with a man named John Hogan. He's a groundskeeper at the zoo."

"Miss Sands—"

"Sams."

"Whatever. My brother's dead, and there's not a goddamn thing I can do about it." Bruce's voice broke slightly at the end of this speech, and Charlotte felt sorry for him. She knew she couldn't bear it, either, if anything happened to her own brother.

Trying to guide the conversation into less emotional waters, she asked, "What will happen to Jerry's car now? I always liked that car."

"It's mine now."

"Oh. He had debt-canceling life insurance on it, huh? Like on a home mortgage?"

"There never was a loan. That car belonged to Jerry, free and clear," Bruce said fiercely. "Now it belongs to me."

Charlotte waited for him to say more about the car, but he didn't.

"My brother was great," Bruce finally said, miserably. "Him and me always stuck together. Our folks were pretty old when they had us, so they raised us funny. But Jerry made everything okay. As long as he was around, we could get through anything. He helped me get started here," he said, gesturing toward the garage, "and didn't even want me to pay him back. That's the kind of guy he was." He paused a moment, and then said softly, "That's the kind of guy they killed."

Charlotte was sorry she had come. She quickly told Bruce again that she was sorry Jerry was dead, apologized for bothering him, and then walked across the street toward her car.

On the way, she heard the sound of metal on metal and looked over at him. He was standing on the pavement where she had left him, using the wrench to beat on the hood of the car he had been repairing. Over and over, he brought his arm and hand high before slamming the tool down, and she could tell by the way his face was screwed up that he was crying.

She got in her car, started the engine, and drove a block north. Then she turned left and down an alley to circle back toward the freeway. It was the alley behind Bruce's garage, and as she passed behind his property, she saw Jerry's white sports car parked there. Impulsively, she pulled her car next to it and got out. She opened the door on the driver's side and stuck her head inside the Corvette, already feeling silly because she knew the police would have searched Jerry's car carefully and what did she think she could find out, anyway?

Having not seen the inside of many sports cars, she was distracted by the electronic dashboard for the first few moments. Then she slowly became aware of a faint, sweet, cloying odor that few people who went to college in the sixties are likely to forget. Hogan may have grown it, but one or both of the Brobsts had smoked it.

Chapter 12

Charlotte squinted into the Saturday afternoon sun as she watched Ty's diving team compete with two other swim teams from the area. Walt had had to go to the office, but she sat with some of the other parents in aluminum lawn chairs around the cement collar of Olympic Pool's diving well. It was unbearably hot, and she felt assaulted by the sunshine as it bounced off the cement. On the other hand, it felt good to be around so many other people. Good and safe.

It was dumb to have forgotten to bring sunglasses. She leaned back in her chair and closed her eyes against the sun, knowing she was missing only the nine- and ten-year-olds' competition, not the big kids'.

Her mind immediately went to events at the zoo. Much of what she had planned to do this past week had been superseded by events pertaining to Jerry's death. But late yesterday she had been able to get from the head of zoo security a copy of a written plan for emergency procedures to be followed if a dangerous animal escaped.

That situation, it turned out, was the basis for a simulation the zoo undertook one weekend day each spring. On that day, the crew trained to recapture the animal swung into action, while the rest of the staff evacuated visitors. After interviewing the security man, she had called the city editor of the *Dispatch* and sold him a yet-to-be-written story on the emergency procedures. If she was going to be threatened for asking questions at the zoo, she might as well get paid for it.

Judging from the kinds of questions he had asked her, Barnes didn't seem to have any suspects in Jerry's murder case. She wondered if the police noticed the odor of marijuana in the Corvette. She had trouble thinking Jerry had smoked much dope. He seemed too energetic, too "wired" for that. Now, uppers might be another story. She had never before considered that his dare-devil behavior might be drug-induced, but maybe that was not too far-fetched an idea.

Finally, she had to laugh at herself, realizing that from a few plants at the zoo and the odor of marijuana in Jerry's car, she had fashioned an elaborate story of employee drug use on the job and a drug deal gone bad. She reminded herself that it was just marijuana, and not the hard stuff, she had uncovered.

Maybe she was just anxious to somehow connect the revolting Hogan to Jerry's death because he *was* revolting and because he was the only "bad guy" she had. She was even beginning to wonder whether she had been too anxious to accuse him of slashing her car top. He had seemed genuinely surprised when she accused him of it the next day. Why had she been so sure he even knew which car was hers, especially since they had met only the afternoon it was damaged? On the other hand, he *was* a weird character and there were plenty of other people at the zoo from whom he could have found out which car was hers. She wondered if—

"Hey, Charlotte, I didn't expect to see *you* here." It was Stevie Kimmel's voice.

Charlotte straightened up and opened her eyes to find Stevie, looking tanned, cool, and collected in teal shorts and matching halter top, standing directly in front of her. Her sunglasses were perched on top of her head, and she held on her hip a four-year-old boy who had performed his first dive earlier as a member of one of the teams opposing Tyler's.

"Hi, Stevie," Charlotte said. "I didn't know you come to this pool."

Stevie explained that she usually didn't. "This is not my home pool," was how she put it. But young Sam was her nephew and she was at the meet with his parents, her sister and brother-in-law. She called Sam "my little eel."

"Of course, everybody in my family swims like a fish," she said. "I grew up on Lake Erie, and we all learned to swim and handle boats before we went to school. My sister and I both spend as much time around the water as we can."

"You must be delighted that the zoo is on the reservoir, then," Charlotte said.

"Well, I would be if I had any time to even look at the water when I'm there. Who are you here for?"

Charlotte said her son was on the Olympic team and pointed Ty out to Stevie.

Stevie said, "I see him. He's cute. One of the older kids," which Charlotte thought was aimed at making her feel like one of the older parents. Or was Charlotte herself being way too sensitive?

The four-year-old fussed, and Stevie said she had to get him back to her sister. Charlotte wasn't sorry to see her go, anxious to get back to contemplating Jerry's killer in peace.

She had to admit that all of her ruminating about pot smoking might be better directed at Bruce. After all, Jerry's car was his now. Maybe he had killed Jerry for it. In a world where teenagers regularly killed one another for their tennis shoes, killing for a Corvette didn't seem impossible. But if he did do it, he was regretting it now, Charlotte thought, still affected by the raw emotion Bruce had shown the day before.

Maybe the most interesting thing she had learned from him was that Jerry's car had never been financed. If he was right about that, then Jerry had lied to Maria. (She refused to even consider that it was Maria who had lied with that story of the house-sized loan.) Judging from the car prices she had read in today's paper, Charlotte thought Jerry's car could easily have cost forty thousand dollars. Pretty fancy car on a keeper's salary, she thought.

The announcer called up the thirteen- and fourteen-year-olds. Time for Ty. As he walked out to the end of the three-meter board, the announcer said softly, "Tyler Sams will be doing a forward one-and-a-half in the tuck position." Charlotte held her breath as she watched him spring, contort his body, and pierce the surface of the water.

The dive looked good to her, and she joined several other spectators in clapping. It must have looked good to the judges, too, because after a few moments the announcer gave Tyler's score: a 6.5. In the two years Charlotte had been attending diving meets, she had never seen a score higher than a 7 on the 10-point scale. Obviously, these judges weren't pushovers.

Everybody clapped again and Charlotte could see that Ty looked happy as Andrew thumped him on the back.

Now it was their friend Aaron's turn to dive. He was to dive from the ten-meter platform—the one she made Tyler promise he would not go off. As she watched Aaron climb the ladder, the familiar fear-of-heights sensations came over her and reached a terrifying, heart-thumping crescendo by the time he stood alone at the edge of the platform. Obviously, it was time to look away. Aaron executed his dive, but Charlotte couldn't bear to look until she heard him enter the water. Then she clapped along with everybody else.

Aaron had survived. He even looked triumphant. Maybe her phobia was getting out of hand if she was affected even when *other* people were in high places. Maybe she *was* being overprotective, she thought. Maybe she should let Tyler use that high platform. She could always attend the meets drugged and blindfolded . . .

Chapter 13

On Sunday, Charlotte slept late, cooked a big breakfast for her family, wrote her feature article on the zoo's emergency procedures, and modem-ed it off to the *Dispatch.* The late afternoon and evening were consumed by a euchre tournament between Charlotte and Tyler and Walt and Andrew. The kids played nearly as well as she and Walt, she thought.

She would have appreciated a replay of all that cozy family activity on Monday, especially since it dawned dark and dreary. But Walt had to go to work, of course, and Ty left on a three-day camping trip with friends.

She herself had a full schedule at the zoo. First was the interview with Stevie that was rescheduled because of Jerry's death a week ago. How long ago that all seemed now.

As she walked to the zoo entrance from the parking lot, she caught sight of the pachyderm building against the northern horizon and suddenly wondered about the method of Jerry's murder. If you were going to murder somebody, she asked herself, would you push him off something that was not high enough to guarantee his death, and then *hope* that the fall killed him? No, of course not. You'd be looking for a sure thing.

Which meant, she suddenly realized, that Jerry's death could have been a horrible, tragic accident. But that theory ignored the little matter of "signs of a struggle" that Barnes had mentioned when he was first interviewed on TV about Jerry's murder. The police must have considered and rejected the tragic accident scenario themselves.

She walked through the administration building toward Stevie's office at the back. As she drew closer, she could hear a rumble of voices coming from Stevie's cubicle. One of the voices was Stitcher's, although it had taken on a whiny, pleading tone that seemed out of place in one who so often bellowed. Charlotte realized with a start that another voice belonged to Detective Barnes.

Never shy about eavesdropping, she stood off to the side and tuned in. Luckily, the secretary that Stitcher and Stevie shared was not at her desk.

"Come on, Stevie," Stitcher wheedled. "All the detective is asking you to do is to look at a lousy piece of paper. It's not like he's asking you to accuse anybody."

"A piece of paper?" Stevie said. "Oh, I'm sorry. I didn't realize . . . I thought it was going to be something gory, the way you were talking."

"Just a piece of paper, Ms. Kimmel," Barnes said. "We're hoping you can identify it for us. Mr. Stitcher hasn't been able to, but we know that far more paper goes through your hands around here than through his."

Charlotte could hear Stitcher chuckling. He probably loved being characterized as someone who was not a paper-pusher.

There was a short silence. Charlotte assumed Barnes was showing Stevie the paper.

"Have you seen this before? Or anything like it?" Barnes asked. When Stevie didn't reply, Stitcher prodded, "Well, have you? For Chrissakes, Stevie, will you help the police? This zoo is dead in the water until we get Brobst's death cleared up!"

"Any thoughts, Ms. Kimmel? Have you seen this handwriting before? Does it look at all familiar?" Barnes asked.

"It's that crazy woman's handwriting," Stevie finally said.

"What crazy woman?" Barnes wanted to know.

"The woman they call Cheetah Rita," Stevie explained. "I'm not sure what this page is, but that's her handwriting on it."

"How can you be so sure?"

"Because I've seen enough of it." Stevie sounded exasperated. "The crazy old thing is forever writing us letters, complaining about one thing or another." She paused. "I guess you can call them letters."

"Complaining about what?"

Stitcher broke in, "*I've* never seen any such letters."

"I take the letters out of Mr. Stitcher's mail," Stevie explained—a bit defensively, Charlotte thought. "You can always tell which ones are hers because there are no stamps on the envelopes. I don't know how she gets them into our mail basket. But, then, we don't know how she slips into the zoo early in the morning, either."

"What do these letters say?" Barnes asked. "You mentioned complaints."

"That's right. She complains about a lot of things, but mostly about our treatment of the animals."

"Let me assure you, Detective, that the woman is completely unqual—"

"Do you have any of those letters, Ms. Kimmel? I'd like to take a look at them."

"No. I just pitch them. Lately, I haven't even been opening them. They never make much sense."

"But if you haven't even been opening them—"

"Lately. I said I haven't been opening them lately."

"Right. If you haven't even been opening then recently, how can you be so certain that the handwriting on the letters matches what is on this page?"

"Because I've seen enough of it to know. I know how she writes. For one thing, she prints all her capital letters. See there?"

"I see," Barnes said. "Now, Ms. Kimmel, do you have any thoughts about what this paper could be part of or be about?"

"It's obviously a page from a three-hole binder," Stevie said, sounding impatient.

Cheetah Rita's notebook! Charlotte fought the impulse to barge into Stevie's office to tell Barnes that Cheetah Rita had been missing her notebook.

"Anybody at the zoo could tell you that Cheetah Rita always writes in that notebook of hers," Stevie said. "She carries it in her briefcase, I guess."

"I can't read the handwriting very well, Ms. Kimmel. Would you mind taking a crack at it for us?"

Charlotte couldn't hear anything and assumed that Stevie was trying to read the paper. Finally, she heard, "I can't make it out either. Nothing that makes sense, anyway. Maybe she was keeping track of something down here. Where this row of single marks are? I don't know. Maybe not."

Charlotte was startled to notice that the secretary had returned to her desk and was watching her, eyes narrowed and mouth open. Who knew how long she had been there?

Charlotte smiled. "Just waiting for Stevie," she said lamely.

"Riiight," said the secretary, making no effort to hide her skepticism.

Unfortunately, this little drama distracted Charlotte from the last of the Stevie-Stitcher-Barnes conversation. In the next moment, Barnes and Stitcher came out of Stevie's office.

Looking startled at seeing Charlotte, Barnes said, "You seem to be everywhere, Ms. Sams."

"Everywhere I have a right to be," she said, quickly taking her reporter's notebook and a pencil out of her tote bag. "Now, I couldn't help but overhear you talk about a notebook page. What does that have to do with Jerry's murder investigation?"

Barnes looked annoyed and said "No comment" as he brushed past her and down the corridor.

Offended, she put the notebook and pencil back in the bag and considered that maybe she would never tell him that she knew Cheetah Rita had been missing her notebook. Why try to help such an arrogant man who obviously felt like he already knew everything worth knowing? It was exactly that attitude that had prevented her from confiding in him about the threatening taped message, too. (She didn't know what had kept her from telling Walt, except that she knew she hated it when he acted like a parent instead of a partner. He just couldn't seem to help it sometimes. On the other hand, Lou had been a pretty good audience for the tape . . .)

Now Stitcher was at her elbow, resplendent today in a green cowboy outfit. It was hard to take someone dressed like that seriously. "You and the detective seem to be acquainted," he said.

"Sort of."

"Well, I'll be glad when he's not hanging around here anymore, so this zoo can get back to business."

"But I've heard that your attendance figures have soared since Jerry's death," Charlotte said.

Stitcher grinned at her. "Dreadful business, isn't it?" he said and walked into his office.

Charlotte found Stevie behind her desk, adjusting the flower vase a half-inch. She asked her about the notebook page, but Stevie, too, was not talking. She told Charlotte that Barnes had told her and Stitcher not to discuss their conversation.

Charlotte conducted the interview only for appearance's sake, finding it difficult to talk about the more mundane aspects of the zoo when all she could think about was what looked like the most important development so far in Jerry's murder investigation: Barnes had a page from Cheetah Rita's notebook. Where could he have gotten it? What could it have to do with the murder? Did the person who stole the notebook kill Jerry? Maybe the notebook hadn't been stolen at all but had been left by Cheetah Rita at the spot where *she* killed Jerry.

Once again, she felt like she herself was inexorably bound up with Jerry's death. First, she had reason to think Jerry was killed to prevent him from telling her something. Now it appeared that a page from a document she had been accused of stealing was considered a clue by the police.

She had to talk with Cheetah Rita. Leaving Stevie's office as soon as she could, she set off for the male cheetah yard. The dank weather had cleared and on the way, she was dismayed to see Hogan scything an area near her own shacklike office in the North American section. He looked creepier than usual with the long-handled scythe, like some Victorian image of the Grim Reaper.

As far as her appearance and location went, Cheetah Rita might just as well not have moved since she and Charlotte had talked six days ago. Apparently concentrating so entirely on the cheetahs that she didn't hear her visitor coming, she looked up, frightened, when Charlotte reached her. Charlotte was momentarily unnerved and felt sympathetic toward the unkempt elderly woman seated before her.

Quickly she blurted out, "I wanted to make sure you know that the police have a page out of your notebook."

"I know it."

"So you must know that I didn't steal it."

"I know no such thing," Cheetah Rita said staunchly. "It wouldn't be the first time that the authorities were involved in the theft of scientific research and—"

"I didn't steal your research findings!" Charlotte shouted. "Why can't you understand that?"

Cheetah Rita looked unperturbed as she made another notation in the notebook open on her lap.

Angry at being so unjustly accused, Charlotte pressed on. "I don't know why the police would be interested in your notebook unless they found it at the scene of the crime, unless they considered it evidence, unless . . ."

"Unless they thought I killed the elephant keeper,"

Cheetah Rita said. She turned on the camp stool until she was looking Charlotte full in the face. Her eyes took on that funny yellow-brown glare that Charlotte had seen the first time they talked. "That's what they think, you know. That I killed him." Then she gave a short laugh that sent a chill down Charlotte's spine.

She was almost afraid to ask. "*Did* you?"

"No, but I'm not sorry he's dead," the older woman said calmly. "He didn't treat the elephants right, and he had no respect for my cats."

She seemed to be at the loony end of the continuum again and Charlotte couldn't tell how seriously to take her startling statements.

"Have the police returned the rest of your notebook?" she asked.

"People like that never give," Cheetah Rita said piously. "They only take."

"Well, would it help if I told them that I know your notebook has been missing?"

"It would help if you told me where the *rest* of it is."

"How would I know? Why don't you tell me where the police found the page they have?"

"That Brown Shirt Barnes told me they found it on top of the pachyderm building."

Charlotte laughed out loud. Regulation-bound though he might be, she had never once considered Barnes to be even slightly tinged with fascism. Maybe Cheetah Rita had realized he liked dogs.

Charlotte said, "Well, you must have an alibi for the night Jerry was killed, or they would have already arrested you."

"I was at home."

"Where's home?"

"None of your business."

She was right, of course. After a moment, Charlotte said, "I've been wondering how you get back and forth from home to the zoo."

"I walk, of course. You drive."

"Of course. How do you get in?"

"The zoo is open every day."

"Yes, but the staff says you get in before it opens in the morning and leave after everything is closed up."

"Drives them crazy, doesn't it?" Cheetah Rita said matter-of-factly.

Charlotte smiled. "I guess it does."

"Well, you can tell them I fly in," Cheetah Rita said. And then she laughed her chilling laugh once more.

"Well, tell me, do you ever fly up to the roof of the pachyderm building?"

But Cheetah Rita had turned back to her cheetahs. Apparently Charlotte's audience was over.

Back in her zoo office and writing with the small computer on her lap and her feet propped up on the old desk, Charlotte realized that she had found Cheetah Rita more likable during this latest conversation—just as nutty, perhaps, but more likable. At least this time she hadn't taken a swing at Charlotte.

She couldn't help wondering, however, whether she had taken a swing at Jerry and sent him over the edge of the roof. Somehow her denial had not been overwhelmingly convincing. Maybe that was because everything about her seemed so eccentric and unreliable. All of which didn't make her a murderer, Charlotte reminded herself. She found herself hoping that Barnes was not planning to arrest her.

Then she wondered about Cheetah Rita knowing that she drove to the zoo. Was that meaningful? Probably not, since everybody did (except Cheetah Rita, to hear her tell it). But what if Charlotte's mode of transportation was on Cheetah Rita's mind because it was *she* who slashed the convertible top last week? After all, during their first conversation, she had said she'd been watching Charlotte. It wouldn't have taken much to figure out which car was hers. And the vandalism *had* happened shortly after Cheetah Rita had accused her of stealing her notebook.

Now Charlotte wondered whether the notebook had ever been stolen at all. Maybe Cheetah Rita had simply forgotten she left it on top of the pachyderm building after pushing Jerry off. Old people misplaced things all the time. And having just pushed someone over the edge *would* have been a distraction. At least, Charlotte hoped it would have been a distraction. She would like to think that killing people was not a usual activity for Cheetah Rita. Maybe the nutty old lady *did* belong in jail.

There was at least one thing wrong with this theory, she finally realized. The police seemed not to have the whole notebook, but only a page. Where was the rest of it? Charlotte wondered.

A few minutes later, Charlotte carried her computer to the pay phone in the gift shop to modem her small story about the notebook page to the *Dispatch*. She didn't think it was enough to run by itself and expected to have the facts of her story confirmed and folded into a larger piece written by a staff writer. That was okay with her: she would receive some compensation for her work, and the *Dispatch's* pressure on the police would have a better chance of flushing out the truth. It had been a productive morning.

Later in the day, Charlotte walked up the broad paved path that separated the yards between Asian elephants and African elephants. She congratulated herself on finally being able to tell one kind from another, the Asians being smaller, lighter in color, and more barrel-shaped than the Africans.

The two Africans were in their yard languidly flapping their enormous, heavily veined ears in the morning sun. She stopped to watch those ears, which she thought were actually shaped like the continent of Africa.

Once she entered the south door of the pachyderm building, she was momentarily blinded as her eyes adjusted to the darkened atmosphere inside. But her nose knew where she was even if her eyes didn't.

Koko, whom Charlotte considered to be a lethal weapon after last week's encounter, was alone in his enclosure. But Barbara Champion, wearing her usual baseball cap, was in with Indy, her ankus leaning against a wall nearby, as she put the great gray beast through some of her paces before her bath. Charlotte was reminded that her interview with Jerry was to have been about elephant training.

She walked over to Indy's enclosure and yelled "Hi" to Barbara.

"How's the arm?" Barbara asked.

"Okay."

"Want to come in to watch?"

"Hah!"

"Maybe it's just as well," Barbara said. "She's a handful this morning." Her eyes never left the hulking Indy as she spoke. "I'll try to keep her close enough for you to see from there."

Barbara guided Indy toward the bars on Charlotte's side of the enclosure. On the way, she skillfully sidestepped an errant foot and leg the size of a tree trunk and spoke sharply to Indy.

"Was she *trying* to step on you?" Charlotte asked.

Barbara laughed. "I think so," she said. "I don't know why she's being so cantankerous this morning."

Nonetheless, at Barbara's verbal commands, Indy stepped forward, stepped back, and lifted one foot at a time by bending her leg at the knee.

Charlotte marveled at the control Barbara had over the huge beast. With skill like this, she wondered, how could Koko's charge on her have caught Barbara by surprise? Maybe it hadn't, she considered for the first time. Maybe Barbara hadn't acted to prevent the charge because she wanted Charlotte to see how dangerous the elephants were and how brave Barbara must be to work with them.

Or, she suddenly thought as her blood ran cold, maybe Koko's charge hadn't been an accident at all but was choreographed by Barbara to scare Charlotte away from the zoo. Maybe Barbara had thought that an elephant charge would be enough to make her stop asking questions about Jerry's death. The possibility nearly took Charlotte's breath away. She resolved to be very careful around Barbara.

A moment later Barbara explained, "The best reason for training zoo elephants is all the foot care they need. If they're trained, we can do it without tranquilizers."

Doing just one foot took about a half-hour, so the keepers rarely did all four feet at once, she said. It was just too exhausting for keeper and elephant. Today's foot was Indy's right front.

In response to Barbara's command of "foot up," Indy bent her right front leg at the knee and lifted her foot. Since Charlotte couldn't see the foot bottom, Barbara described the sole of Indy's foot to her as consisting of flat and roughly calloused pads, with deep cracks through them.

She explained that her first task was to remove anything, like pebbles, that was caught in the cracks. Then she would carve away the edges of the tough pads themselves with hoof knives that had been invented for horses.

As she talked, Barbara inspected the bottom of the huge foot and occasionally spoke soothing chatter to Indy.

"Well, would you look at that?" she said after a little while.

Charlotte gladly would have, but couldn't see the foot bottom from where she stood. Barbara reached down for one of her knives and told Charlotte she'd have to use its tip to pry something out of a crack in Indy's sole. Turning a few moments later, she held the object out to Charlotte.

Charlotte refused to put her hand between the bars to take the object. Barbara laughed and tossed it to her. It was the top to an expensive fountain pen.

"Didn't this hurt her?" Charlotte asked.

"In the place where it was lodged, yes, although not all of what an elephant picks up on its feet has to hurt. But she's got a bad bruise there now from that thing."

"Maybe that's why she was acting nasty earlier."

"That was nothing, Charlotte," Barbara said seriously. "Believe me, you haven't seen nasty from an elephant yet—even from Koko the other day. But you could be right that that pen top was bothering her."

Then Barbara said, "You know, you could help us a lot if you wrote about that pen top in one of your articles. You could show a picture of it and tell people to stop throwing such things into the animals' cages. Indy's lucky she stepped on it rather than ate it. Something like that could get lodged in her intestine and kill her."

Charlotte pocketed the pen top and agreed to make a plea that visitors restrain some of their thoughtless habits.

After Barbara had finished Indy's bath and could take a break, she and Charlotte left the pachyderm building, bought some coffee at a concession stand outside, and sat down at one of the tables. Barbara had offered to get both coffees and bring them to a table, but Charlotte insisted on getting her own. She felt she couldn't be too careful around Barbara.

Once they were seated, and in an effort to keep things light and not reveal her suspicions, Charlotte asked her if the similarity between her name and that of Babar the elephant in the children's books had inspired her to work with elephants.

Barbara treated the question very seriously and said that she had never read those stories. "But that's probably the only thing about elephants I haven't read," she said. At thirty-eight, she had been working with the elephants at the Columbus Zoo for twenty years.

"I appreciate you showing me your routine with Indy today."

Barbara said she enjoyed demonstrating her skills. "You know, I've been here at the zoo so long that I was here to show Jack Hanna some of the ropes with our elephants. But when the former head elephant keeper retired, I had to threaten to file a sex discrimination suit to get my job."

Barbara was warming to her subject. "There's always somebody around that doesn't think you can do the job unless you have a dick," she said, surprising Charlotte with her directness. "What does having a penis have to do with whether you can do the work with the elephants here?"

What indeed? thought Charlotte.

"You have to study and learn and use your brain. I know those elephants are big, but human muscles aren't going to save you from elephant damage. You have to use your head."

Unaccustomed to many keepers opening up to her like this, Charlotte wondered whether it was only coffee that Barbara was drinking. "I bet you miss Jerry," she said.

Barbara snorted. "Jerry Brobst? Nah. He thought he was God's gift to elephants as much as he was God's gift to women. Although I will have to admit that he could really work well with them if he wanted to. The elephants, I mean.

"Women, too, I suppose," she said wryly. "It was just that most of the time he thought he could do what he wanted, not what needed to be done—especially not what I told him needed to be done. I know he didn't like working for a woman, but I earned this job through long years of hard work. He should have been able to respect that."

"Didn't he?" Charlotte asked.

"Oh, no. Not Jerry. He thought a smile and a wink were all he needed to get his own way with any female that walked the earth, and when that didn't work with me, he just tried to ignore me. He used to make me furious by ignoring me and going over my head to my boss when he didn't like what I told him to do. He was not an easy man to like."

"Who do you think pushed him off that roof?" Charlotte asked.

"Who knows? Maybe one of his women, ticked off because he was spreading himself thinner than usual."

"I guess you weren't at the zoo that night," Charlotte prompted.

"I was not one of Jerry's women either, Charlotte," Barbara said sternly. Then she went on. "I was hardly here that whole day because I had to get out to the 4-H camp to do a presentation. Hanna always taught us never to give a presentation without taking an animal along. Luckily for us elephant keepers, it doesn't have to be our own animals." Barbara smiled. "I took a ferret with me."

"How difficult would it have been for someone to get up on the roof?"

"Not very. Just about anybody could have gotten into that interior stairway and then on up, especially if Jerry had let that person in."

Suddenly Barbara looked contrite. "I really am sorry he's dead," she said, sounding serious, and Charlotte believed her. But then Barbara finished, "I'm going to have to replace him, and people who can work with elephants are hard to come by."

So much for heartfelt grief, Charlotte thought.

Chapter 15

That evening Lou called Charlotte, bubbling over with news about a weekend jaunt to Marietta to see the melodrama on the paddlewheel steamboat.

"You would have loved it, Charlotte," she said. "Cheering the hero, hissing the villain . . ."

"Let me tell you about hissing the villain," interrupted Charlotte. "Barbara Champion, the head elephant keeper—"

"Who was going to show you the elephant manicure today?"

"Pedicure, Lou. Well, Barbara found a pen top embedded in one of Indy's feet, which was interesting all right, but not the most interesting thing I found out today. She says she and Jerry did not get along *at all*."

"Did she hate him enough to kill him?"

Charlotte suddenly realized that Barbara hadn't exactly said she *hated* Jerry, and disliking a person enough to kill him did not seem to be a serious possibility. Maybe she had jumped to conclusions about Barbara.

"Are you still there, Charlotte?"

"Sorry. I was just thinking. To tell you the truth, I was surprised that Barbara mentioned anything at all negative about her relationship with Jerry, given that he's dead and the police are looking for his killer. I mean, I wouldn't let people know how heartily *I* disliked someone who had been murdered, would you?"

"Oh, I don't know. If other people knew about it, maybe it would seem funny if she acted as though everything was fine between them. Maybe *that* would seem incriminating." Then Lou asked, "Exactly what didn't she like about Jerry?"

Charlotte told her some of the things Barbara had said.

"Hmmm. Interesting, isn't it?" Lou said. "Sounds like she thought Jerry's actions belittled her, which can be humiliating. And getting revenge for humiliation can be a powerful motivator."

"For murder?"

"For lots of behavior. All of us are sensitive to anything that smacks of humiliation. But some people's egos are so damaged by it that they seek to punish the humiliator and, when possible, insure that he can't humiliate them again. Sometimes they're willing to do that at all costs."

"Like push the humiliator off the roof, I'll bet."

"That's the hard part: in all but the most obvious cases, we can't really predict who's likely to become violent."

"Well, it's become difficult for me to predict who I'm going to suspect next of Jerry's murder since I received that threatening message on my tape."

"Poor Charlotte. I wish you'd shown that tape to Detective Barnes."

"And have him dismiss me like he did when I told him about Jerry wanting to talk with a reporter? No thanks. The only thing worse would have been to show the tape to Walt and have *him* take my plight *too* seriously. I swear, that man would have forbade me to set one foot inside the zoo again." She paused a moment, then said cheerfully, "Not that I would have paid any attention to him."

"I was about to point that out. But you know you have to be very, very careful at the zoo, don't you, Charlotte?"

"Sure. I'm getting so careful that I wouldn't even let Barbara carry my coffee to the table today, lest she slip me some poison on the way."

"A little healthy paranoia can be a positive thing, I always say."

"Do you think it's paranoid for me to wonder whether Barbara could have staged Koko's charge at me—you know, to scare me away from the zoo? She usually has extraordinary control over the elephants."

"Didn't that happen right after Jerry's body was found?"

"Yes."

"Then it seems like Barbara or anyone else wouldn't have known at that point you were going to investigate Jerry's death."

"Unless they thought I already knew Jerry was very anxious to talk to a reporter."

"Does Barbara have an alibi for the night Jerry was killed?"

"She says she gave a presentation at a 4-H camp."

"The one in Delaware County?" Lou asked.

"I don't know, really, but that's the closest one."

"If so, then I know the guy who runs the place. His wife was a colleague of mine at the research center at Ohio State. If you'd like, Charlotte, I could call him tomorrow and ask about what happened that night."

"I guess it is about time that we check out Barbara's alibi."

The next morning, Lou put in a call to the 4-H camp in Delaware County. She caught Pete, the director, just as he was sitting down for his coffee break. As he already had his mug of coffee and a doughnut, he was willing to chat.

Lou explained that she was working on career programs for one of the local junior high schools and that they were trying to line up speakers for the fall. She said, "Somebody told me that you invited one of the keepers from the Columbus Zoo to talk to your kids recently. How did that go?"

"Shoot, Lou, I thought you were going to ask me to tell those kids about my job—tell them how they could go to summer camp forever."

Well, why not? She could probably find a school that would be interested. "Of course, we'd love to have you if you're willing to do it," she said. "Sometime in November. I'll call to set a date after Labor Day. But tell me, how did the zoo keeper work out? Could you recommend him as a speaker?"

Pete's guffaw prompted Lou to hold the telephone receiver a foot away from her ear. "What?" she said. "What was so funny about him?"

"Not him. Her. The zookeeper was a female. Barbara Champion. She's the head elephant keeper, in fact."

"That's funny, is it? I guess Vi wasn't able to talk you out of renewing your MCP license, was she?"

"Now, Lou, you know my wife loves me in spite of my chauvinistic tendencies."

Patience, Lou said to herself, you need to find out what happened. "Was her presentation funny? Is that why I'm going to need a hearing aid?"

"No, her presentation was fine," he said at a normal decibel level, sounding chagrined. "Fine. No complaints there. She brought a ferret with her that she took out of its cage. She let the group come up and touch it and ask questions and so on. She really did a beautiful job on the presentation."

"Then what was so funny?" Lou persisted.

"While we were eating supper one of those seventh-graders opened the ferret's cage and, of course, the thing skedaddled. Unfortunately, it skedaddled right into the swimming pool. Barbara saw it happen, got up from the table, and dove right in after it with all her clothes on."

"Can't ferrets swim?"

"It seemed to be staying on top of the water, but of

course it couldn't have gotten out of the pool unless it could climb the ladder. And I don't know whether ferrets can climb ladders, do you?"

"I have absolutely no idea," Lou said, wishing he'd get on with the story, for God's sake.

"Turns out that it was the chlorine that was bothering Barbara. She wanted to get the ferret out of the pool before the chlorine made it sick. Or killed it, probably."

"And that was funny?" There was disbelief in Lou's voice.

"No, but you didn't see her, Lou. She wasn't Venus rising from the foam, it was more like a whale sounding." A chuckle or two escaped him.

"I see," said Lou. "Not just sexism, but sizeism as well. Barbara Champion was too big to suit you?"

"Sizeism? That's a new one on me. Whatever you do, don't tell Vi about this new one."

"I hope the ferret was okay."

"She scrubbed that thing with soap just like you would one of those ratty little dogs, wrapped it in two of our bath towels and rushed off back to the zoo. Didn't even stay for our sunset bonfire."

"It sounds as though she'd be a good bet for one of our programs. Very responsible. Thanks for your help, Pete. Say hello to Vi for me."

"Will do." Pete hung up, happy with his memories.

Fuming, Lou immediately called Charlotte at her office. "I don't know why I let him get to me—*I* don't have to live with him," she said as soon as Charlotte answered. "It's just that he influences all those kids."

"Are you talking about Mr. 4-H?"

Lou said she was and described the conversation she had just completed, still annoyed at the way Pete had disparaged Barbara's size. But Charlotte was more interested in her timing.

"If she left the camp before the sunset activities, she

couldn't have been there after ten," she said. "Most likely, she left before nine, maybe even earlier, since they were eating supper when the pool incident happened. So the camp stuff really doesn't explain Barbara's whereabouts between ten and midnight, when Jerry was killed, does it?"

Chapter **16**

That afternoon Charlotte headed south on High Street from Clintonville, her destination City Hall on West Broad Street. She'd been summoned by a call earlier in the day from the director of the Columbus Recreation and Parks Department, Sigrid Olson. The call had come while she had been reading the *Dispatch* story about Cheetah Rita's notebook page having been found on the pachyderm building roof.

She knew Sigrid only slightly. They had met when Charlotte had been trying to find out who murdered her cousin's husband, and she could not imagine that Sigrid remembered their interaction with any fondness. Why was she so eager to chat now?

Charlotte decided she would risk parking at a one-hour meter while she was in City Hall, but was unable to find an open spot on the street within three blocks. Giving up, she pulled into the parking garage located under the state capitol building in the center of downtown. At least it was cheaper than the surface lots operated by local tycoons who, because of the state of the economy, had blacktopped several downtown lots of prime real estate, rather than put up buildings.

She was only about three blocks from City Hall as she came up the garage stairwell, which smelled of urine and who knew what else, on the corner of Broad and High. She waited to cross High with the light, a habit developed when the city's annual budget had seemed to be based entirely on fines for jaywalking. She would be willing to wager that the people who lived in Columbus during those years were more likely to wait at red lights than pedestrians in any other American city.

She headed west, noticing that the marquee at the Palace Theater was dark as she walked past on the other side of the street. Midsummer was not a good time for stage shows in Columbus, at least indoors. The Picnic with the Pops series with the symphony orchestra was thriving on the lawn of the Chemical Abstracts complex just north of the Ohio State University campus, and the new series of star attractions at the zoo seemed to have caught on. Last year, Mandy Patinkin had won the competition against the peacocks by incorporating their noises into his show.

The twenty-foot-tall metal statue of Christopher Columbus, a gift from the city of Genoa, gazed out on Broad Street from the front of City Hall. Its green patina was well advanced, giving Chris a slightly seasick look.

City Hall had been built in the early 1930s, at first an opulent building with lots of polished stone, brass doors, dark wood, and gracious open spaces. Now, it was jammed to the hilt with not-so-temporary dividers cutting into the spaces and fake wood paneling applied to the lower parts of walls that had been painted an institutional green.

Just inside the southwest doors, Charlotte noticed that the seal of Columbus had been carved into the coconut fiber floor mat laid into the stone floor. Didn't anybody but she think it was odd for city government to encourage people to deliberately wipe their feet on this symbol of the city? she wondered. But then, how much confidence could one have in a government whose first door inside was engraved with the message "Trustees of the Sinking Fund"?

On the way to Sigrid's office in Room 127, she passed through the Columbus Hall of Fame, which consisted of photos and brief descriptions of the exploits of well-known Columbusites. Most of the people represented there were male sports figures, including the fired but now venerated football coach Woody Hayes, boxer James "Buster" Douglas, golfer Jack Nicklaus, and two of Ohio State's four Heisman Trophy winners. Women appeared to have contributed to Columbus chiefly by having won four Miss America titles.

She read the bio for Harry Preston Wolfe, whose family owned the *Dispatch* and had started the Columbus Zoo with the gift of two reindeer housed in old Beechwold, the neighborhood just north of Clintonville. His family had remained interested in the zoo and continued to hold seats on the nonprofit corporation called the Zoo Association Board that ran it.

Moving past a wall of student-created posters on the left, Charlotte entered through beautiful old brass doors that led to a room filled with dividers. Sigrid's secretary popped out from one of the spaces and told her that Ms. Olson wanted her to go right in. So she tapped lightly on a solid dark oak door, opened it, and walked in.

Sigrid was busily scribbling on a typed sheet that lay on the blotter in front of her. She looked up at Charlotte, smiled, and said, "I'll have this finished in a minute. Please sit down, Charlotte."

Charlotte sat in an armchair by the desk, which looked as though it had been there for a least half a century. She took advantage of the wait to appraise Sigrid and her surroundings. Sigrid looked the same as before: tall, athletic body; perfect, even features in a slightly heart-shaped face, with bright blue eyes and long pale blond hair curled at the ends. She was beautiful, quite unlike her current surroundings.

Heavy dark oak bookcases with glass fronts held city reports, computer printouts, and an assortment of athletic equipment. Above the bookcases were what appeared to be sample cases with leaves, flowers, butterflies, and insects pinned to the backs. Fortunately, there were no buffalo heads or champion fish mounted on boards. Nevertheless, Charlotte, who was used to working in an amiable clutter, felt almost claustrophobic.

There was a tiny backboard mounted on the wastebasket next to the desk, its hoop and net waiting to receive whatever was tossed that way.

Sigrid raised her head, crumpled a couple of sheets of paper into a ball, and tossed them at the wastebasket. "Two points," she announced. "Charlotte, I'm so glad you could come today."

"I'm very curious about why you wanted to talk with me. I assume it has something do with my zoo series for *Ohio Magazine*?"

"Sort of. I remember how well you went about finding out what really happened when Phil died at that art exhibit, and I wanted to ask you to help me with what's going on at the zoo."

Flattered, Charlotte asked, "What *is* going on at the zoo?"

Sigrid looked upset. "I think they're going to arrest Jane Wilcox for murdering the elephant keeper, and that's just— out of the question. I can't let that happen."

Charlotte was surprised that an arrest seem imminent, but then a look of total bewilderment crossed her face. "Jane Wilcox? Who's Jane Wilcox?"

"She's the one the zoo people call Cheetah Rita. I'm surprised you don't know her."

"Oh, I know her. I just didn't know her real name," Charlotte said, feeling a little guilty that she had never even asked about it. "How do you know her?"

"Miss Wilcox was my high school biology teacher in Youngstown."

Charlotte waited for more. When it didn't come, she prompted, "She must have been a very good teacher for you to be so concerned about her now."

"She was. Very good." Sigrid swallowed, took a deep breath, and then went on. "But more important than that, she helped me understand that I was a worthwhile person, even though I didn't look like Goldie Hawn or Sally Struthers. Remember how popular the look and style of those two stars were? Dumb blonde? And short?"

Charlotte nodded encouragingly, even though she had never once considered the height of Sally Struthers or Goldie Hawn. Now, how thin and tanned they were was another story . . .

"I was six feet tall by the time I was a high school sophomore. For obvious reasons, some people called me 'Stretch.' Of course, I hated that. To make matters worse, I tended to be clumsy.

"But Miss Wilcox was different, too—smarter and unmarried and more focused than the other teachers. She knew how I felt. So she helped me a lot, by pointing out that I could do many things that short girls can't, for instance." Sigrid paused and looked down at her desk for a few moments. "Charlotte, I was just so appreciative that somebody paid a little extra attention to me that didn't have to do with sports."

This was obviously difficult for Sigrid to talk about. It was certainly difficult for Charlotte to imagine the beautiful and confident Sigrid of today as a gawky high school girl. Her tall, photogenic person was often interviewed on local television news shows, and when she had worked for Columbus Power and Light, she had made frequent commercials to pitch the notion of wise power use. All of that had followed her career as a leading scorer on Ohio State's women's basketball team in the late 1970s.

Now she went on. "Miss Wilcox was from the Columbus area and had gone to Ohio State. So she was very influential in my deciding to go there, too. And you know what a good decision that turned out to be." She looked at Charlotte, seemingly for confirmation.

Charlotte nodded. "She must have been very proud of your basketball playing."

"I suppose so," Sigrid said in a small voice. "Several years after I graduated from high school, I heard that Miss Wilcox's father had gotten very sick with diabetes and that she had had to give up teaching and come back here to Columbus to take care of him. But I didn't hear any more about her until I moved into this job and she started sending me notes."

Ah, the notes again. Cheetah Rita's paper trail. "What kind of notes?" Charlotte asked. "And how did she even know you were here?"

"I suppose she read in the paper about me taking this job. And maybe she thinks that the Department of Recreation and Parks supervises the zoo. A lot of people think that, you know. They don't know about the Zoo Association Board."

"Right," Charlotte said.

"They don't know that I have only one seat on that board."

"Of course. But what are the notes like?"

"They were just—notes. About problems she sees at the zoo. I haven't received one for quite some time now."

"Did she seem lucid in the notes?"

"Not entirely. But I'm sure she's just slipped a little, Charlotte. And slipping a little isn't a crime. After all, she's well over sixty.

"I'm very upset that anyone would think that such a kind, productive person—she taught one of the *life* sciences, for heaven's sake!—could actually kill someone," Sigrid said, visibly holding back tears. "She's really very gentle, and I think the police are concentrating on her just because she's handy. It's easy for people to think that someone who is a little different, maybe even a little senile, could do something that is *really* different—like murder someone. But I'm certain she didn't do it."

"I still don't know what all this has to do with me," Charlotte said.

"I want you to keep your eyes open," Sigrid implored. "Talk to people. See if anyone else had a motive to kill the elephant keeper and let me know if you turn up anything. Maybe if the police had someone else who could have done it, they'd stop concentrating on Miss Wilcox."

"What makes you so sure they're concentrating on her?"

"Well, I read the article in this morning's *Dispatch* about a page of her notebook being found near where the elephant keeper was pushed off the roof. And since then I've talked with the police detective in charge of the investigation."

"Did Detective Barnes actually say he's ready to arrest her?"

If Sigrid was surprised that Charlotte knew the name of the detective in charge, she did not show it.

"My conversation with him was completely confidential, I'm afraid," she said. "I'm sure he was willing to speak with me about the investigation only because I head a city department. I don't think he'd want me to share our conversation."

"Oh, come on, Sigrid," Charlotte said. "You drag me down here and ask for my help, and now you're pulling rank on me. What did Barnes tell you?"

Sigrid looked down at her desk and Charlotte let the silence stretch out.

Finally Sigrid said, "Well, I don't remember everything he said."

Charlotte kept still.

"Well, maybe just a few things. I know he said that the elephant keeper's fingerprints were on the notebook page, as well as Miss Wilcox's."

"Does that mean Jerry was the one who stole Cheetah Rita's notebook?" Charlotte demanded.

"I didn't know it had been stolen. Oh, that poor woman!" Sigrid wailed.

"Why is Barnes so short of suspects? *Lots* of zoo employees could have been at the zoo at some point on the Sunday Jerry was killed. Do all of them have alibis?"

"I guess so. I remember him saying that it is taking a long time to verify who was there late. They still hope Bob will remember."

"Bob? Stitcher, you mean? Remember what?"

Sigrid looked stricken. "I shouldn't have said that."

"But now you have. So give, Sigrid."

"It's just that the director was one of the last to leave that day at dusk, when the zoo closed. But he can't remember whose cars were still in the parking lot when he left."

"What makes them think he might eventually remember?"

"They say it happens all the time—that we forget relatively minor things but are able to recall them eventually by not concentrating on them. The memory just sort of floats to the top of our awareness—if we let it. The police psychologist has given him several relaxation exercises to do, which they think might help."

Charlotte had a mental image of Stitcher listening to relaxation tapes and practicing deep breathing while dressed in his cowboy togs. Her laughter broke the spell with Sigrid, who refused to share any more information she had picked up from Barnes.

Finally Charlotte asked, "Have you talked with Miss Wilcox? Recently, I mean?"

"Only once. I was visiting the zoo about six months ago and there she was by the cheetahs—Miss Wilcox. She looked about the same, although she was dressed a little more informally than she did when teaching."

I should hope so, thought Charlotte, thinking of Cheetah Rita's camo outfits and rubber boots.

"I stopped to talk to her and she told me her father had died and that now she finally has the time she has always wanted to study cheetahs."

"She's studied them all right—almost constantly for two years. Have you talked to anyone at the zoo about her?"

"Only that Kimmel girl. She thinks Miss Wilcox is crazy. The rest of the staff probably does, too, but she's not. I'm sure she's not. Maybe she's a little eccentric, but she's very smart."

"When you talked to Miss Wilcox," Charlotte couldn't

resist asking, "did she happen to mention the kingdom of the cats?"

Sigrid ignored the question, so Charlotte assumed that the subject of the cat kingdom had been broached. Or maybe something else just as interesting. Perhaps Sigrid had made the unfortunate mistake of declaring herself to be a dog lover.

"You've got to help her, Charlotte."

"She's made it plain that she wouldn't accept help from me."

"Then help me. Do it as a favor to me."

Charlotte considered Sigrid's pleading facial expression.

"I don't for a moment think it's normal to believe in the kingdom of the cats," she said, "but I don't know that that makes her dangerous, either. And I have sympathy for someone who is obsessive about finding out things—I can get that way myself. Just not for two years at a time."

Sigrid quickly said, "When I talked with her at the zoo, she told me she had a lot of time to make up for in her study, time that was spent taking care of her father full-time."

"She still might be crazy."

"Please, Charlotte," Sigrid said, getting up from her desk and walking over to shut the door. "The thing is, I feel very guilty about Ms. Wilcox. She practically saved my sanity when I was in high school, but then when I went away to college, I never kept in touch with her. Not once did I send her a letter or even phone her. I just got too busy, being away from home for the first time and feeling that I had made a place of my own at last. You know how it is. But I never really thanked the person who had made it all possible for me. Who made all this possible for me."

She waved her arm expansively to take in the crowded conglomeration in the room. Apparently, Sigrid had found a home, and Charlotte was touched that it was in this very modest city government office rather than in her sleek, expensive office at CP&L.

In the end, and against her better judgment, she agreed

to let Sigrid know if she turned up anything that could have been a motive for Jerry's murder—held by someone other than Cheetah Rita—as she researched her articles. At the same time, she would keep a protective eye on Cheetah Rita. However, she warned Sigrid, she would not let their agreement get in the way of her reporting accurately and fairly.

"I have to call them like I see them," Charlotte said.

"Of course, of course," Sigrid said. "I wouldn't expect anything else. But I'm so relieved that you've agreed to help keep me informed about the zoo."

Charlotte left soon after, cutting off Sigrid's complaints about how difficult it was for her to get information from Stitcher even though she had been on the search committee who recommended that he be hired.

Chapter **17**

After receiving the taped threat, Charlotte had been reluctant to resume her exercise regimen, somehow connecting the threat with her walk, since that was when it had been delivered. But she knew that was silly. There was no reason to think that she was any more vulnerable on a walk around her neighborhood than anywhere else. She had managed to convince herself to resume walking but still hadn't the nerve to put on the Walkman earphones again. Who knew what revolting message could come from them next? So the next morning she took her walk without music or mystery.

It was just as well, given how much she had to think about. Yesterday she had taken Sigrid's emotional request at face value, but in the clear light of a new day, she wasn't so sure. Was Sigrid simply asking her to look after Cheetah Rita, who had been Miss Wilcox in a previous lifetime? Or was that merely an excuse to get Charlotte to help Sigrid in another way? Would Charlotte find out later that Sigrid really wanted something else—maybe to learn what Charlotte knew about some other situation at the zoo, not necessarily the murder investigation?

For instance, now that Hanna was gone and Stitcher couldn't exactly be called an overnight success, maybe Sigrid could use some zoo "intelligence" because her Department of Recreation and Parks was trying to wrest control of the zoo from the Zoo Association Board. Charlotte wouldn't mind helping Sigrid protect an elderly friend who was eccentric—if that's all Cheetah Rita was. But she had no intention of becoming Sigrid's "mole" at the zoo.

Briefly she considered whether Sigrid's involvement could be more sinister. Could she have known Jerry Brobst and what he had wanted to tell a reporter about? Charlotte didn't have any evidence of that. In fact, she couldn't remember Sigrid even using Jerry's name during their conversation yesterday, referring to him only as the elephant keeper. But, of course, something like that could be quite purposeful.

On the other hand, having all these suspicions was exhausting and Charlotte was tired of them. Maybe Sigrid wanted exactly what she said she wanted: to help an old friend—someone who had helped her, someone who was in trouble. And it certainly looked like Cheetah Rita was in trouble. Charlotte wondered whether Sigrid would pay for Cheetah Rita's legal defense if she was arrested.

Now *that* would make for an interesting story: the head of a city department paying for the defense of a woman against whom the city police department had brought murder charges.

If Sigrid's motivation was on the side of the angels, then Charlotte had truly misjudged the woman. Although she had not known Sigrid well, before yesterday she had pegged her as completely self-absorbed and interested only in her own career.

It would be wonderful if Sigrid was not as self-centered as she thought. But Charlotte didn't like the idea that she might have so seriously misjudged her. It brought up other possibilities.

Stevie Kimmel, for instance. Had Charlotte misjudged her as well? Was there more to Stevie than she had given her credit for? Stevie obviously cared for her nephew—that had been easy to see at the swimming pool. But even then, her appreciation of him had seemed keyed to what he could *do*—go off the diving board at a tender age, for instance—rather than that he just *was*.

Charlotte didn't think the notion of unconditional love was part of Stevie's emotional repertoire. She just seemed too competitive. Of course, that was by Charlotte's own standards, she realized. And who had appointed her Ms. Quality Control?

She knew it was just as well that she was on her walk, for if she had been working in either office, thinking this hard would have required that she pace around quite a bit, as was her habit.

She circled back toward home by using a route that took her past a particular house at the end of her street. She had watched this house with fascination for years. Today it seemed to be a metaphor for her life at the moment.

The house was in a perpetual state of becoming. Its owners had systematically added multiple bay windows, added rooms on the back, changed the lines of the house by adding wide overhangs, put up balconies, constructed a turret, built a garage out back, added an apartment on the top floor of the garage, built a play yard for their children, and as the children got older, a fenced basketball court. And all of this had been accomplished on a conventional city lot.

Now they were building an elevated walkway from the house to the apartment over the garage. But it wasn't just a walk with a roof over it. No, it was entirely enclosed, with wide windows all along both sides.

Every time she thought there was nothing more the owners could do to the house, they started another project. She loved that house because it was what the people who lived in it *made it become*. Perhaps, she thought, she should regard herself as a work in progress, too.

•   •   •

She went to the zoo that afternoon, full of good cheer and tolerance, anxious to give Stevie and even the strange Cheetah Rita a break—as well as to ask Bob Stitcher about the cars in the parking lot the night Jerry was killed.

She attended to business first. Stevie's and Stitcher's secretary was away from her desk, so Charlotte just knocked lightly at the acoustical screen that helped frame Stitcher's doorway. Sitting at his desk, he waved her into the office. But as soon as Charlotte said she wanted to ask him a couple of questions about the cars in the parking lot, he put both hands over his ears and yelled, "Get out! Get out! I'm not supposed to think about that. You'll set me back a week of listening to those stupid tapes! Get out!" She got out.

Cheetah Rita was next on her list. Charlotte found her, seated on her camp stool outside the female cheetah yard this time, staring at the spotted cats behind the metal openwork fence. When Charlotte got close, Cheetah Rita looked over her shoulder and said belligerently, "Leave me alone!"—an action that even someone in Charlotte's benevolent frame of mind found hard to view sympathetically.

In an effort to put herself more on Cheetah Rita's level, she seated herself on the ground near the camp stool. As usual, she could barely see the cats lying in the grass. But she could see quite clearly the path they had worn right inside the fence around the perimeter of their yard. It made her feel sad to think of the cheetahs spending a lifetime in a fruitless search for a chink in the fence that stood between them and freedom. It seemed even sadder that the freedom they were compelled to seek probably would have amounted to being struck by a car on Riverside Drive.

Cheetah Rita, Charlotte thought, must have made her peace with the cheetah's situation long ago. Right now, it was obvious that she saw more than Charlotte did in their behavior, as she watched them intently and then periodically wrote things in her notebook. She was nothing if not methodical about the cats, Charlotte thought.

"Miss Wilcox," Charlotte finally said, "I talked with one of your old students yesterday. Sigrid Olson."

"You mean Stretch?"

Charlotte winced. "She told me you were a good teacher."

"Hah! I bet she told you I was a tough old bag. Mean to the kids."

"No, she said you were very nice to her, that you helped her."

"Well, she won't help the zoo animals."

"She doesn't supervise the zoo, Miss Wilcox."

"It doesn't matter now."

"What do you mean?"

"Stop trying to get me to say amusing things for your readers!"

"Sigrid told me Jerry Brobst's fingerprints were on the notebook page the police found. Do you think he could have stolen your notebook?"

"You don't say!"

"What would he have wanted with it?"

"The research! I keep telling you it's the research that's valuable. No one else is doing this kind of observation and analysis."

As though to show Charlotte the kind of observation and analysis she was referring to, Cheetah Rita tipped the notebook open on her lap toward her. But then she abruptly stood up, tossed the notebook into her briefcase, and gathered it up with the camp stool as though to leave.

As she walked by the seated Charlotte, her briefcase swung violently toward Charlotte's head. Charlotte ducked and avoided the blow, but she felt certain it was no accident—that Cheetah Rita had been trying to hit her. She swore under her breath and yelled something vulgar at the elderly woman's retreating back. Then she got up, thinking that Sigrid's belief in Miss Wilcox's gentleness was based on very dated experience.

In an effort to not let her happy and tolerant mood dissipate entirely, she walked over to the petting zoo. The antics of children and the barnyard animals should revive her spirits.

When she got there, she was surprised to find Stevie in the outdoor enclosure with the animals, helping a young man stroke the muzzle of the petting zoo's long-suffering donkey. Several other people were in the area, three of whom seemed to be in charge. It took Charlotte a moment to realize that everyone but Stevie was blind. As Charlotte watched, Stevie seemed happy and relaxed. She was focusing her single-minded attention on helping the folks enjoy themselves, ignoring, for instance, the animal droppings that littered the area and threatened her expensive shoes. Charlotte laughed as Stevie gave the goat who tried to eat the hem of her skirt a sharp rap on the nose.

So it was Saint Stevie after all, she thought, leaning over the fence to wave and feeling better than she had all day.

But suddenly John Hogan was standing at the fence, too—much too close to Charlotte, his left arm grazing her right. He seemed to have materialized out of nowhere. She stepped away, frightened, and said, "What do you want?"

"Just thought I'd say hello," he said in a low voice. "See if you had recovered from those . . . delusions you were having."

"Delusions, my eye," Charlotte said. He gave her the creeps, and she was glad they were outside and in a public place.

Hogan laughed softly and walked away, leaving Charlotte feeling shaken.

Looking after him, she decided that she had been foolish to let down her guard even for a minute. She'd better figure out who she had to fear at the zoo before it was too late.

Chapter 18

Thankfully it was time for lunch. Charlotte bought hers at one of the concession stands on the west side of the zoo and joined Barbara Champion and some other staffers who were already seated at a long table nearby. Their topic of conversation turned out to be Stevie, whom they generally seemed to dislike.

Trying to maintain her more forgiving or at least balanced attitude toward Stevie, Charlotte felt compelled to describe Stevie's seemingly out-of-character experience with the blind folks at the petting zoo. Everybody laughed when Barbara dismissed it as an out-of-*body* experience for Stevie, and they remained clearly unconvinced of her redeeming social value.

One of the commissary workers boastfully told how his boss had handled Stevie shortly after she began working at the zoo. He said Stevie frequently came into the commissary to help herself to a piece of fruit several times a week "just to tide me over until dinner."

Eventually the commissary director let her know that she couldn't throw her weight around like that, that all the food in the commissary belonged to the animals.

Everybody else seemed to think it was funny, his correcting the top administrator's assistant like that—especially over something as small as an occasional apple. Charlotte thought it would have made a more interesting story if Stevie had requested some of the more interesting tidbits—she knew the commissary stocked earthworms and hairless baby mice called pinkies, for instance—instead of a fruit fix.

Hogan joined the table, so Charlotte quickly excused herself. She could feel his eyes on her back as she walked away and tried all the harder to concentrate on her destination—the commissary, which she decided she had perhaps overlooked as a site of interesting information for her stories. On the way she saw Stevie, apparently walking back from the petting zoo, and received a friendly wave from the director's assistant as though Stevie knew she had a new defender. Or maybe she was just in a good mood. Exhibiting a little kindness can do that to a person.

Up ahead stood the commissary, a two-story cement block building painted a pale yellow with green trim. As the zoo's grocery store, the commissary received and stored all the food consumed by the animals. Each animal house ordered food for its charges from the commissary by the week, based on menus made up by Maria Pickard, and the commissary delivered it every morning because so much of the food had to be fresh.

Inside, it appeared to be one large room stocked like a crowded warehouse, with narrow aisles running between tall shelves that were hard to see around or through. Expecting to come across the commissary director or his staff at any moment, Charlotte strolled among bags of dry dog food and towers of huge cans of sweet potatoes and kale stacked to the ceiling. Today's deliveries had already been made by this time, but she had expected to find staff members still working. Everybody must still be at lunch.

The high shelves created canyons between them and it occurred to her that it would be easy to get lost in there. She hadn't yet found any exotic food, but was already convinced that she could make an interesting story out of what the zoo had to go through to feed its multispecies brood.

She looked into refrigerators packed with carrots, turnips, and green beans, and walked between bins of coconuts and onions. Along one wall were bins of apples, oranges, and bananas. She was looking at racks of eggs in a refrigerator when a man's voice right behind her made her jump. Guiltily she closed the refrigerator door and turned around, expecting to have to explain her snooping to a staff member.

"Sign here," a man in a delivery uniform said, handing her a pen and a form on a clipboard. She did her best to appear to know what she was doing and nonchalantly signed the delivery slip.

He dropped the clipboard on top of a stack of cardboard cartons on a dolly behind him and tilted the dolly, prepared to wheel it away.

"Where to?" he asked.

"What's in there?" Charlotte asked, realizing that she had not even skimmed the delivery slip.

"Crickets."

"Well, then," she said confidently, as though that made a difference, "just stack them on that counter there."

The delivery man stacked the cartons and left. Charlotte approached the counter, wondering which zoo animals ate crickets and how long before these specimens would go down some greedy gullet. She didn't really care, except that having signed for them and now hearing the endearing little chirps they were making inside the cartons somehow made her feel involved in their fate.

It occurred to her that she could set the crickets free— just carry the cartons one by one to the door of the building and open them up on the ground. The crickets would jump away and no one would be the wiser. Until the delivery slip was checked, of course. Luckily, she had signed Lou's name.

But if she freed the crickets, then some other animal would go hungry. She didn't know what to do. Obviously, she was not suited for a job where she'd have to make life-and-death decisions like this, she realized, and decided to bring her commissary visit to a close. It was about time, anyway, since the crowded atmosphere was making her eyes play tricks on her: a tower of canned goods had appeared to sway as she walked past it.

On the way out, she passed the doors to a walk-in freezer along one wall. Opening the door and looking into the cold and foggy atmosphere inside, she was able to make out stainless-steel racks and wheeled carts but was not able to identify the wrapped bundles they contained. And what were those four-foot-long objects hanging from hooks in the ceiling? Carcasses, she supposed. Beef carcasses, probably. Taking no chances, she propped the door open with a handy giant can of chicken broth and walked into the freezer.

She shivered. The only light was from the open door but she could read the labels on the wrapped packages, which all seemed to contain beef, horse meat, and various kinds of fish. And it was carcasses that hung unwrapped from the ceiling hooks. They just didn't look like they would yield cuts of meat she was familiar with. She'd have to ask Dennis, the commissary director, if they were the carcasses of horses, she decided. She turned to leave just as the door swung shut.

She screamed, ran to the door, and tried unsuccessfully to work the handle. Then she pounded on the door with her fists for a long time, but nobody opened it. She was trapped.

That door didn't close itself. Someone had made good on the taped threat.

Trying not to panic in the frigid darkness, she frantically ran her hands along both sides of the door, looking for a door lock release or at least a light switch. She found the light switch and turned it on. But the pale light did not reveal any way to get out of her frozen cell. Ten minutes before, she had been contemplating rescuing crickets and now she was in desperate need of rescuing herself.

She was furious and more than a little frightened. Who would do this to her? Most important, how was she going to get out?

It was cold in there. She could see her breath in the frosty air. All she was wearing was a jumper over a short-sleeved blouse. Even her shoes were flimsy. How was she supposed to know she'd be needing a parka and mukluks when she dressed for work that July morning?

Recalling that keepers occasionally froze fish in blocks of ice so that the polar bears would have the challenge of working to get at their food, she had a sudden image of her own body encased in ice and providing an afternoon's entertainment for the bears.

She began rubbing her arms and stamping her feet to warm them, but soon that was not enough. She decided she'd have a better chance of not freezing if she kept moving. So she began walking around and around the freezer, between the carts and racks containing bundles of meat and fish and among the carcasses hanging from the ceiling. The floor had frost on it, and sometimes she would slip and lurch a little to one side or the other and would brush up against the carcasses. It was disgusting.

On she walked. She tried to calculate how long she could stay alive in the freezer. She figured she'd freeze to death before she suffocated. But surely someone would need to open the freezer before the end of their work day!

How long would it take Walt to realize she was missing? she wondered. He knew she was coming to the zoo today, but how long might it take for anyone to think to look for her in a freezer? Boy, what she wouldn't give to see Walter coming in that door—to see anyone coming in that door.

She had a pretty good idea of when she had entered the commissary but had totally lost track of time since then. It seemed she had been walking around and around the freezer forever, and her watch was worthless because moisture had fogged up its crystal.

Periodically, she would panic. But after a few such painful

episodes, she learned that it helped to take deep breaths and to try to think of something other than how long she was going to be trapped, such as who could have locked her in. That, at least, was enough to raise her blood pressure and probably her temperature as well.

Charlotte was getting very tired. Maybe it wouldn't be so dangerous to stop walking for a while. The skin on her arms and face felt tight and her joints began to ache. Her toes felt like Popsicles. She kept walking but she was moving a lot slower now. She didn't know how much longer she could keep it up. She'd have to stop walking soon and sit down on the floor. It probably wouldn't hurt to take a short nap.

After an eternity, the door opened and a stocky man wearing a butcher's apron and carrying a tray full of wrapped packages came through the door. He was just an ordinary man doing an ordinary job, but Charlotte had never been happier to see anyone in her life. However, that didn't keep her from charging the open door, knocking into him, and causing him to drop his tray as she barreled out into the commissary.

He left the mess on the floor and followed her out, demanding, "Who the hell are you?"

Charlotte blew on her hands and stamped her feet. In a few moments, she blinked her frosty eyelashes, pushed back the stiff strands of hair that had fallen into her face, and explained who she was. Then she asked his identity.

"I'm Dennis Wolf, and this is my commissary. Now, what are you doing in my freezer?"

"I've been in there forever, beating on the door and yelling at the top of my lungs," she said. "Why didn't you let me out?"

"How was I supposed to know you were in there? I've been gone since about eleven-thirty," Dennis said, explaining that he had enjoyed a lengthy lunch with a dog food salesman. "On his expense account," he said.

"Then who was it that locked me in?" Charlotte demanded. "I had the door propped open, so it wasn't an accident."

"You're right about that," Dennis said, reaching into his pants pocket and pulling out a matchbook. "I found this wedged in the door handle from this side—had to take it out to open the door. I didn't know why it was there, but one of my workers thinks he's quite a prankster. I just thought it was something he had cooked up."

"How did it work?" Charlotte asked.

To show her, Dennis pushed the matchbook back into the door handle on the outside, where it lodged the catch in place. Then he tried to turn the handle. It didn't budge.

"See?" he said. "That's how it was. And you couldn't have moved it from inside, either. I would imagine that you're not in any mood to go in and try it."

"That's right," Charlotte said firmly.

After a moment, she asked. "Could your worker have locked me in there as some kind of joke?"

"Nah. He's pretty goofy, but he's not mean. Locking somebody in a freezer so long strikes me as more than a joke—even for him."

Dennis pulled the matchbook out of the door handle, but Charlotte took it out of his hands before he could put it back in his pocket. The cover advertised the Riverview Restaurant where she and Lou had lunched recently. The matchbook didn't look special, but it could have killed her. She shuddered.

She thanked Dennis for his help and left the commissary, hoping she'd feel completely thawed out by the time she got home and saw Walt and Ty. She had no intention of letting either one of them know how close she had come to becoming a frozen dinner. And she had absolutely no intention of letting whoever locked her in that freezer get away with it.

Chapter **19**

Recalling her cold and frightening experience in the freezer was enough to send icy shivers down Charlotte's spine the next morning as she lay in bed. She found herself clutching the uninformed Walt, who misinterpreted her, and then things heated up quite a bit.

Still lying there, she tried to figure out a way to remain in that warm cocoon all day. However, she knew that if she didn't find the person who was trying to shut her up, nobody would. And besides, Walt—admittedly one of the cocoon's chief attractions—had to go to work.

After he left, she skipped her walk and got out the phone book while she ate breakfast. The only John Hogan listed lived on Early Road, west of the zoo, in Delaware County. That area was fairly rural, as she remembered, but she knew things must have changed since she was last there.

So she set out that hot, sunny morning, not exactly sure what she expected to find out about Hogan from looking at where he lived. Maybe she'd find a suspicious-looking green-house on his property and be able to turn him in to Detective Barnes. A whole greenhouse of marijuana wouldn't connect him to Jerry's murder, but maybe it would put him out of commission while she and the police looked for other evidence against him.

She found Early Road easily enough. It ran east and west and was almost devoid of traffic at that hour of the morning. The surrounding flat countryside was recently rural but now contained housing developments every few miles, bedroom communities for Columbus. The land in between housing developments contained no crops but seemed to lie fallow, waiting to be platted off.

Charlotte located Hogan's address and the name "Hogan, JN" on an aluminum mailbox where a long driveway met the road. The mailbox and driveway were for a white frame farm-house set back from the road about forty yards. She drove past the property twice to look it over, so she'd know what she was getting into. There was a chain-link fence around the house and yard, but the driveway was outside the fence. An old barn, which looked like it now served as a garage, was at the end of the driveway. There were two houses across the road out front, but the nearest neighbors on either side were about a half-mile away.

She turned into the driveway and drove slowly toward the house. The property was flat and grassy, with few trees. Small, neat shrubs were planted against the foundation of the house. She didn't see any flower beds but there was a small child's swing set in the yard, and for the first time she realized that she had never considered that Hogan might be married. Since she found him so repulsive, she had assumed everyone else would, too.

Once she was at the end of the drive, next to the house, she got out and knocked on the door to see if anyone was at home—a wife and child, for instance, or an ancient mother for whom John Hogan was the sole support and caretaker. The existence of any such dependents would improve her opinion of Hogan, she realized. But no one answered her knock.

She stood at the door and wondered what to do next. She wanted to look in the front picture window, but dared not do so in full view of the neighbors' houses across the road. So she walked around back, asking herself whether there were no limits to her nosiness.

Apparently not. There was also no suspicious-looking greenhouse back there. She climbed the steps to the back porch and looked in the window pane that was the top half of the door. Inside was a spotless kitchen. Hogan *must* have somebody living with him, she thought, because someone as sloppy about his person as he was could not possibly keep house so well.

She spotted cellar doors—the kind that could have sheltered Dorothy and Toto—at the foundation of the house. She left the porch and walked over to the cellar doors. She bent down and tried to raise one, but they were locked from the inside. She had visions of a cellar full of marijuana growing in long neat rows under grow lights hanging from the ceiling.

But, she realized, Hogan didn't need a cellar or basement for that. Just recently the Columbus police had arrested two marijuana farmers that police said grew the stuff in a townhouse apartment they rented only for that purpose near OSU's campus. Kitchens and bedrooms and living rooms apparently worked just as well as basements and cellars. Or barns.

She walked to the barn and tried the door, but it, too, was locked. Inside a dog set to barking and growling. It sounded large, and Charlotte thought it was time for her to leave before the dog managed to find a way out.

Back in her car, she lamented the fact that she hadn't found out much about Hogan on this little trip. When you got right down to it, she couldn't even be sure that the person living at this address was the John Hogan she was interested in.

She backed out the driveway and drove the short way to

one of the two houses opposite the Hogan house. She got out of her car and knocked on the door of the house. No one was home. She drove the few yards to the second house. As she walked up the front porch, she saw the curtain at the window move and felt sure her arrival was not a surprise. That was good. Maybe the same person had been watching her over at Hogan's house and regularly kept an eye on the neighbors' property.

A short, plump elderly woman answered Charlotte's knock. She looked like something out of a Norman Rockwell illustration, all gray hair, ruddy cheeks, and cheerful smile. There was even flour on her apron. She opened the screen door a little to hear what Charlotte had to say.

Charlotte introduced herself as a friend of "a John Hogan who works at the zoo." She asked whether the woman knew whether the John Hogan who lived across the road was that John Hogan.

"I do believe he works at the zoo, yes," the woman said. "But we don't neighbor much."

Hoping for evidence of drug-dealing, Charlotte asked, "Could you tell me whether he gets a lot of company? A lot of different people coming to visit with him?"

"Can't say that that's true. He and his family keep to themselves a good bit."

A family. She had been right about Hogan not living alone.

"Well, thank you. I'm sorry I missed John, but at least I know I have the right house now," Charlotte said, conscientiously keeping up her ruse. "I'll come back sometime when they're home." She turned to leave the porch.

"About the only one who came with what you could call any regularity would be the fellow in the white car," the elderly woman said to Charlotte's back.

Charlotte turned around toward the door.

"One of them little, low-to-the-ground jobs," the woman said quickly. "Until about a month ago, every Thursday morning. Like clockwork."

Before Charlotte could say anything, the screen door

closed and even the front door clicked shut. She could hear the lock being turned. There seemed to be no point in trying to get the woman to say more after she had barricaded herself like that.

Standing on the porch and looking across the road at the Hogans' house, Charlotte wondered just how long the woman had longed to tell someone that bit of information about her neighbor.

Chapter **20**

A few hours later, Lou Toreson opened the back door of her dusty maroon, nine-year-old Ciera and pulled out the folded-up lawn chair and her canvas carryall. She sneezed as the breeze blew some of the rock dust from the gravel of the zoo's crowded parking lot into her face.

It was the middle of Thursday afternoon and somnolent seemed to Lou to be the best word to describe the scene. Although the day had started with the brightest of sunlight, by now there were enough white cumulus clouds to keep the sun from striking directly most of the time.

The cicadas had started their annual sawing hum, although they were not as insistent as they would be in another couple of weeks. Lou smiled as she remembered that, growing up on a farm in Iowa, people always said "Six more weeks until frost" the first time the persistent locusts started their songs.

Although this had not been a particularly hot summer, the humidity had been bad. Frost would sound pretty appealing if the moisture percentage went any higher.

Charlotte had called last night to tell her about her horrible freezer episode and her understandable desire to find out who wanted to shut her up—perhaps permanently, as he had Jerry Brobst. Lou had insisted that she report her entrapment to the police, but Charlotte had adamantly refused. Instead, she had told Lou, she was going to step up her investigation of both Hogan and Cheetah Rita, and about then was when she had had her brilliant idea that Lou should diagnose Cheetah Rita.

"It would be so easy for you, Lou," Charlotte had said. "You're a psychologist, after all. All you'd have to do is observe her a while, talk to her a little bit."

"Just a smidgen of 'park bench psychoassessment,' is that what you're asking for?" Lou responded. "No reputable psychologist would be willing to identify a person as psychotic or neurotic on the basis of a peek and a chat."

"I'm not asking for something that would stand up in court, for heaven's sake. I'd just like to know if you think this woman could be violent."

"No psychologist could tell you that for sure, Charlotte, even with a lot more observation than you're asking for."

"I realize that. But I don't know what to think about her. Sigrid is certain that she couldn't have shoved Jerry Brobst off that roof, but I know she has been capable of hurting me."

"Not a good sign, is it?"

"No. And long before Jerry died, I heard that she spanked a visitor's child for throwing a rock at the cheetahs."

"Personally, I've always thought that the only thing keeping all of us from spanking other people's misbehaving children was the fear of being sued."

"So you don't think that means anything?"

"It may just mean that Cheetah Rita feels she doesn't have anything to lose in a lawsuit. Maybe because she doesn't have many material goods. What do you know about her financial situation?"

"Nothing, really." Unwilling to give up so easily, Charlotte went on. "I told you about her believing in the 'kingdom of the cats,' didn't I?"

"Yes. You even said she took on a reverential tone when she used the phrase."

"That's right. She sounds downright religious when she talks about it."

"Maybe it would better to talk with her family."

"I don't think she has any family, and I was serious about her sounding religious about the cats. I think she might really think they're divine."

"Oh. Well, then, it's all the more true that her cat-kingdom statements don't necessarily indicate a thing about her sanity."

Charlotte groaned in exasperation.

Lou continued. "Listen to me, Charlotte. I know that you have pretty conventional religious beliefs—conventional for the last part of the twentieth century, anyway. Right?"

"Sure. But what does that have to do with Cheetah Rita?"

"I just want to point out that you would have just as much trouble proving *your* religious beliefs as Cheetah Rita would have proving hers. Think about it. How would you go about proving your religious beliefs?"

"But surely it matters that my beliefs *are* conventional."

"It may indicate how in tune you are with much of society, but it really doesn't tell us much about your sanity. My point is that she can't be considered delusional on the basis of having strange religious beliefs. We have too much historical evidence of religious beliefs changing over time and how strange some of them seem later."

"Okay. But what if her beliefs aren't really religious in nature? What if she just believes that cats of all types—or at least cats of the cheetah type—are actually going to take over? I don't know. Maybe they're finally going to learn how to turn doorknobs and then will eventually figure out how to rule the earth."

"Is that what she has in mind, do you think? Their ruling the earth?"

"I don't know. What else could she mean by the phrase 'the kingdom of the cats'?"

"Ever hear of the phrase 'the animal kingdom'? Remember your biology? Kingdom, phylum, class, order, family, genus, species?"

"Cheetah Rita *taught* biology," Charlotte said in a small voice, wondering what other connections she could be missing, what other information she could be overlooking.

They were quiet for a long time. Finally, Lou said, "You've always been in favor of marching to a different drummer, Charlotte. Maybe Cheetah Rita has just found her different drummer."

"Maybe so."

"She's obviously eccentric, but that doesn't make her psychotic. Somebody would have to do a full diagnostic workup on her before we started throwing words like 'paranoid schizophrenic' around in a meaningful way."

"I'm not looking for labels, Lou. And you know I'd be the last person to want to consider an elderly woman crazy just because she's finally found the time to devote herself to something she's intellectually excited about. I'm just trying to understand her. And I'd like a little more assurance that the old lady really didn't kill my friend and try to kill me."

Lou told her she couldn't provide that assurance. "You're asking too much from a chat."

"But you should be able to tell if she is completely 'round the bend, shouldn't you?"

"That's such a good professional term, isn't it?" Lou said. " 'Completely 'round the bend.' " Then she laughed and reluctantly agreed that she would try to talk with Cheetah Rita today.

Unfortunately, way too many other people in central Ohio had also decided on a day at the zoo. Lou trudged through the parking lot to the entrance, carrying her chair and her bag. Clusters of chattering children surrounded the refreshment kiosks and spilled out of the souvenir shop. Several small ones who were too tired and too hungry rivaled the monkeys with their high-pitched shrieks. As usual, the example of one had been picked up by several others. But as Lou neared the female cheetah yard on the west side of the zoo, a blessed silence seemed to settle over the late afternoon.

She walked halfway around the yard before spotting the cheetahs under the scraggly-looking evergreens toward the back of their fenced area. Just as she had hoped, Cheetah Rita was settled close by on her camp stool, a three-ring binder open on her lap. She looked exactly as Charlotte had described her.

Lou stopped on the paved path to watch the cheetahs for a couple of minutes. Two of the smaller ones were struggling over what appeared to be a large bone. What exactly did the zoo feed these animals? she wondered.

She moved a little closer to where Cheetah Rita was sitting, paused tentatively, and then moved past her to set her lawn chair on the grass between the path and the high fence around the cheetahs.

Lou relaxed into her lawn chair and watched the two young cheetahs join the adults in a late afternoon nap. After there had been no movement for about five minutes, Cheetah Rita closed her notebook and Lou was afraid she was going to pack up and leave. She decided to make her move.

Quickly she reached into her carryall and pulled out a colorful postcard. Then she turned to Cheetah Rita and asked her the date. To her relief, Cheetah Rita quickly told her. Lou said, "Thank you. Isn't it peaceful here this afternoon? People our age, I think, particularly appreciate afternoons like this. Don't you agree?"

Perhaps because she saw Lou as an age-mate (which wasn't really true, given that Lou was probably ten years younger than she), Cheetah Rita responded "Indeed" and seemed to relax a bit. After a only little prompting from Lou, Cheetah Rita and she were soon chatting amicably about the weather in a way she would have not expected Cheetah Rita to be capable of from Charlotte's description of her.

But before long, Cheetah Rita had made two references to "that elephant keeper who mistreated the animals" and Lou was no longer sure where the conversation was headed.

"Mistreated them in what way?" Lou inquired innocently.

"He jabbed them with his ankus!" Cheetah Rita fairly shouted, waking up the cheetahs and causing zoo visitors walking nearby to stare. To Lou's surprise, she grabbed an ankus out of her briefcase and jumped up to demonstrate Jerry's behavior. She looked like a fencer as she moved back and forth with her right arm extended, holding the ankus, and shouting, "Jab! Jab! Jab!"

Having found what she thought was a sympathetic audience, she continued discussing and imitating Jerry at some length, and eventually Lou wondered how she could turn off the torrent of words from Cheetah Rita.

About an hour later, in Charlotte's Clintonville office, Lou set the scene for Charlotte. "I said I knew it was Thursday, but wasn't sure of the date and asked if she knew what the date was. She popped the correct answer right out. That's a pretty standard diagnostic question in mental hospitals, and she passed with flying colors."

"Really? If you don't know the date, you're crazy? Then I'm in trouble most days."

"Are you looking for a diagnosis, Charlotte? Actually, knowing the date is only one indicator that diagnosticians look for. By itself, it doesn't mean a whole lot."

"What else did you find out?"

Lou took a deep breath. "She really seemed irrational about Jerry Brobst. I mentioned that it seemed so peaceful there by the cheetahs and before long she went into a harangue about how much more peaceful it would be now that that dreadful elephant keeper wasn't around to mistreat the animals."

"She didn't say she shoved him off the roof, did she?"

"No, nothing like that. But she did repeat several times how he used to jab the elephants with the ankus and how badly it must have hurt the elephants to be jabbed with the ankus, and asked how would he have liked it if somebody had jabbed *him* with the ankus."

Lou started describing in some detail Cheetah Rita's demonstration of how Jerry jabbed the elephants.

"She just happened to have an ankus in her briefcase?" Charlotte asked incredulously. "Perhaps she took it from the elephant keeper we all know who doesn't need his now—the one she pushed off the roof."

"It sounded to me as though she would have been more likely to go after him with the ankus. But, of course, it just might have been easier to give him a push."

"Then you think she did kill him?"

"I don't know, Charlotte. She certainly was very angry with Jerry and continues to express that anger even though he's dead. But that doesn't mean she killed him. And it doesn't necessarily mean she's crazy either. Anger may be a very appropriate response. But it might not be appropriate to continue the emotion after the target of the anger is unavailable."

"In other words, maybe she is and maybe she isn't; maybe she did and maybe she didn't."

"Exactly."

"Sounds a long way from exact to me."

"I warned you not to expect too much, didn't I?"

"Yes."

"Really, it would take a lengthy diagnostic process to figure out exactly how Cheetah Rita is functioning. But there did seem to be an awful lot of anger in her."

"Did she say anything about the possibility that Jerry stole her notebook?"

"No. Did he?"

"I guess I forgot to tell you that Sigrid said Jerry's fingerprints are on the notebook page Barnes found on the roof."

"Why would he have stolen it?"

"I've been trying to answer that question myself. Now, what strikes me as a possibility is that Cheetah Rita's notebook contained what Jerry was so anxious to tell a reporter. To tell me."

She and Lou were quiet for a moment as they thought this over. Finally Charlotte said, "I don't have a clue about how to check out that hypothesis—especially with the notebook still missing—but I *do* have new information about Jerry and Hogan."

Lou leaned forward in her chair to listen and Charlotte thought, not for the first time, how nice it was to have a friend like Lou who was so definitely on her side and as interested as she in getting to the bottom of things. She said, "To make a long story short, I went to see Hogan's house today and asked a neighbor whether a lot of people seemed to visit him—you know I've wondered if he was selling his marijuana."

"Didn't it occur to you that prowling around Hogan's house could be dangerous?"

"Stop sounding like Walt. Anyway, the neighbor said, no, there weren't many visitors. But get this—she said the only person who showed up with any regularity was the man who drove a white sports car, one of those 'low-to-the-ground jobs,' she said. In other words, Jerry Brobst!"

"I'm amazed."

"So maybe Jerry wasn't getting marijuana for his own use; maybe he was selling it for Hogan. You know I've never thought Jerry used pot. But maybe he was the middleman."

Lou nodded her head and said enthusiastically, "And that would explain why he could afford that car at two times his yearly salary."

"Right. I think we're really on to something here," Charlotte said. "Incidently, the neighbor said Hogan is married and—"

"Wait a minute. Do you have any idea *when* Jerry visited Hogan?"

"Every Thursday morning, the neighbor said. Why?"

"Well, what makes you so sure that it was Hogan he was visiting? Maybe it was Hogan's wife."

"You don't know a thing about these people, so—"

"Right, but I know neighbors. There's a man who lives across the street from me who watches my every move. I swear he uses binoculars. Neighbors like that are most interested in gentlemen callers, if you get my drift. That's the kind of thing they would be guaranteed to bring up. And Jerry visited on a *weekday* morning."

"I didn't think about that. In fact, I've been pretty muddled about this: I didn't worry much about Hogan answering my knock this morning because I assumed he would be at work on a Thursday morning. But later, when the neighbor said Jerry visited on Thursday mornings, it didn't occur to me that Jerry would not be home but at work. But Mrs. Hogan wasn't at home this morning, either."

Lou suggested that while they didn't know where Mrs. Hogan worked, they could at least find out whether her husband really worked at the zoo on Thursday mornings.

Charlotte looked at her watch to verify that it was not yet five o'clock. Then she picked up the phone and dialed the zoo. In an officious voice, she asked to speak to Groundskeeper John Hogan and was told that he was working outside and unable to come to the phone. But she could leave a message if she liked. Instead, she asked the operator whether Hogan worked Thursday mornings as well as afternoons. The operator did not reply for a moment but then confirmed that all day Thursday was a workday for John Hogan.

Charlotte said thanks and hung up before letting out a whoop of congratulations for Lou. "You were right! If Jerry visited the Hogan household on Thursday mornings, it wasn't John he came to see. And what a fine motive for murdering Jerry Hogan would have had!"

"If there is such a thing as a fine motive for murder," Lou said thoughtfully. "I wonder what Mrs. Hogan is like?"

"I have no idea, although how cool could a person be who married John Hogan?" Charlotte still had trouble thinking that *anyone* had considered Hogan marriage material. "I guess what argues most in favor of Jerry and Hogan's wife having an affair is my knowing that any woman would be desperate to get away from Hogan."

"But we shouldn't really jump to conclusions, should we?"

"Right. We'll just have to find some evidence of their relationship," Charlotte said, before adding, "which I'm sure existed."

They speculated about Mrs. Hogan for a few minutes until Charlotte suddenly jumped up and said, "Oh, I've stayed too long. I have to get home. Ty's coming home from camping and I'm cooking a big dinner for us. Want to come?"

"No thanks. I've got lots of things to get done tonight—things that I would have finished today if I had not been out watching elephant-jabbing demonstrations, I might point out."

"Oh, I don't want to hear it," Charlotte told her as they walked out to their cars. "You loved finally getting to talk with Cheetah Rita, and you know it."

Driving home, Charlotte realized that if the affair checked out, she may have done exactly what Sigrid wanted her to do—uncover a motive someone other than Cheetah Rita may have had to murder Jerry. But she decided not to share that information with Sigrid until she was a little more certain of the park director's motives.

The dinner was a big success, with the Samses happy to all be together again. Tyler was full of tales of his self-sufficiency at the campsite and looked taller and more tanned than he had just three short days ago. At times like this, Charlotte had trouble pushing away the realization that he would be going off to college before they knew it. His absence during the camping trip having been bearable, she wondered whether she could convince him to do college three days at a time.

Chapter **21**

Charlotte sought out dietician Maria Pickard in her office at the zoo the next day. She was looking for confirmation of an affair between Jerry and Hogan's wife and had no idea who else to ask, particularly since Stevie hardly seemed to know Jerry and always seemed anxious to avoid talking about the seamier side of things.

She chatted with Maria and then watched her print out menus for the following week on her laser printer before finally blurting out, "Have you ever heard anything about an affair between Jerry and John Hogan's wife?"

Maria didn't hesitate. "Sure," she said. "It began in the spring, I guess. Then it cooled off."

Bingo! thought Charlotte. A possible motive for Hogan to have murdered Jerry. "Did it stay cooled off?"

"I don't know. The last time I heard John talking about it was in mid-June. He said he and Naomi were going to—"

"Naomi?" Charlotte interrupted, wondering where she

had recently heard that name. "Her name's Naomi Hogan?"

"What's wrong with that?" Maria asked. "Are you okay? You seem a little stressed today, Charlotte."

"Nothing's wrong with that. It's just that you don't hear that name very often." Unable to come up with a better explanation, Charlotte decide she must have been thinking of Lou's sister. "What were you saying about Hogan?"

"Just that he said he and his wife were going to get back together, that he was willing to let bygones be bygones. He was playing Mr. Magnanimous. But I still didn't like him. You know how he is."

Charlotte nodded.

Maria said, "I heard that the police talked to both the Hogans right after Jerry was killed, so they must have known about their relationship."

Probably talked to the neighbor across the road from the Hogans, too, Charlotte thought. But they still hadn't arrested Hogan for Jerry's murder, so they must not have been able to prove the affair was relevant to the murder.

"Tell me, Maria. Did Jerry and Hogan have a fight at some point?"

"You've been busy, haven't you?" Maria laughed. "Who told you about the knock-down, drag-out they had?"

Thinking it unwise to admit she had read about it in Jerry's personnel file, Charlotte said she couldn't remember.

"That's okay. I know you have to protect your sources," Maria said, but Charlotte thought she sounded miffed. The mention of protecting sources had probably reminded Maria that Charlotte was not just a colleague with whom she was trading information but a reporter whose intent was to gather information regardless of whether she was willing to share any.

Perhaps as a consequence, she was also not as forthcoming about the fight between Hogan and Jerry as Charlotte would have wished. About all that Maria was willing to say about the fight was that, as Charlotte had expected, the larger Jerry had gotten the best of Hogan. To Charlotte, it looked like more of the kind of humiliation Lou had talked about as being a possible motivator for murder.

"Have you ever heard of Hogan or Jerry using or selling drugs?" she asked.

Maria looked surprised and said, "Are you working for the police these days, Charlotte?" and promptly clammed up.

When Maria went to deliver her menus, Charlotte sat on the steps outside Maria's building and tried to collect her thoughts about Jerry. Since his death, there had been quite a lot she had found out about him that was news to her. This affair was just one item. The fact that he was having an affair with Naomi Hogan made it seem less like he was visiting the Hogan household to buy drugs, although she had to admit there was nothing that said Naomi wasn't involved in the marijuana business, too. And there still was that little matter of his car smelling like he was at least a user.

She wondered whether her theory about why Jerry could have stolen Cheetah Rita's notebook was true. She wasn't even sure he *had* stolen it. But why else would his fingerprints be on the page the police found? And if he stole it, what better reason than that it contained what he wanted to talk to a reporter about? Whatever could be in Cheetah Rita's notebook that would be so interesting to a reporter?

Charlotte was disappointed with Lou's assessment of Cheetah Rita. She didn't exactly know what she had been looking for, but certainly something more substantial than "maybe yes, maybe no." Her reading about zoos had uncovered information about a woman called the "Wolf Lady" who spent years observing wolves at the Philadelphia Zoo. She sounded as obsessive as Cheetah Rita.

On the other hand, the Wolf Lady had eventually started publishing a newsletter for other wolf aficionados. That certainly made her seem more than merely competent, she thought, always willing to consider writing of any kind as evidence of superior mental faculties. Was Cheetah Rita capable of putting out a newsletter? She didn't know about her capability but felt certain that the antisocial woman would not be interested in communicating that way.

Charlotte sought out Stevie in her office. Behind her well-organized desk, Stevie looked stylish and immaculate, as always. Unconsciously, Charlotte smoothed back her own hair.

"How can I help you, Charlotte?" Stevie asked.

"I was just curious about something: Cheetah Rita's accusations that Jerry Brobst mistreated the elephants."

"Must you write anything about her? Until the police arrest her—if that's what they intend to do—we'd much prefer you ignore her. We don't want the public thinking we have crazy people running around the zoo."

"Why are you so convinced she's crazy?"

"Aren't you? The woman has spent two years watching cheetahs, for God's sake. Does that sound like a normal life to you?"

"Different," Charlotte said, aware she sounded exactly like Lou. "Not average. But I don't know about crazy."

"Well, I think she's deranged. And if she killed Jerry Brobst then she's obviously dangerous and should be locked up. Until she is, I'd just as soon have the public believe that all the dangerous creatures here are already behind bars."

"But exactly what accusations did she make in her notes?"

"I told you Detective Barnes said I can't talk about that."

"But you must have read the article in the *Dispatch* about the notebook page. Barnes himself told the reporter about it. Now everyone knows that the police found a page from Cheetah Rita's notebook on top of the pachyderm building. Surely it won't matter what you say about it now."

"Honestly, Charlotte, you do hang on, don't you? Well, all right." She sat back in her chair and primly folded her hands on the blotter on her desk. "Cheetah Rita was forever sending notes to Mr. Stitcher," she said. "Sometimes she wrote about the cats, sometimes about the elephants, sometimes about the bears, sometimes about the ferrets and the otters, sometimes about the birds. You name it, Cheetah Rita had a complaint about it. I don't know how she had time to observe the cheetahs, with all the checking up she did about the other animals."

"Is there any reason to think that her complaints were somehow documented in her notebook?"

"I don't know. I just identified her handwriting, I don't have a clue as to what she keeps track of in that notebook. Probably witches' potions," Stevie said disdainfully.

"What exactly did she complain about?"

"*Everything.* Elephants not getting the exact diet she felt they should have, for instance. Although how she could even have an opinion about that, I don't know."

"What changes did she want in their diet?"

"I don't remember. Believe me, her notes were all rambling drivel, Charlotte."

"Was diet all she complained about with the elephants?"

"Let me think a minute." Stevie seemed to concentrate. Finally she said, "She also mentioned that Jerry physically abused the animals. Poked them or something with that little club all the elephant keepers carry. I forget what it's called."

"An ankus."

"Is that it? Well, anyway, she thought he used it too much. Oh, and she also thought he talked to them too much."

"To the elephants?"

"Right. See, I *told* you she was crazy."

"Can you do that? Talk to them too much, I mean?"

"I have no idea. And how could Cheetah Rita know? She doesn't know anything, Charlotte. She's a crazy person and I resent your acting as though she could make valid accusations against this zoo. I warn you, we better not see any of this in your articles."

"I'm just trying to figure out whether she could have hated Jerry enough to kill him."

"That's the police's job."

"Sure, but a person can't help but wonder. And I don't want my stories to take advantage of someone who is mentally ill."

"Well, it's a safe bet that she is."

"If the police think she killed Jerry, how come they're letting her run around loose at the zoo?"

"Detective Barnes says that she's not going anywhere, that they're just as sure where she's going to be—right here at the zoo—as if they had arrested her. They don't seem to think she's dangerous on a daily basis."

"I guess they're right."

"Tell that to Jerry Brobst," was Stevie's opinion.

Charlotte left Stevie's office and, having been reminded by Stevie's mention of a ferret, sought out the ferret keeper to ask when Barbara Champion had returned the animal she had taken with her to the 4-H camp right before Jerry was killed.

The keeper asked why she needed to know, and Charlotte told him her next article going to be about the day Jerry died and the effect his death had on the zoo. That seemed to satisfy the keeper, who looked in a ledger where zoo staff signed animals in and out.

He reported that Barbara had returned Figaro, a male ferret, at 8:45 that Sunday night. Immediately Charlotte realized that that meant Barbara was back at the zoo near the time Jerry was killed. Of course, she could have left the zoo again right away without having been the one to push Jerry off the roof.

It would be helpful if Stitcher could revive his parking lot memories. Without that information or something similar, Barbara didn't really have an alibi for the crucial time period.

She thanked the ferret keeper and then went to have lunch at one of the concession stands. As she ate her salad, she wondered about Cheetah Rita's complaints on behalf of the elephants. The fact that she thought Jerry talked to the elephants too much made the rest of her complaints sound a little suspect. Of course, for all Charlotte knew, it *was* possible to talk too much to elephants.

She could ask Barbara Champion's opinion about Cheetah Rita's accusations, but Barbara could hardly be considered an unbiased source. Although she had heartily disliked

Jerry, there was no doubt about her loyalty to the Columbus Zoo. Barbara had a vested interested in making everyone believe that the zoo treated its animals royally.

Having finished her salad, Charlotte sat wishing there was a pastry concession at the zoo. Her cholesterol level obviously needed to be readjusted. She fought the impulse to make the short drive into Dublin to get a napoleon at the French restaurant there.

The last time she had been in that restaurant, she remembered, was with Deborah Mancini after they met at the funeral home. Suddenly she knew who she'd ask about Cheetah Rita's accusations.

Annoyed as always that there was no phone in her zoo office, she decided to call it a day at the zoo. She walked back to the shed to pick up her computer and a few other things and drove to her Clintonville office to make the call.

Deborah turned out to be unavailable when Charlotte phoned, so she left a message for her to call back, collect. Before the afternoon was out, Deborah did just that. Charlotte was happy to accept the charges, happier still when she eventually learned the interesting information Deborah had to share.

Chapter **22**

"Have the police caught Jerry's killer?" Deborah demanded when she called.

"I'm afraid not. Did they call you about Jerry saying he wanted to talk with a reporter?"

"Yes, they called with some questions, but they didn't seem very interested in the answers."

"Well, I'm interested in your answers. Could you spend a few minutes talking with me about elephant care? I may quote you in some articles I'm writing."

"I'll be glad to tell you what I know, but your keepers in Columbus know as much as I do."

"Yes, of course. But I wanted to get the perspective of someone from another zoo."

"It's your nickel."

"First, what does your zoo feed your elephants?"

"Well, all we have is four adult Africans right now. In the mornings we give them a bucket of herbivore pellets and . . ."

Deborah explained the rest of the elephants' diet of timothy, alfalfa, and hydroponic grass in some detail.

"Is that all they get?"

"Isn't it enough? You wouldn't ask that question if you had to lug all that food around to each of them. Each of them gets about three hundred pounds a day, Charlotte. And that's not peanuts." She laughed heartily at her little joke.

"I just wanted to make sure I had everything," Charlotte said, thinking about how much more confident Deborah seemed now than when they met at the funeral home. Maybe it was because she was back home in familiar territory or because she was talking about things that she was an expert on. Or maybe Charlotte had just met her at a time when her grief over Jerry's death had made her seem in need of mothering. She wondered exactly what Deborah's and Jerry's relationship had been. She had always assumed it had been romantic. Now she wondered whether Deborah knew of the Jerry/Naomi Hogan liaison.

To Deborah she said, "Do you have to use your ankus much with your elephants?"

"Well, I'll tell you, I never approach our elephants without it. Any keeper will tell you that the elephants are about the most dangerous animal at the zoo."

"That's what I've heard."

"Our Africans weigh about twelve thousand pounds apiece and are ten or eleven feet tall at the shoulder. We have to get in their enclosures with them every day, and we have to be able to control them. Our ankus is the symbol of our authority. Sometimes it seems almost funny that the only thing we have to protect ourselves with is this dinky two-foot-long club with two points on it, one of which is blunt."

"Tell me, did you ever have any reason to think that Jerry Brobst used his ankus too much or that he otherwise mistreated the elephants?"

"Who's saying that?" Deborah said angrily. "Jerry loved those elephants. Anybody who'd say that doesn't know what they're talking about."

"I was just checking, that's all. Let me ask another question: Do elephants like to be talked to by their keepers?"

"Ours do. One in particular. But I suppose that it depends on the elephant."

"Have you ever heard that talking—or too much talking—is bad for elephants in any way?"

"No, I never heard that. Is it?"

"Is it what?"

"Bad for them."

"How would *I* know? *You're* the elephant keeper," Charlotte reminded her, momentarily exasperated.

"I just thought that maybe you all had discovered something new in Columbus. Most of what keepers learn never gets written down. We just pass it along amongst ourselves. Jerry always called it our 'oral tradition.'"

Deborah fell silent for a moment, but before Charlotte could ask another question, she said, "So the police aren't any closer to solving this, are they?"

"No, not really."

"I bet old Stitcher is pitchin' a fit about having a murder at his zoo. It can't help the numbers."

"Actually, attendance numbers are way ahead of last year's at this time. But how do you know Bob Stitcher?" she asked, then said, "Oh, of course. Stitcher's last job was at Tulsa, wasn't it? I forgot about that."

"Everybody here would like to forget *him*."

"He was not well liked there, either?"

"He had friends, he had enemies. Just like anyone else in a position like his, I guess. It was after he left that people here got wise to him."

"What do you mean?"

"As often as he and Stitcher fought, I would have thought Jerry would have made it common knowledge at the Columbus Zoo."

Charlotte's heart beat faster. "Made *what* common knowledge?"

"Well, I don't want to say too much. . . ."

"What did Jerry know about Stitcher, Deborah?"

"I don't know all the ins and outs of it, but it seems Stitcher was doctoring the books while he was here."

"Are you saying he embezzled money from the Tulsa Zoo?" Charlotte asked incredulously.

"No. That's the strange part. And the part that really made it hard for people to find out about what he had done. He didn't take a penny."

"So why would he cook the books?"

"To make it look like the zoo was doing better than it was. To make *himself* look more successful. And it worked, didn't it?"

"Meaning . . . ?"

"Well, he got the Columbus job, didn't he? That was quite a step up, coming from a zoo as small as this one."

"So, he inflated the attendance figures. I don't—"

"No, it was more than that. Jacking up the attendance numbers was only part of it. Some of it involved fixing up the accounting, but he didn't embezzle money. I'm sure of that much. If he had still been here when all this was discovered, he would have been fired. It would have been a real scandal. As it was, everybody was just glad he was gone."

"Who's 'everybody'?"

"All of us keepers, for instance. And probably most zoo employees. You can't keep a secret in a place like this. And, of course, the board of directors knew all about it. I even know the woman who discovered what she called 'the irregularities' in the accounting system."

"Is she on the board or in the zoo administration?"

"She's an accountant here at the zoo. But she told her boss and he had her talk to the board at one of its meetings. Then they called in some auditors, and they did the official investigation."

"Did anybody consider filing charges against Stitcher?"

"I don't know. But, believe me, his name is *mud* at *this* zoo."

After getting the names of members of the board and the

name of the accountant Deborah had mentioned, Charlotte thanked her and was about to hang up. Then she said, "Oh, one more thing. You said that Jerry knew all this?"

"Yes. We talked about it a couple of times."

After the call, Charlotte sat thinking that Deborah's information had opened up an exciting new possibility concerning who could have murdered Jerry. Maybe it was blackmail money from Stitcher that had paid for Jerry's car, and Stitcher who had pushed Jerry off the roof to end the blackmail.

Even if Charlotte was wrong about all of that—meaning no blackmail, no murderer—Deborah's major allegations against Stitcher would make a whale of a story. *If* they were true. She needed to verify what Deborah had told her. Until then, she had no reason to believe any of it. Deborah could be mistaken. Or perhaps she had some ax to grind against Stitcher. Who could tell at this point?

She tried to phone Lisa Hatch, Deborah's friend in the zoo's accounting department, but Lisa was in a meeting. So she tackled members of the Tulsa Zoo board, calling them, one by one, in a fruitless attempt to shed some light on Deborah's allegations. After she had tried to reach all twelve members, the score stood at four members who were unavailable, seven who would comment only in the blandest platitudes about their former zoo director, and one who threatened to sue her if the Tulsa Zoo was ever mentioned in any article she ever wrote for the rest of her life.

Luckily, she was able to reach Lisa on her second call. It was obvious that Deborah had told her friend that Charlotte might try to contact her. She seemed willing, even eager, to discuss Stitcher.

"Bob Stitcher really did a job on this organization, I'll tell you," Lisa said. "I don't mind at all if the public finally gets a glimpse of what he did. If your article can do that, then I'll be glad to help you."

For about a year before he left the Tulsa Zoo, she said, Stitcher directed her to start using several accounting practices that collectively made him look like a most effective director of an extremely successful zoo, all the while they created serious financial difficulties for the zoo.

"For instance, by stretching out the payables," Lisa said, "he made it look like the zoo had cut costs dramatically."

"What do you mean, 'stretching out the payables'?"

"Just paying the bills after sixty days instead of thirty. It made the zoo seem like it had more cash on hand than it did."

"But surely many institutions do that," Charlotte protested. "My husband complains all the time that contractors don't pay him on time."

"That's true. And sometimes families do it when things are tight in a particular month. But when institutions do it as a matter of policy, it's a bad idea. Not only is it unfair to their creditors, but more importantly, it gives those examining the books of the institution the wrong picture of the institution. And it hurts in another way, too; it invariably results in late payment charges that you have to pay anyway. Of course, if you have enough clout with your suppliers, you can just ignore those late charges. And that's what Stitcher told us to do. But they all caught up with us after he had gone."

"What else?" Charlotte prompted.

"He kept absolutely every receivable on the books, no matter how remote the possibility of collecting it. Sixty-dollar pledges from ten years ago were still carried as long-term receivables."

"Organizations don't usually do that?"

"Only those who are trying to look like they are in better financial shape than they are," Lisa explained. "It had the effect of artificially inflating the assets of the zoo."

"Not smart, but not really a crime, is it?" Charlotte asked.

"Well, it is a form of fraud," Lisa assured her. "But maybe the worst thing he did was direct me not to pay the zoo's industrial compensation insurance for the three quarters immediately before he left. The Oklahoma attorney general's office actually sued the zoo after Stitcher left. We owed them over a hundred fifty thousand dollars!"

"What did Stitcher do with that money?" Charlotte asked.

"If you're asking whether he embezzled it, the answer is no. I've never found anything that would indicate Bob stole a dime. But expansion decisions were based on how the zoo looked on the books, and that dug a pretty deep hole for us. He was raising his own profile not for the Tulsa Zoo, but so he could snag a prestigious job like Columbus."

"It worked, didn't it?"

"Like a charm. And part of why it worked was that he grossly inflated the attendance figures. He looked like the king of zoos there for a while."

"How could he do that? Doesn't anyone keep count of how many tickets you sell? A computer tally or something?"

"We've got tickets automated, but with so many free passes given for the zoo and with different groups of people—like senior citizens, for instance—paying a variety of prices for tickets, you can't just divide the gate by the ticket price and know how many people attended. He was in charge of coming up with attendance figures, and they were always way, way high."

Lisa paused a minute and then asked, "By the way, Charlotte, do you know whether the attendance figures that are being set in Columbus are legitimate, now that Stitcher is there?"

"That's a good question, isn't it? It bears looking into, and I'll do it. But tell me, could Stitcher serve prison time for any of this?"

"I'm not sure. But I think they could have gotten him on public malfeasance, so even though he may never have gone to prison, he would at least have lost his job and never been able to hold a public job in the future."

"Why didn't the board go after him?"

"Everything was a mess after he left. Our new director was hired when the board thought the zoo had a great deal of cash on hand—which we didn't. He soon discovered that he was facing a mountain of bills, a blizzard of late charges, that suit from the attorney general's office, and no reasonable chances of reaching Stitcher's attendance figures for at least five years minimum. He was angry and almost quit. We all were angry. We had to work hard just to stay even. Several people had to be laid off because we had to cut back expenses."

"How are things now?"

"Much better. It's been ten months and we're getting closer to having things under control. We don't have to worry anymore about going under."

Before hanging up, Charlotte couldn't resist asking whether Stitcher had ever done anything violent while he was at Tulsa.

"What do you mean?"

"Well, he yells at people here all the time," Charlotte said, "says some terrible things—"

"Sounds familiar."

"I just wondered whether you ever knew it to escalate to anything physical."

"No. I think he's all mouth. And dirty tricks like this accounting stuff."

And perhaps taped threats and locking a person in a freezer for a while but not long enough to kill her, Charlotte thought. Stitcher could have wanted to scare her away from the zoo so that she couldn't find out that he killed Jerry or that he had nearly killed the Tulsa Zoo. Now that she had found out about Tulsa, what would he do?

After her conversation with Lisa, Charlotte reached a board member who had been unavailable earlier. He reluctantly confirmed Lisa's charges. But the reason he gave for the board not prosecuting was somewhat different than Lisa's; the board did not prosecute because they feared bad publicity from a public who could, with some justification, wonder how the board could have let this happen in the first place.

"Your story may force our hand," he said. "We may have to prosecute once the truth is published."

Chapter **23**

Charlotte got Bob Stitcher to agree to an interview with her the next day, Saturday. She figured his sudden willingness was due to her mentioning that she had talked with officials of the Tulsa City Zoo. However, because of already scheduled activities, he said, at least part of the interview would have to be "on the run," by which she assumed they would be walking around the zoo as they talked. That was fine with her. In fact, she should probably not meet with any of the people she suspected unless it was in a very public place. Besides, she thought the allegations she had to discuss with Stitcher would stop him dead in his tracks.

Walt got to sleep in that morning, a rare occurrence for someone in his business on a summer Saturday. But he would be available to take her to the airport that evening for her flight to Tulsa, where she would spend Sunday meeting with Deborah and Lisa Hatch.

She woke Tyler and told him to hurry if he expected her

to drop him off at the pool on her way to the zoo. He did hurry and fifteen minutes later they were on their way.

As he got out of the car at Olympic a few blocks north of the house, he said, "No, Mom, I won't go off the high diving platform. No, Mom, I will not spend too much time playing video games. No, Mom, I will not eat junk for lunch. Yes, Mom, I will be home by dinnertime." He smiled and headed in the door to the pool complex.

How much easier it was, she thought wryly, if you trained them to answer your questions before they were asked. If only the people she interviewed would be just as cooperative.

She arrived at Stitcher's office in the administration building five minutes early. This being Saturday, his and Stevie's secretary was not on duty. As she stood in the waiting area outside his office, Charlotte could hear Stitcher shouting, ". . . and then I'll strip you of every shred of human dignity! I'll humiliate you! I'll eviscerate you! I'll . . ." Since no one responded, she assumed that he was shouting into the phone. But in a few moments, the coordinator of volunteers came out of Stitcher's office, blushing and with his eyes downcast.

There was an eerie silence in the little waiting area. Finally, Charlotte decided it was safe to go in, although considering the topics she had to bring up, who could be sure?

She rapped on the edge of Stitcher's acoustical screen at the doorway to his office.

"Come in," he said. He sounded testy, but he wasn't shouting.

His office decor looked as though he had tried to bring the Southwest to the Midwest. There were Native American paintings of horses on the wall, a Navajo blanket draped across the back of a couch, several pottery pieces scattered about, and a cow skull, complete with long horns, mounted on the wall behind his desk.

"You seem to have brought Tulsa with you to Columbus," she said. "Are you a collector?"

"No, not really. These are just a few things I picked up. I

went to school in New Mexico and started off working for
zoos in southern California."

"Where did you start in zoo work?"

"A tiny zoo in San Bernardino. I worked mostly with the
hoofed stock—zebras, antelope, that sort of animal. I had always been around horses a great deal and the other hoofers
seemed just like horse variations to me so I really got into it.

"Then I moved down to San Diego to work in its public
education program. I was there for several years, working my
way up to heading that program. It was during those years
that I really came to believe that people need to understand
that zoo animals are not pets, but wild animals."

"I've heard that you don't believe in anthropomorphiz-
ing the animals."

"That's right. All of this naming business, for instance,
has got to stop."

"But doesn't naming some of the animals help the public
feel closer to the animals and then shell out more money for
their care? And I know you need the money for their care."

"Without a doubt. But instead of making people think of
the animals as human, we ought to be educating the public so
that people can appreciate the animals for what they really
are. I resent our having to tart them up as furry humanoids
or other kinds of entertainers."

Not unlike Cheetah Rita, Charlotte thought. She bet the
zoo director and the zoo groupie had more in common than
either one of them knew.

"It sounds like this is very important to you," she said to
Stitcher.

"You bet. I'm sick to death of seeing zoo visitors oohing
and aahing over the more beautiful animals like those dumb
bears and ignoring our less photogenic animals. Especially
since the public puts its money on the pretty animals, too.
Do you know that koala bears sleep about twenty hours a
day? I think we all ought to just attach a stuffed koala to a
branch and tell everyone we have a koala exhibit. Nobody
would know the difference, since the live koalas rarely move

anyway. Every zoo in the nation could have a koala exhibit! We'd all be rich!"

Charlotte laughed and said she thought he had hit on some very creative zoo financing, which encouraged Stitcher to continue in the same vein.

"And the pandas. We can't forget the pandas. People go ga ga over pandas even though it is so easy to see that nature has set us up to love them."

"What do you mean?"

"Well, we tend to appreciate animals that look like human babies. For instance, those that have heads that are large in proportion to their bodies and eyes larger in proportion to their heads. Like human babies do. And pandas are a textbook case."

"There's research evidence for our preferring those kinds of animals?" Charlotte asked.

"Of course. Do you think I make this stuff up?" Stitcher said defensively. "Scientists think those preferences reflect a characteristic that has evolved because it helps us humans remain viable as a species. The characteristic is that we feel protective of our young—those big-eyed, big-headed babies we humans have—which is very important, given how long human babies have to remain under the protection of adults before they can survive on their own. The same features in animals trigger the same emotional response in us. That's why so many of us love animals like pandas. Personally," he said, "I prefer turtles any day."

"But if we've evolved that way, what chance do we have of changing?"

"Well, we can stop efforts that encourage people to think of animals as humans," Stitcher said. "In fact, I would be in favor of abolishing zoos altogether if they weren't the only thing standing between wild animals and extinction."

"In spite of the fact that people can learn a great deal from coming to zoos and participating in educational events?" Charlotte asked.

"Yes, in spite of that. People would be better off learning

about animals from books or movies or TV programs. They don't need to see animals in the flesh to learn what they look like and how they live."

"But isn't it disruptive to the animals to have camera operators moving in on their home territories? How can that be better than having the animals in the zoo?"

Stitcher snorted. "The operative word there is 'home.' These habitats we put together for the animals here are very artificial. They can't move around the way they would if they were at home in Africa or Asia or even here in this country. They get fed regularly every day so they lose all their hunting skills. It's such a fake environment."

"If that's how you feel about zoos, why do you continue to be involved with them?"

"Because there is no wild left. Other than in zoos, there is no place left for wild animals to live. That's why zoos are important," Stitcher said. "Biodiversity."

He looked at Charlotte and smiled for the first time in the interview. "Don't you agree?"

"Certainly," she said. "Except for snakes. I wouldn't care if every snake in the world became extinct."

"That's silly," he said.

"But honest."

"Entomologists say that the cockroaches will outlive us all. It's a truly frightening thing to picture the earth with nothing on it except vegetation and bugs, but we do seem to be aimed in that direction without much concern for the consequences."

How could he reconcile saving the animals with cheating them out of proper care and maintenance? Charlotte wondered. That was really what he had risked in Tulsa. It was time to ask Stitcher about the Tulsa situation, but before she could bring it up, he said, "I'm due over at the Gorilla Villa. If you want to continue our talk, you can join me."

Charlotte stood up and Stitcher came out from behind his desk. He was wearing his usual Western-cut shirt and pants with the curved yoke and curved pockets. And his usual cowboy boots.

She had to ask. "Why do you wear those boots? They seem inconsistent with your views on preserving animals."

"If you had been paying attention to what I said, you'd realize that I'm interested in preserving animal *species*, not every animal that draws breath," Stitcher said. "These boots are cowhide. Did you think they were some sort of exotic leather made from a rare animal? Of course I wouldn't wear anything like that. Cattle are not an endangered species. As far as I can tell, they never will be. So I wear cowhide boots."

Once outside, he stopped to take a deep breath. "Always did prefer fresh air," he stated. Then, ignoring the golf cart parked next to the administration for his and other administrators' convenience, Stitcher set off for the gorilla compound at a brisk pace, with Charlotte struggling to keep up with him.

"As I said on the phone," she said, "I've been talking to some people at the zoo in Tulsa. They say you created serious financial difficulties during the last year you were director there."

"That's bullshit!" he denied hotly. "Who says that?"

"An accountant and at least one member of the board."

"What accountant? What board member? I want names!" he demanded, his voice rising.

She told him, adding that "You can read all about it in my story in Monday's *Dispatch*. I'll be out in Tulsa myself tomorrow," she said, steeling herself for his reaction.

"Your story! Hah! What about *my* story?" By now he was nearly running and she was puffing along beside him, thinking that perhaps reporters had not evolved enough to conduct interviews on the run.

"That's why I'm here," she said. "To get your side of it."

She made him slow down and eventually sit with her on a bench near the gorillas while she asked him about every one of Lisa Hatch's allegations and recorded his answers. He denied all wrongdoing, repeating periodically that he hadn't stolen from the Tulsa Zoo and that he had left that zoo in far better shape than he'd found it in.

"They're all just a bunch of lousy ingrates," he said. According to him, the allegations stemmed from professional jealousy on the part of the director who replaced him. "He's not done squat for that zoo. I can't believe anybody'd put any credence in a smear job like this."

He stood up, signaling the end to the interview. Charlotte braced herself for a threat—of evisceration, at least—if she wrote the story, but Stitcher merely looked down at her and then waved his hand as though to dismiss her. "What the hell," he muttered and began to walk away.

"Wait," she cried after him. "Jerry Brobst knew about what you did in Tulsa. Was he blackmailing you?"

Stitcher just walked on, and she had to admit that he didn't seem upset enough about her story to have fallen victim to blackmail. But maybe he was just resigned by now.

She sat there a moment, watching and listening to a gorilla pounding his chest with both fists, just like in the movies. It reminded her of the kind of male posturing Stitcher usually did but that was strangely absent during her interview with him.

Charlotte wandered over to the office of zoo dietician Maria Pickard and found her friend sitting at the computer, surfing through the Internet. She moved a stack of journals off a folding chair and sat down beside her.

"I came in to download some files the National Zoo sent," Maria explained, "but some of this other stuff is fascinating. Anymore, I'm so afraid I'll miss something important on the Internet that I cruise around here almost every day now."

Following a discussion about how computer networks and databases were changing workplaces like the zoo, Charlotte asked Maria if she had any idea what Jerry could have wanted with Cheetah Rita's notebook.

"Not unless he planned to write a paper based on her research," Maria said. "And that would have been highly unlikely."

"Because it would have been stealing?"

"Yes, but Jerry was never one to put too fine a point on

things like that. I really meant because he wasn't much interested in the scientific aspects of animal keeping. However,
there's some pressure on all our keepers to conduct research,
of course."

"It sounds like you think Cheetah Rita could be coming
up with legitimate findings."

"You never know. She gives me the creeps, but I don't
know of anyone else who's spending more time observing
cheetahs. She knows when every one of ours gets a new
whisker."

Then she said, "But science isn't the only thing that's important with keeping animals. I've heard other keepers say
that Jerry had more intuitive 'feel' for animals than anyone
else they had ever seen. He was really something with the
elephants."

When Charlotte rose to say good-bye and leave, she
mentioned that she was flying to Tulsa that evening to visit
the zoo.

"Whatever for? That's where Bob Stitcher worked last,"
Maria said, as though that fact should disqualify Tulsa from
everyone's list of places to visit for all time.

"I just thought it would be interesting to see how his last
zoo is doing these days," Charlotte said, making no mention
of the dirty tricks she was investigating.

"Well, I've met some people at conferences who have
worked there. None of them acted as though it's any great
shakes as a place to work."

"I'll let you know," Charlotte said as she walked out the
door.

Chapter 24

Early that evening, Walt dropped Charlotte off at the airport for what turned out to be an uneventful flight to Tulsa. That was flying at its best, as far as Charlotte was concerned.

Once in Tulsa, she took a cab to her hotel and settled in for the night. She was grateful that Walt had understood that she would have felt irresponsible if she did not see with her own eyes the evidence against Stitcher before writing the story.

Unfortunately, the trip was made at the Samses' expense, although she had tried to get the city editor of the *Dispatch* to foot the bill. He'd said that if the paper was going to pay for travel, it was going to be a staff writer, not a freelancer, who made the trip. Charlotte wouldn't hear of him assigning the story to someone else.

About dawn the next day, a man wearing a zoo uniform arrived at the Tulsa Zoo's administration building on a staff golf cart. He carried a burlap bag out away from his body and by its neck, which was closed with a short length of twine. He unlocked the front door, walked in, set the bag on the floor, turned on lights in the reception area and front offices, and finally unlocked a storage room at the back of the building.

Inside the room were orderly rows of metal shelves on which heavy cardboard banker's boxes sat. Reading the labels on the outside of the boxes, he located the two he wanted and carried them one at a time to a small meeting room at the front, grateful when he could plop each heavy box onto the rectangular table that took up most of the space in the room.

He looked at his watch and decided he'd better hurry. He walked quickly to the reception area, picked up the burlap bag, and carried it back to the table in the meeting room, where it began to move with a slow undulation.

"Shit!" he said softly. How he hated snakes.

Quickly he opened one of the boxes and looked in. It contained three neat stacks of paper accounting records. He pushed the outer stacks toward the short sides of the box, blocking the openings cut for sticking in your fingers to carry the box. That freed up some space in the middle.

Then he gingerly picked up the bag and placed it in the open box, among the papers. He worked at the twine until he got it loose and then, not daring to touch the bag now that it was open, gave the whole box a shake.

A few moments later, the snake poked its nose out of the neck of the bag and it wasn't long before the colors of a coral snake showed brilliantly against the white papers. The snake slithered between two stacks of paper to the bottom of the box. As soon as he saw the tail of the snake flick out of view, the man took out the bag and quickly closed the box. He was shaking as he left the building and drove away on the golf cart.

Deborah came right on time to pick up Charlotte that morning. They stopped and ate breakfast on the way and Charlotte was pleased to find the young woman as likable as before. They arrived at the administration building at the same time Lisa did. Lisa turned out to be a tall redhead who looked about thirty-five years old. Together they went inside and into the small meeting room.

"I asked Ray Oreste to bring out the files for the time period we'll be talking about," Lisa said. "That's what's in these boxes. We do all our work on computers but make paper copies of each month's and year's records, too."

Deborah told Charlotte that Ray was the zoo's handyman. As an afterthought, she added that he was one of the few Tulsa Zoo employees who remained loyal to Bob Stitcher.

Charlotte reiterated that she wanted to see and make copies of documentation for the accusations against Stitcher that Lisa had made over the phone. Lisa assured her she would have no trouble providing that. Deborah went off to make coffee, while Charlotte and Lisa got down to work.

Lisa opened the first box and they methodically worked their way through the contents, examining relevant copies of electronic ledger pages for the last year or so Stitcher directed the zoo. Lisa handed the records to Charlotte, who handed off to Deborah the papers she wanted copied. Deborah operated the copier in the next room, and the stack of Charlotte's "evidence" that she would take home with her grew larger.

At one point Charlotte asked Lisa whether her boss knew about her helping with the story about Stitcher. "Sure," Lisa said, "he knows all about it. I wouldn't be surprised if he stopped in today. He's as anxious as I am to let people know what Stitcher did to our zoo."

Late in the morning, Charlotte phoned two board members and got good quotes from them, now that they realized that publication of the story was inevitable.

The zoo director who succeeded Stitcher came in about the time the zoo opened to the public and was only too helpful—unseemly in his eagerness, Charlotte thought, to pin as many of his zoo's woes on Stitcher as possible.

Eventually Charlotte asked Lisa whether Stitcher had ever directed her in writing to do the screwy accounting.

"Well, by the time he asked me not to pay the Workman's Comp, I had become suspicious and, of course, not paying Workman's Comp is pretty serious, anyway. So I asked him to write me a memo, asking me not to pay. I was surprised, but he wrote one."

Lisa stood and quickly rifled through the papers remaining in the first box. "It's here somewhere," she said. After a moment, she said, "I don't see it. Must be in the other box. Open it up, Charlotte, and see if that memo is lying anywhere near the top."

Charlotte stood and pulled the box toward her across the table. She opened the lid and reached in to take out a handful of papers. More accounting records. Laying those aside, she reached in again. As she brought out the next handful, she felt something move within her grasp. Frightened, she flung down the papers and then screamed as she saw the snake come from between the papers and slither toward her.

In her panic, she knocked over her chair as she backed away and ran for the door, only to collide with Lisa and Deborah, who were also trying to leave the room. After what seemed like an endless period of jostling, they were finally able to sort themselves out and put a closed door between them and the snake.

In their relief after getting out of the room, they slumped against the wall and hung onto one another while the terror they had felt so strongly started ebbing away. In a moment they were able to laugh a bit, everyone feeling a little punchy from the experience with the snake.

Finally, Charlotte said, "I *hate* snakes!" as though she were seriously trying to enlighten her listeners.

"Well, you could have fooled me," Lisa said sarcastically.

"Maybe the first clue was how she dropped those papers—"

"*And* the snake—" interjected Charlotte.

"—and let out that absolutely *blood-curdling* scream," finished Deborah.

"Oh, and I noticed how you professional zoo people conducted yourselves," Charlotte shot back. "You're supposed to protect the public, but I had to nearly knock you out of my way to get out that door. We must have looked like the Three Stooges."

"There's absolutely nothing professional between me and snakes," Deborah said. "I'll take my chances with four-footed creatures. It's not so easy to hide an elephant."

"How do you think that snake got in there?" Charlotte asked.

Deborah and Lisa looked at one another. Deborah spoke. "I wish we could convince you that accidents like this happen all the time at zoos, but I don't think we could. The truth is that extraordinary safety precautions are taken with danger-ous animals like that coral snake."

"I should hope so. So you don't think the snake was an accident, either."

"Believe me, Charlotte, we usually don't have deadly snakes slithering around in our files," Lisa said.

"Before I left yesterday, I mentioned how I hated snakes to Bob Stitcher," Charlotte said. "It's hard to believe that someone would actually do this, but maybe he asked that handyman to put the snake in the files in hopes it would bite me and I couldn't write the story about him."

"But who says the snake was intended for you? Maybe Ray the handyman put the snake in there to get back at Lisa and me for helping you with the story. He could have been acting alone or maybe Stitcher hired him to get back at us. Ray was a big fan of Stitcher's."

"A unique individual, I'm sure," Charlotte said.

It was Deborah who finally rallied, saying, "I'm calling the snake people to come get that thing," which she did.

Charlotte wanted to call the police, too, but before they could, the current zoo director came in and nixed the idea as too likely to produce bad press for the zoo.

"Just think how bad it would have been if one of us had died from snakebite," Charlotte pointed out. "Whoever did this should be punished."

But she was unwilling to push so hard as to put Deborah

and Lisa's jobs at risk with the director. The director agreed to have the head of zoo security interrogate the handyman and let Charlotte know anything they found out. If Stitcher turned out to be involved, then, of course, she should press charges, the director said. Charlotte was amused that he acted as though she needed his permission.

Unfortunately, things got more complicated when the two reptile keepers arrived to catch the snake and return it to wherever it belonged. The keepers, a man and woman, caught the snake without much trouble while Charlotte, Lisa, and Deborah remained outside the room. Then they quickly identified it as a harmless colubrid rather than the deadly coral snake the three women had been certain it was.

"Both kinds of snakes are the same colors," the male keeper explained. "They both have rings of red, black, and yellow encircling their bodies, but the rings are in a different order, depending on whether the snake is a coral or a colubrid. On the coral snake, the red ring is bordered by rings of yellow. On the colubrid, the red ring is bordered by rings of black instead."

The female reptile keeper chimed in, "I always think 'Red and black, venom lack. Red and yellow, kill a fellow.' "

"Yours is clearly a colubrid," the male keeper said to Charlotte, who corrected him with certainty, "No snake is mine."

He apparently thought she was doubting his identification and started to take the snake out of the bag until all three of them yelled, "Don't do that!" and "Stop!"

The female keeper said, "There's another funny thing about this snake. Its fangs have been removed."

"That snake couldn't have bitten us if it had wanted to?" Charlotte asked.

"That's right."

"You mean we have here a nonpoisonous snake that couldn't bite at all?"

"Exactly. Looks like someone was taking no chances of hurting you."

"A regular model citizen," said Charlotte.

Chapter **25**

Charlotte's article containing the allegations against Bob Stitcher and his side of the story was on the front page of the *Dispatch*, complete with byline and photos of some of the documentation she had gathered from Lisa. There was no mention of what Charlotte would forever call the "snake attack" against the reporter.

On page two was a sidebar by *Dispatch* reporter Chris James that was a historical look at the attendance figures at the Columbus Zoo, including the months since Stitcher had become director.

She and Walt exulted over her story before he left for work. Then she showered and dressed and considered waking Tyler so he could comment on this major coup by his mother. But she decided to let him sleep a few more minutes and went back downstairs to the kitchen.

Ty appeared soon after, yawning and stretching. "Let me see the paper," he said. "Are you in there?"

She handed him the *Dispatch* and he sat right down and read the story.

"Pretty exciting stuff," he said. "I'm impressed."

"Well, thank you," said Charlotte, pleased. "Would you like pancakes for breakfast?"

With the two of them working together, breakfast was on the table in no time and polished off just as quickly. They left the dishes piled in the sink. Ty left for Andrew's house, and Charlotte went into the den to read the rest of the paper.

Perhaps because she was at the back of the house, she did not hear a vehicle pull into the driveway. It turned out to be the Channel 4 television van with reporter Ned Ellison and a camera operator as passengers. The camera started taping when Charlotte answered the doorbell.

Looking straight at the camera, Ellison said, "This is Charlotte Sams, author of this morning's *Dispatch* article about allegations against Columbus Zoo Director Bob Stitcher. The allegations were made by members of the Tulsa Zoo community, where he worked before coming to Columbus."

Turning to a startled Charlotte, he said, "Ms. Sams, tell us your reaction to the fact that Mr. Stitcher may have committed suicide last night or early this morning."

"What?" she squawked. "Stitcher is dead? I have no idea what you're talking about. I have nothing to say. No comment. Turn that thing off."

Ned told the camera operator to stop and then said, "Sorry, Charlotte. We were just trying to get an unrehearsed reaction. I thought for sure you knew about Stitcher."

"No," she said. "No, I didn't. Tell me."

"Well, his wife found him when she got home from a meeting in Toledo. It was after two o'clock this morning. In the garage, with the car running."

"Oh my God," Charlotte breathed.

"Yeah, I know," Ned said sympathetically. "Nice job on the story, though."

She wanted to push him off the porch. The TV people left, and Charlotte went inside. She found it hard to believe that Stitcher was dead. Just yesterday she had believed he had tried to kill her with a snake, and now he was dead by much less exotic means.

It was almost noon, so she turned on the small portable set on a kitchen counter to wait for the midday newscast. The usual noon anchor was doing the lead-in promo. "Stay tuned to this newscast to find out what's happened to the director of the Columbus Zoo. Our own Ned Ellison will have the details along with an interview with Jack Hanna, the former director, interviewed after Stitcher's death."

The first of a string of commercials appeared on the screen. Finally, the anchor said, "And now here's Ned Ellison with this late-breaking story. Ned."

Ned reported what he had already told Charlotte and added that no suicide note had been found. Of course, there would be an autopsy, he said. A story in this morning's local newspaper about allegations made by officials at the Tulsa Zoo could have had something to do with Stitcher's death, he said, adding that the reporter who wrote the story had no comment to make at this time.

Jack Hanna was on tape with a few remarks about how sorry he was that Bob Stitcher had died, but that the zoo was the important thing. People should continue to come out and support the animals at the zoo. In fact, today would be a particularly good day to visit a zoo, any zoo, but particularly the one in Columbus, Hanna said.

Charlotte envisioned hordes of zoo visitors, their appetite for the macabre whetted, getting in their cars for the trek to the zoo. Stitcher would have loved it.

Ellison followed up his interview with Hanna with a prediction that the Columbus Zoo Association would be taking a very careful look at what had been going on at the zoo in the last few months. He then closed the story by saying he would have additional information on the early evening news.

Charlotte snapped off the TV just as the phone rang. It was Sigrid Olson.

"Would you explain to me what is going on here!" Sigrid shouted into the phone. "All I asked you to do was to make sure nobody railroaded Jane Wilcox for the Brobst murder, and now the zoo director is dead and I don't know what the hell is going on.

"We did a national search to find Stitcher for the director position less than a year ago and now we're going to have to do it all over again. Well, Charlotte, tell me. What happened? I need to know why the zoo team is losing."

"I don't know," said Charlotte. "I don't know what's going on. The TV reporter was here about forty-five minutes ago, but he only told me that Stitcher had probably committed suicide. I don't know any details except what everyone heard on the newscast. I can't stand thinking that my story could have resulted in Stitcher killing himself."

There was a pause in the conversation. Charlotte could hear Sigrid breathing into the phone.

"Why didn't you tell me about the Tulsa problems before you put it in the paper?" Sigrid finally said. "As head of Recreation and Parks and certainly as a member of the Zoo Association Board, I should have known about this before it went into the paper. You let the team down, Charlotte. This is a real air ball. Why is it always so hard for me to get the information I need about the zoo!" She paused, but Charlotte had nothing to say, so Sigrid plowed on.

"We had no idea that Stitcher might be padding the attendance figures. I suppose I should pressure the Zoo Association to bring in a team of auditors to check everything at the zoo now. But do you have any idea how much that is going to cost us? We can't afford to do it and we can't afford not to.

"Actually," Sigrid said, sounding a little calmer, "maybe it was a good thing you found out as soon as you did. What if this had been going on for years before anybody figured out what he was doing? Maybe you didn't let the team down so badly after all, Charlotte. Good defense! I'll talk to you later."

She hung up, leaving Charlotte listening to a dial tone. She felt totally confused, certain only that she was glad she had not supplied Sigrid with information about the motives of anyone at the zoo.

She sat back down at the kitchen table. Stitcher hadn't struck her as being the kind of person to give up easily. Having the things he did in Tulsa made public must have been difficult, but she didn't think they presented an insurmountable problem for him. He could have left town, changed his name, gone into some other line of work. Or he could have stayed in town and faced the music. Fighting back seemed like Stitcher's style, whereas committing suicide struck her as completely out of character.

Besides, while the allegations from Tulsa were serious—enough to embarrass him and even maybe cost him his job—he wasn't likely to go to jail over them. It wasn't as if he had been accused of embezzlement or of killing somebody. *Killing somebody*, she repeated silently. Maybe that was it. Maybe he really did kill Jerry and knew that once people started poking around, the truth would come to light.

Well, if that was the case, then she had just solved another of Detective Barnes's murder cases for him, Charlotte thought. Not that he'd ever admit it.

Still, after finding out that he might have sicced a snake on her (harmless though it was), she found it difficult to think she knew Stitcher well. What kind of person would make doubly sure that a snake couldn't hurt someone but still use that snake to scare her? Did that sound like someone who could have killed Jerry? Even if she heard from the Tulsa Zoo that it was Stitcher who was behind the snake attack, she expected to have trouble making up her mind: Should she be furious with him or feel sorry for him because he obviously felt so ambivalent about his mission?

By this time she was pacing around the kitchen. Having decided that she needed more information, she stopped long enough to call the zoo and ask for Maria. Maria didn't want to talk at first, blaming Charlotte for her boss's suicide.

"First Jerry and now Stitcher," she said. "Maybe it's not safe to have anything to do with you, Charlotte."

"Oh, please be reasonable, Maria," she said. "You know I didn't have anything to do with Jerry's death, and if my story caused Stitcher to kill himself, then I'm very sorry. But my story was accurate and fair. *I* didn't do anything wrong—*he* did."

"I still don't like it," Maria said.

"I thought maybe you could tell me what you know about Stitcher's death or what he was doing yesterday or anything else that you think might be relevant."

"Why? Are you going to put this in one of your articles?"

"No. I promise. Right now I'm just trying to make sense of his death."

"Well, all I know about how he died is what's been reported on TV. The last time I saw him was last evening at a picnic we had for Zoo Association members."

"What time was that?"

"The picnic didn't begin until after five. Most of us staffers were there, and the bigwigs from the association, of course."

"Anyone else? Anyone out of the ordinary?"

"No. Sigrid Olson was there from the city's Recreation and Parks Department. But she's on the association board, too, so she often comes for events. She did talk with Stitcher alone for a long time before we ate."

"What about?"

"I don't know. But before he left her, I heard him say, 'You women are driving me crazy!' He sounded upset. But being upset was a way of life for Bob."

"How did Stitcher act otherwise?"

"Like always. He did his share of yelling—at John Hogan, for instance—"

"So Hogan was there, too."

"Yes, but that's not unusual, either. He helped set up the tables, and when Stitcher didn't like how they were arranged, he really let Hogan have it."

"As you said, he was his usual self."

"Until he got sick."

"When?"

"He seemed like always until after most people had eaten, say, seven o'clock or so. Then I overheard him telling Stevie that he didn't feel good. I never saw him after that."

"What did he say was wrong?"

"He said he felt light-headed and kind of clammy. I could tell he was sweating a lot because his shirt was soaked. But it was hot and I thought he had just gotten overheated."

"What did Stevie do?"

"I think she suggested he sit down in the shade for a while."

"Do you know when he left?"

"No."

"How did he get home?"

"They found him dead in his own car. He must have felt well enough to drive himself home."

"Mrs. Stitcher wasn't at the picnic, I take it."

"No."

"Was that unusual?"

"No, she rarely came to the zoo or to zoo functions. I think she just wasn't interested, and she seemed to have her own things to do. She's an accountant, you know."

Charlotte hadn't known, and immediately wondered whether it was from his wife that Stitcher had gotten the ideas he put into practice in Tulsa. How come she hadn't turned up the fact that he was married to an accountant when she was doing the story on the allegations against him? She hated it when she found out relevant information when it was too late to use it. It also made her worry about what else she might have missed.

"Maria," she said, "doesn't it seem funny to you that Stitcher was feeling sick earlier in the evening before he committed suicide? Doesn't that make it seem possible that it wasn't suicide at all?"

"You mean that maybe he died from spoiled potato

salad? Or some other illness? Ha! They found him in his car, with the car running in a closed garage, Charlotte. You just don't want to think that your article made someone feel bad enough to kill himself. And I don't blame you."

"Thanks a lot," Charlotte said and hung up the phone.

Chapter **26**

The phone rang again almost immediately. It was Lou. "You must feel terrible," she said. "That newscaster couldn't quite bring himself to say it was all your fault, but it seemed like that was the story to him."

"Not you, too," snapped Charlotte. "First the TV guys show up, then Sigrid Olson bawls me out, and then Maria Pickard isn't all that sure she wants to talk with me."

"Come on, Charlotte," Lou said. "Reporters like you write hard-hitting, responsible stories all the time without their subjects committing suicide over them. Besides, I think it's a real stretch to think of Stitcher as a candidate for suicide."

"Thanks. It helps to know that *you* don't just assume my stories mean death."

Lou laughed until she noticed that Charlotte did not join in. Becoming serious herself, she asked, "Think about it. Why would Stitcher take his own life? He took stuff out on other people, not himself. Maybe—I'm sure you've considered this—it was murder."

"I've been hoping that he just got sick from the food at the zoo, although I don't know of any food allergies that make you drive home and hook yourself up to your car's tailpipe."

"Face it, Charlotte: he must have known too much about Jerry Brobst's murder," Lou said decisively.

"Without having committed it himself, you mean?"

"Yes."

"For the last couple days he was high on my list of suspects for having killed Jerry himself," Charlotte said. "Either Jerry was blackmailing him over the Tulsa allegations, I thought. Or else Jerry wasn't blackmailing him but was threatening to make the allegations public. They still seem like good motives for murder to me."

"Me, too."

"But I have so much trouble thinking that he killed himself. And I have trouble thinking of him choosing Jerry's method of murder. I think he would have chosen a more certain method. Like shooting or drowning."

"Or hitting him over the head with a blunt instrument," Lou said. "Like his tongue."

"Yes," Charlotte said, chuckling. "Something like that. Or maybe, Lou, I just don't want to think my story caused him to turn on his car inside his garage and sit there, alone, gulping in huge lungfuls of carbon monoxide until he died."

Neither of them spoke for a few moments. Then she asked Lou to accompany her that afternoon to talk with Stevie and Mrs. Stitcher. "It would be helpful to have a friend along while I talk with all these people who probably hate me."

As soon as Charlotte ended her conversation with Lou, the phone immediately rang again. This time it was Walt, who said in an exasperated tone, "We've got to get Call Waiting. I've been trying to reach you for over an hour."

"What's wrong?" Charlotte said, bracing herself for more bad news.

"I heard about Stitcher and just wanted to make sure you didn't feel your story was responsible."

About an hour later, Charlotte and Lou were caught up in the midst of the traffic jam on its way to the zoo. Charlotte didn't much care how long it took them to get there because she was using the time for thinking. Of course, she acknowledged, that probably made her boring company for Lou. But after having been filled in on Sunday's snake attack in Tulsa, Lou seemed to welcome the silence.

The flag at the gate was flying at half-mast when they entered. They parked and elbowed their way along through the mobs of single-day ticket holders to reach the quieter entrance for season ticket holders and employees.

Lou waited outside the administration building while Charlotte sought out Stevie, lest Stevie remember Lou as the one who had taken her on the wild goose chase to find Stitcher.

Charlotte found Stevie in her usual neat-as-pin cubicle. However, Stevie herself was looking a little disheveled today, with her hair standing as though she had run her hands through it several times and the collar on her blouse flipped sideways.

When Charlotte knocked on the door frame, Stevie looked up from the papers she had been poring over and said through clenched teeth, "Charlotte Sams. How dare you come here after what you've done to this zoo? I think you had better leave. Right now," she said, rising from her desk chair.

Charlotte walked on into Stevie's cubicle. "I just wanted to ask about Stitcher's illness at the picnic last night," she said. "And how he got home if he wasn't feeling well."

"How should I know? I think your questions are in bad taste. The man felt so bad about your story that he committed suicide. *Everything* you could do at this point is in bad taste."

Perhaps, in Stevie's mind, being in bad taste was the greatest crime of all, Charlotte thought.

"I need to know how Stitcher got home," she repeated.

"How should I know? He kept giving me orders all evening. Go here. Do this. Do that. All I know is, he sent me to his office to get a file that took me a half-hour to find and, then, when I came back with it, he was gone."

"What file?"

"What?"

"What file did he ask you to find?"

Stevie looked confused. "The USDA file, I guess. Or something like that," she said. "Now get out of here."

And then the unflappable Stevie Kimmel sat back down in her chair, laid her head down on her arms on the top of her desk, and sobbed.

Charlotte quietly backed out of the office.

A USDA file? Charlotte had asked the question just because she thought it might be helpful to know what Stitcher was thinking during his last few hours. But what connection would the zoo have with the USDA? The USDA meant food to Charlotte, so she and Lou walked over to zoo dietician Maria Pickard's office to ask about the connection.

Perhaps because she didn't want to make a scene in front of Lou, who was a stranger to her, Maria seemed a little friendlier than she had over the phone.

"Oh, so you've found out about our little problem with the Department of Agriculture, have you?" she said. "You are uncanny, Charlotte."

Pretending that she was not totally ignorant of the entire situation, Charlotte said, "And I'd like to know more about it."

Maria obligingly explained that the USDA inspects zoos and this year had fined the Columbus Zoo for not providing enough shade for the elephants.

"Actually, the fine was for late filing of the reports that explain why we don't have enough shade. But the fact remains that the USDA thinks we don't have enough shade."

"How come this hasn't been reported?"

"Because Stitcher was trying to keep it under wraps, of course."

"Well, he did a good job," Charlotte complained. "I've been talking with people here for two months and this is the first I've heard about elephant shade. Who all *does* know about it?"

"Not many of us. Stitcher and Stevie, of course. The elephant keepers. That's probably all."

"And you."

Maria laughed. "And me. But I know everything, haven't you noticed?"

"So Jerry would have known about it?"

"Of course."

On the way to the car after leaving Maria's office, Lou said, "You're thinking that this elephant shade business is what Jerry wanted to talk with a reporter about before he died, aren't you?"

"That's right. But it doesn't seem to account in any way for his having stolen Cheetah Rita's notebook."

"Not yet. But who says it has to? His having wanted to talk with a reporter and his having stolen her notebook—if he did—may be entirely two separate incidents."

"Maybe."

"Or maybe you'll turn something up that connects them," Lou said. "I think you're doing a great job with this whole situation."

"It's nice of you to say that, but so far two people have died, and both deaths seem connected to me or my job."

"That's what I always like about you, Charlotte: your ability to see the silver lining in every cloudy situation."

Lou and even Charlotte laughed.

In a moment Lou said, "That Maria seemed to be quite a gossip."

"In my business, we like to call such people 'good sources,' especially since I've not known her to lie."

"Well, I didn't mean that I thought she was a *malicious* gossip. She just seemed willing to tell you a lot."

"Some people actually trust me, Lou, believe it or not."

"I think I'll just stop here before I put my foot any further into my mouth."

Charlotte had gotten the Stitchers' address out of the phone book before she and Lou had left for the zoo. Of course, Mrs. Stitcher might not be home, but Charlotte still did not want to phone ahead. After all, if she gave Mrs. Stitcher the chance, she might very well refuse to see her. Who could blame her? But over the years Charlotte had learned that it is much harder for people to get rid of you if you are standing in front of them in the flesh rather than merely a disembodied voice on the phone.

The Stitchers' house was on the west side of the O'Shaughnessy Reservoir, opposite the zoo. Many of the houses along there were very expensive, with wide lawns going right down to the water. Stitcher had lived in one like that.

Walking up the driveway to the house, Charlotte and Lou could see between his house and the next, all the way across the reservoir to the zoo. From there, it looked like a peaceful and colorful small town. Stitcher would have been able to keep an eye on things from his back porch.

Mrs. Stitcher answered the door herself. After Charlotte introduced herself and Lou, they were welcomed into the house so warmly that she worried that perhaps the grieving widow was luring them in so she could club them over the head for having contributed to the death of her husband. Mrs. Stitcher remained warm and polite once they were inside, but Charlotte decided she should still stay on her guard.

Mrs. Stitcher was a tall, large-boned woman of about fifty, with auburn hair and fair skin, wearing pale yellow pants and a navy silk blouse. She had on what looked like ballet slippers.

As the three of them walked to the living room, Mrs. Stitcher glanced out a window that faced the reservoir and stopped.

"Well, look," she said, pointing. "Our canoe is gone. Bob

always kept it on that stand out there by the bank." She smiled sadly. "It's a funny thing, isn't it? A couple of days ago, I would have been furious that anyone would steal something from us. But now that Bob's been stolen from me, I doubt I'll even report the canoe to the police."

She invited Lou and Charlotte to sit on the couch and then hurried to pick up some plastic toys that lay on the cushions before they sat down. Her daughter and grandchildren had been visiting for the entire summer, she explained.

"But as luck would have it, they, too, were away last night when Bob got home," she said. "Otherwise, someone would have been here to help him. I regret that I was not."

She did not cry, but Charlotte thought that she had never seen anyone look so sad as Mrs. Stitcher. Tears welled up in her own eyes, and she looked away, regretting any part she had played in the death of this woman's husband. First Jerry and now Stitcher. It didn't matter that she hadn't much liked Stitcher or even that he might have been behind the snake attack. All this death was just too much.

She looked around the living room, which bore no resemblance at all to Stitcher's office. The colors were soft pastels, the furniture was contemporary, and tasteful reproductions of abstract expressionist prints were framed on the walls. If Stitcher had longhorn cows on the walls at home, they were in another room. She wondered whether Mrs. Stitcher's good taste had merely prevailed here or whether Stitcher had put on the cowboy routine only for public consumption.

Now Charlotte explained that she wanted to apologize if her story about Stitcher's accounting had had anything to do with his death.

To her surprise, Mrs. Stitcher said, "Oh, I don't think your story had anything at all to do with it. I can't imagine how it could have. I know he wasn't the least bit upset about that story."

"Well, I'm glad to hear that. I've been very worried."

"There's no reason you should be concerned," said Mrs. Stitcher, smoothing the pale fabric of her pants with manicured fingers. "But he didn't break the law in Tulsa, you know," she said abruptly, giving Charlotte a defiant look. "Nobody has ever accused Bob Stitcher of doing anything illegal."

Charlotte changed the subject by saying, "It must have been terrible to have found him like that."

"It was. I felt guilty that my meeting had run so late. But the police seemed to think that he had been dead for some time when I found him."

"I understand you're an accountant. Do you work full-time?"

"Yes, I'm the executive director of a statewide professional association of accountants. I can do most of the work out of my home here, but every so often we have a lengthy meeting somewhere else in the state, like the one last night in Toledo."

"Had Mr. Stitcher been ill lately?"

"No."

"I've talked with the zoo dietician. She said that he seemed to become ill at the picnic last night."

"I've heard that, too, and I've made the police aware of it."

"You said that he was not very upset about my article. Was he worried about anything else?"

"Bob's been very happy here in Columbus."

"He did a lot of shouting at the office," Charlotte pointed out.

"Why does everybody feel they have to keep bringing that up?" Mrs. Stitcher said impatiently. "He yelled a lot here, too. Haven't any of you ever known a 'yeller' before? That was just his way."

Charlotte asked whether she knew if her husband was upset about the zoo being fined for not having enough shade for the elephants.

"How did you find out about that?" Without waiting for an answer, Stitcher's widow hurried on. "Bob knew those animals needed more shade, too. He did! But getting it was going to require changing the structure of the pachyderm building, and his hardest fights with the Zoo Association Board were always over changing the physical plant of the zoo. Because doing that is always so expensive. You have no idea how expensive it is."

"Had he begun fighting for that shade yet?"

"He was always fighting for the best interests of the animals. You should know that!"

Charlotte was getting uncomfortable, aware that Mrs. Stitcher had become more and more upset as the conversation progressed. She was glad when Lou said sympathetically, "All of this has to be a terrible shock. Did he leave a note for you?"

"No, no note or message of any kind. And I have to say that I'm not surprised. I don't believe for a moment that he committed suicide."

"How interesting," Lou said quickly, after glancing meaningfully at Charlotte. "Who would have wanted him dead?"

"I think it had to be whoever killed the elephant keeper— someone whose car was in the parking lot the night that poor man was killed."

"We heard Mr. Stitcher was trying to remember those cars," Lou said, "I guess now we'll never know."

"On the contrary. Bob remembered."

Charlotte gasped. "Whose cars were there?"

"He told me it would be better that I didn't know, and now it looks like he was right," Mrs. Stitcher said. "You'll have to ask the police. I'm sure he told them."

Suddenly she rose from her chair and crossed the room to stand in front of the couch, with her fists clenched at her sides.

"Suicide is completely out of character for Bob," she said passionately, pounding her fists in the air. "I'll *never* believe that he would kill himself."

She leaned over until her face was very close to Charlotte's, and Lou wondered whether she should knock the widow down before she did something violent. Charlotte didn't flinch but stared right back into the depths of Mrs. Stitcher's dark blue eyes.

"Are you married, Ms. Sams?"

Charlotte said she was.

"Do you love your husband?"

Charlotte said she did.

"Well, do you think your husband could do something so much out of character as kill himself without you knowing that he was even unhappy? Do you?"

Charlotte admitted she thought she would know, and Mrs. Stitcher backed off.

"Well, I loved my husband, too," she said, straightening up. "I know he was not unhappy. And I know he did not take his own life. He was murdered!"

She returned to her chair, took a deep breath, and said, "The only question now is, who's going to be next?"

"Why should there be anyone else?" Charlotte asked.

"Because I don't believe Bob could have been the only threat to the killer."

Oh. Charlotte was sorry she had asked.

"You must have told the police how you feel," Lou said.

"Yes. They don't believe me, of course—they think I'm just unwilling to admit that I wasn't able to keep Bob happy. But I've demanded an autopsy, and that should prove I'm right."

Mrs. Stitcher now looked entirely spent. In a few minutes, Charlotte said, "We appreciate your talking with us," as she and Lou got up to leave. "Is there someone I can call to come be with you? We could wait until they get here."

"Oh, no. I'll be fine. My daughter and grandkids will be back at any moment. And the neighbors have been wonderful."

Chapter **27**

Charlotte woke up the next morning with the phrase "Two at the zoo," "two at the zoo," running through her head, over and over. Apparently her mind had gone on working even while she slept. Or tried to.

Two deaths of zoo employees. More like two murders, if she and Mrs. Stitcher were right. She had a vested interest in making sure the number did not climb to three.

Walt was already sitting at the breakfast table when she went downstairs. She sat down and, without preamble, said to him, "One of the oddest things about my talk with Mrs. Stitcher was that as I sat there in that pretty room, listening to her loving description of a reasonable man, it was easy to forget that Bob Stitcher was not like that—not like the pretty room, not the way she described him, not reasonable."

"And good morning to you, too, Charlotte."

She leaned over and gave him a quick kiss but then went right on thinking out loud. "I have to keep in mind how

Stitcher *really* was and remind myself that he probably sent a snake to scare me to death. Remind myself that he liked to humiliate the coordinator of volunteers. Remind myself how he hurt the Tulsa Zoo." She paused. "Remind myself that he wore those ridiculous outfits."

"That's our man," Walt said, pouring himself and Charlotte some coffee.

"Now," she said, "I think that whoever killed Jerry did it impulsively, on the spur of the moment, because no one would actually *plan* to kill someone by pushing him off the pachyderm building roof. Because you couldn't be sure that he would die."

"Okay by me," said Walt, beginning to skim the newspaper.

"And I think that means that he was killed by someone who did not have a long-standing reason to hate him."

"Sounds good," said Walt.

"I think that's why nobody's been able to come up with any decent suspects. The best I've been able to uncover is that dumb Hogan, who had his wife stolen by Jerry and who got into a fight with him."

Walt looked up from the paper long enough to remind her that Hogan was a pretty good suspect, given that he was violent enough to have slashed her car top.

"Maybe, but I have no proof of that."

"But you do know he was willing to risk his job and possible charges for growing marijuana."

"All right. Anyway, the police haven't done any better than I have. All they have is Cheetah Rita, and even though she may have left her notebook page at the scene, they apparently don't have enough to charge her. Then there's Barbara Champion."

"The elephant keeper," he said from behind the paper.

"She really didn't like Jerry at all. And she may have orchestrated Koko's charge on me to scare me away from the zoo."

Walt perked up and lowered the paper. "I didn't know

you felt that way about it," he said quite seriously.

Whoops. No point in telling him more than he could handle. "Not really. It was just a thought."

"You haven't mentioned Stitcher," he said. "Even if he was murdered, he may still have killed Jerry in order to stop him from blackmailing him. And stopping blackmail is a very good motive for murder in my book."

"Okay," she said, "but then who would have killed Stitcher? I can't believe these murders aren't related. It's two at the zoo. Who would have wanted both Jerry and Stitcher dead?"

"Obviously, Jerry's killer," Walt said before ducking behind the paper again. "If he thought Stitcher was going to turn him in."

"I've thought of that, of course. Maybe the killer found out that Stitcher had remembered whose cars were in the lot that night. Or, think about this: What if Stitcher really had not suffered from memory problems at all but had just been protecting someone by not telling the police?" She paused to butter some toast and then resumed.

"But then why would he have stopped protecting them? Was it just coincidental that he stopped when my article about the Tulsa allegations came out? Unless—get this, Walt—the blackmailer was not Jerry at all but someone else who was still alive, in which case my story made public what the blackmailer was holding over Stitcher. How's that? Was the blackmailer afraid that Stitcher would then go to the police to turn him in? For blackmail? Or for the murder of Jerry Brobst? Walt?"

"What?"

"Oh, never mind. I'm going in circles anyway. Just pour me some more coffee, will you?"

Later that morning, Charlotte went to her Clintonville office, mostly because she didn't know what else to do. Trying not to take unnecessary chances, she locked her office door once she was inside, instead of leaving it wide open as she usually did.

She sat at her desk and listed everything she could think of to do to try to prove that Stitcher did not commit suicide as a result of her article. The entire list consisted of two items: "Call Deborah to see whether Stitcher arranged for the snake" and "Ask Barnes about whose cars were in the lot." Then she crossed out the second item as being impossible. She was not likely to even see Detective Barnes anytime soon.

Idly, she looked through a stack of glossy 8" x 10" photographs that Stevie had said she could use in the series. They had been taken by the zoo photographer and some of them were very good, including a shot of Teak and Amber, the twin gorillas born at the zoo. She'd find a way to use that.

There was also a good shot of four adult cheetahs, with no sign of Cheetah Rita skulking anywhere in the background. She couldn't tell whether the picture was taken at the male or female enclosure. She wondered what effect Stitcher's death would have on Cheetah Rita. Maybe the next director would not work so hard at having her bounced from the zoo. Wasn't it interesting that the two people who gave Cheetah Rita the hardest time had so recently lost their lives?

The photos made Charlotte remember that Barbara Champion had asked her to include a photograph of the pen top she had pried out of Indy's foot pad. So she dug the marbleized navy blue pen top out of her tote bag and laid it on the board over which her camera was suspended on a tripod. She looked through the lens to focus.

It would be a pleasure to make the plea for visitors to keep all their possessions out of enclosures, especially after Barbara had regaled her with stories of animals who got sick from eating such things as belt buckles, containers, and wristwatches that had been thrown to them. There was even a story about an elephant at the National Zoo having eaten a child's backpack, but she didn't know whether to believe that one or not.

It was while she snapped the picture that she realized the pen top might be more than a symbol of humans' inhumanity to animals. It could also be a symbol of someone's inhumanity to Jerry Brobst. The pen top could have been lost there by Jerry's killer.

Excited, she realized it could be every bit as incriminating as Cheetah Rita's notebook page. It could be evidence or at least a clue. She could turn the pen top over to Barnes and while she was there, she could ask him about the cars Stitcher remembered being in the parking lot the night Jerry was killed. To her surprise, she found she could even imagine telling Barnes about the taped threat and being locked in the freezer. Maybe it would help to unburden herself to Barnes. She was certainly getting tired of looking over her shoulder all the time.

So she put the pen top in her purse and drove downtown to the new police headquarters, which sat catty-cornered at Marconi and Gay, with a sleek cement lioness crouched on each side of the front door. Cheetah Rita should get a look at these cats, Charlotte thought.

The new headquarters building had been open for less than a year. Apparently, the architects and the heating and cooling people had not been putting together the same building, so the whole thing, especially the large open lobby, was too cold in the winter and now, in the summer, unbearably hot. As soon as she got inside, she saw a number of fans trying to cool things down.

She told a perspiring officer behind the desk that she wanted to talk with Detective Barnes and he, after making a couple of phone calls, directed her to the elevator and told her Barnes's office was on the second floor.

When she found his office, Barnes stood to greet her and motioned to the chair next to his desk. Almost immediately she was sorry she had come.

"I read your article about Bob Stitcher's alleged actions in Tulsa, Ms. Sams," he began.

"Oh, that . . ."

"Since you had to have realized the implications your story could have for the Brobst murder case, I'm surprised you didn't let me know what you had found out."

"I don't work for the police," Charlotte said demurely.

"My point, exactly," Barnes said, glowering at her. "Stay out of this business at the zoo."

"I'm just doing my job," Charlotte said, "which is more than I can say for you, if I keep finding out things before you do. Like this pen top. I think it might be evidence."

She took out the pen top and put it on Barnes' desk. "I would have used gloves, but by this time it's ridiculous to think any of the owner's prints would still be on it."

He barely looked at the pen top. "I haven't a clue as to what you're talking about here, Ms. Sams. Enlighten me."

"Well, this is obviously the top to an expensive fountain pen. One of the elephants at the zoo picked it up in a crack in her foot pad. She had to have gotten it from the enclosure, and *I* think it could have been left there by Jerry Brobst's killer."

"Foot pad?" Barnes said.

Patiently, she explained the elephant foot care regimen and how the pen top had been discovered. "So you think that this pen top could have been left by the person who pushed Jerry Brobst off the pachyderm building?"

"That's right, Detective."

"How do you know it wasn't thrown into the yard by one of the zoo visitors?"

"Well, I don't, of course. But you considered Cheetah Rita's notebook page to be evidence that she could have been the killer."

"Mostly because it was found on *top* of the building, Ms. Sams, to which the public does not have access. And nothing makes me think that a zoo visitor could have wadded up that notebook page and hurled it thirty feet up onto the roof. Whereas, this pen top," he said, looking at it as he held it at both ends by the thumb and index finger of one hand, "easily could have been thrown into the yard by a visitor. I understand they throw all kinds of trash into the cages. Someone even told me about a backpack being tossed in."

"You heard that one, too, huh?"

"Yes. So you see, Ms. Sams, I can't put much credence in your little theory. Not only is there no way to tell who left this pen top, there is no way to tell when it got left. It could have been there long before Brobst was murdered—or long after, in fact."

Bristling at his tone, Charlotte said, "Well, as I said, it *could* have been left by the killer. I didn't say it had to have been. But surely you'll want to check it out."

"I don't think that will be necessary," he said, handing the pen top back to her.

Insulted, Charlotte opened her mouth to protest, but Barnes, with a smug smile, didn't give her a chance. "And, frankly, Ms. Sams, if you don't mind my saying so, I think you're slipping. You were much sharper the first time around."

"The game's not over yet," she said and stomped out of the office.

Chapter **28**

Back in her car, an angry Charlotte headed for the zoo. She didn't doubt that what Barnes said was true; she *didn't* know when the pen top had gotten into the enclosure. But she had been under the distinct impression—however naive that seemed now—that figuring out such information was the police's job. Well, you learned something every day, didn't you?

So much for being angry at Barnes. She was angry at herself for not asking about the cars Stitcher remembered being in the lot. Now she'd have to figure out some other way to get that information.

Once at the zoo, she hunted up Barbara Champion. Not that Barbara was hard to find. She was right there in the African elephant enclosure, rinsing off the big male.

Charlotte reminded her about the pen top and asked if she remembered when that foot of Indy's had last been cared for *before* Barbara found the pen top. Barbara said that she kept records of all animal care—Stitcher, like Hanna before him, had required it of all keepers. She'd have to look it up.

"If you come back after lunch, I'll show you the pedicure schedule," she said. "Even though you *did* check up on me—what time I got back to the zoo the night Jerry died, I mean."

Charlotte didn't say anything.

"You talked to the ferret keeper," Barbara said accusingly.

"I'm just trying to do a good job with my stories."

They talked a bit about Stitcher's death, and Charlotte was relieved to find Barbara did not seem to hold her responsible. She also asked Barbara about the USDA fine, which—both the fine itself and the fact that Charlotte knew about it—seemed to make her angry.

"So now you know our little secret, don't you?" she said. "For over twenty years I've worked here, trying to do what's best for the elephants. We all tried to get Stitcher off his butt to get more shade, but he wouldn't move. Brobst—over my objections—even put up that silly-looking metal parasol out there in the Africans' yard, thinking that maybe that would cast a shadow big enough to help."

"Is that what that ugly thing is supposed to be for?"

"Yep. And now we're going to have to go public with our shade problems because of the fine. I'm going to have to skip zookeepers conferences this year, just because I don't want to hear everything that's going to be said about us and the care I give our elephants."

Charlotte told her she'd be back after lunch for the pedicure schedule and then bought a sandwich at one of the concessions. On the way to her zoo office to eat it, she saw Hogan trimming a hedge by himself.

Anxious to change the balance of power that had accompanied most of their meetings, this time *she* approached *him*. A good offense is the best defense, she thought, and if she couldn't even ask the police to protect her, she'd have to become offensive herself.

"I'm on to all your tricks, Hogan!" she yelled as she walked up to him.

"What's bugging you now, Ms. Sams?" he said with a sneer.

"Oh, so you know my name now, do you? Well, I know all about you, too—about your fight with Jerry Brobst and even about your wife's affair with him."

"Shut your mouth about my wife!"

"It's only a matter of time until the police figure it out that one of you killed him."

"You bitch!"

"No, on second thought, I can't imagine somebody as wimpy as you having the guts to do anything like that. Your *wife* must have killed him. That's what the police will figure out."

Hogan threw his hedge trimmers in her direction, where they landed harmlessly at her feet, and stalked away down the path.

Charlotte watched him go, feeling confident she had won this round.

At about 1:15 she returned to the pachyderm building to join Barbara. But she couldn't find her. She walked inside, outside, and around the entire structure. The animals were all in their yards outside, but there was no sign of Barbara. The other keepers for that building were apparently still at lunch, so there was no one to ask where she might be.

Charlotte hadn't asked where the records were kept. Maybe there was an office or offices in the building that she didn't know about. She went back in and walked the entire length of the building, down the wide aisle between the huge cages for their huge occupants. At the far end, right before the door to the outside, she found a door off to the right. She opened it and stepped into a short hallway.

"Barbara?" she called out.

Two black metal doors were closed on either side of the hallway. Offices, she thought. She tried the first, but it was locked. The second was slightly ajar and opened onto a set of steps going up. They must be the stairs to the rooftop, she thought. The stairs Jerry and his murderer must have used. What had someone called them? The internal stairway. She thought that had been Barbara.

Charlotte had assumed the police would keep these stairs blocked. Maybe they had, but there was nothing blocking them now, not even that yellow plastic tape they put up to keep people out of a crime scene. There was probably a locked door at the top of the stairs so that you couldn't actually get out on the roof, which was the real scene of the crime.

She climbed the stairs with no real expectation that the door at the top would be unlocked. But it was. What good luck, she thought, her heart leaping at the wild possibility of actually finding the bottom to the pen on the roof. That would show that patronizing Barnes.

She opened the door and walked a few feet out onto the wide flat roof, feeling she was on top of the world. That made her feel sick, of course, afraid in this high open place that gravity would momentarily fail her and she would float off the roof and then plummet immediately to the ground. Her heart pounded in her ears, and she began sweating. Her knees felt like they could not support her. She fought her panic with all her might, hoping not to let her fear of heights paralyze her now.

She slowly inched her way toward the part of the roof above where Jerry's body had been found. If only she had something to hold onto! But the roof was empty, being only a flat expanse that sloped slightly toward its gutters along the perimeter.

She was almost to the edge when a voice behind her said, "I knew you'd come up here if you found the door open."

Charlotte jumped, which made her think she was on her way off the roof. She sat down, her hands clutching fruitlessly for support from the flat, dirty surface of the roof.

Barbara walked over. "Trying to imagine how Jerry died?" she said.

Charlotte suddenly remembered how Barbara had asked her to reach into the elephant enclosure to hand her the ankus—right before Koko charged. Consequently, she could feel herself about to start hyperventilating and could not answer.

"What's the matter? You're going to get dirt all over your clothes." Barbara leaned down to look at Charlotte. "Are you all right? You look a little green."

Charlotte didn't doubt it. All she wanted was to get off this infernal roof.

Barbara offered her a hand up, but Charlotte, in a panic, shouted, "Don't touch me!"

Barbara laughed. "Don't tell me," she said. "You're not one of those bozos who's afraid of heights?"

"Just leave me alone, Barbara," Charlotte spat out. "Get out of here."

"Well, I'll be damned. This is a riot. You can't even stand up, can you?"

Charlotte ignored her and started scooting on her hands and butt toward the stairway. Barbara walked silently along beside her. Finally Charlotte got into the stairway and was able to stand on the third or fourth step down. All of her body was safely within the building.

Barbara said, "There, you made it," but Charlotte ignored her. She paused there briefly until her breathing became normal and then she walked down the stairs with her hand on the rail and Barbara following.

On the way, Barbara took a piece of paper out of her pocket. "I looked up when anybody last did Indy's right front foot before we found that pen top."

Charlotte did not answer.

"It hadn't been done since the Friday before Brobst died," Barbara said, "because we were so short-handed after that."

At the door to the outside, Charlotte muttered "Thanks" and set off for her zoo office. Behind her, she heard Barbara laugh. "Any time," she said.

Chapter 2

For the first time that summer, Charlotte welcomed the confined space in her zoo office.

Chapter **29**

For the first time that summer, Charlotte welcomed the confined space in her zoo office. How much safer its hot little atmosphere felt than the wide world at the top of the pachyderm building.

Her anger at Barbara had slowly subsided, and now she felt silly to have been so frightened on the roof. It hadn't just been the height; the thought had actually crossed her mind that Barbara was considering pushing her over the side. Of course, she reminded herself, the fact that she hadn't pushed Charlotte didn't mean that she hadn't pushed Jerry. She had to stay on her guard. It wasn't so silly to keep in mind that Barbara appeared not to have an alibi for the time Jerry was killed.

After recovering a bit, she thought about the pen top. She loved the idea that it was a clue, perhaps because it argued against most of the zoo staff being Jerry's killer. After all, this was a place whose concessions did not even provide soda straws, for fear that the plastic straws would end up in the animals' enclosures. She hadn't seen a keeper use so much as a Bic pen, let alone a fountain pen, since she'd been there.

The only zoo employees she could imagine using such a writing instrument were all in the administration building, and Stitcher was the only one of them that seemed to go anywhere near the animals' yards—or their keepers, for that matter. But maybe she should add Maria to the list of possible fountain pen users.

She got out her calendar and considered what Barbara's information about the foot care meant. The foot in question was trimmed on a Friday; Jerry's body was found the next Monday; and Barbara pried out the pen top exactly a week later. That meant that Indy could have picked up the pen top for just a short time *before* Jerry was murdered. No matter who left it there, they did not do it more than two days before Jerry was thrown off the roof.

No, unfortunately, that was not true, she realized. She was confusing when Indy actually picked up the pen top with when she had opportunity to pick it up. The pedicure schedule really only told her the ten-day period during which Indy must have picked it up. But for all Charlotte knew, the pen top could have *been there* forever before it found its way into Indy's footpad.

So the pen top might be evidence but it didn't have to be. Sort of like Lou's maybe-she-is, maybe-she-isn't diagnosis of Cheetah Rita.

Oh well. Maybe it was time to call it a day at the zoo and go home and wash her slacks, which were filthy from her rooftop escapade.

She gathered up her tote bag, purse, and the folder on the zoo's history that Stevie had loaned her earlier, which she would return on the way out. With any luck, Stevie would be dealing better with Stitcher's death than she had yesterday and wouldn't throw Charlotte out of her office.

As it turned out, neither Stevie nor her secretary were in.

Charlotte walked on into Stevie's cubicle, laid the folder on her tidy desk, and turned to go. Then, thinking that it would be politic to leave a thank you note, she tore off a page from a note pad on the desk and pulled a pen from a mug stuffed with assorted pens and pencils that was sitting on a file cabinet.

As she did so, she couldn't resist casually pawing through them to look for the mate to the fountain pen top in her purse. No navy pen bottom.

But a mug was the place for more informal writing instruments, she realized. An expensive fountain pen would be kept in a desk drawer. She sat down at Stevie's desk, pulled open the drawer, and looked inside.

She almost laughed out loud. The desk drawer, in dramatic contrast to the desk top in public view, was a chaotic mess. Stevie's pristine desk had a slobbish underbelly composed of old candy bar and mint wrappers and a hoard of small office supplies such as rubber bands, paper clips, and at least three staplers.

There was also a small clear plastic pill box containing white, diamond-shaped tablets, a tablet shape she had never seen before. Trust Stevie to have designer drugs. Designer *prescription* drugs, she reminded herself, since Stevie would be the last person she would suspect of using anything messy, anything illegal.

In the shallow bin at the front of the drawer lay three or four fountain pens and an uncapped pen bottom of marbleized navy blue. What a jolt! She could hardly believe that Stevie appeared to be the owner of the pen top picked up in the elephant yard—Stevie who seemed to actively avoid the animals.

She heard a noise outside the cubicle and decided the secretary had returned. In her excitement, she fumbled getting the pen top out of her purse. Then she took out the pen bottom from the desk drawer. The bottom leaked onto her fingers, which was surprising. She didn't think that was supposed to happen with the new ink cartridges out now. Maybe this was an antique fountain pen. Maybe Stevie was a collector.

She snapped pen bottom and top together. They were a set.

"Find what you were looking for, Charlotte?" came Stevie's voice; she was standing just inside the doorway.

Startled, Charlotte gasped and then felt herself blush as she leaned back in Stevie's chair.

"Oh. Hi, Stevie," she managed. "I was just going to write you a note, thanking you for the history materials."

Conscious of being in Stevie's chair, behind Stevie's desk, with Stevie's drawer open in front of her, Charlotte put the pen on the desk, closed the drawer, and stood up. "Now I can thank you in person," she said.

As she and Stevie exchanged places, Charlotte pointed to the pen lying on the desk and said she had returned its top.

"Oh, well, thanks. I don't even remember losing it, to tell you the truth. Wherever did you find it?" Stevie asked casually.

And Charlotte, realizing she was frightened of the efficient young woman in front of her, tried to sound just as casual as she lied, "Just outside the administration building door. Off to the left, in the grass."

Stevie looked at her closely and then said, "Well, thanks for getting it back to me."

"How long have you been without that pen top, Stevie?"

"Like I said, I don't even remember losing it."

The two of them eyed one another a moment as the pen lay between them on the desk.

Then Stevie picked it up and slipped it into the right pocket of her suit skirt, a motion Charlotte had seen her make a hundred times that summer.

Stevie briskly asked Charlotte whether the history materials had been helpful. They discussed them for a moment before Charlotte walked out of the office. She was glad to get out of there and all the way home could not shake her ugly feelings about Stevie.

While Charlotte was bringing about the reunion of pen top and bottom in Stevie's office, Lou was having a late lunch down the road at the Riverview. She had enjoyed the meal she'd had there recently with Charlotte, and today seemed like a good day for a reprise.

She was amused that her waitress's name tag read "Naomi," since it meant that she must be the one whose absence the manager complained about the last time. Lou smiled as she recalled Charlotte's silly little performance about that name and Lou's sister.

Unfortunately, today was not a good day for Naomi, either. Although present in body, she was apparently not there in mind, and Lou kept having to ask for things that should have been on the table, like ketchup, a glass of water, and even a plate. Where *was* this young woman's mind? Lou wondered.

She tried to be understanding when Naomi spilled salad in her lap, but it was difficult. Just wait 'til the cashier asks, "Was everything all right with your meal, ma'am?" as Lou paid her bill!

But then tears spilled down Naomi's cheeks as she cleaned up the salad, and Lou felt compelled to say, "There's no real harm done, dear."

"I'm sorry," Naomi said miserably. "I just seem to be doing everything wrong today. I've done everything wrong for a long time, I think."

"It's just salad."

"I was thinking more about sins of the flesh."

A surprising association, Lou thought.

"My religion teaches that we have to be punished for our sins."

Seeing how troubled Naomi was, the counselor in Lou moved her to say soothingly, "Now, now. I'm not one to talk much about religion, but it seems to me that it's almost never too late for us to take responsibility for our mistakes and make them right."

"If only I could," Naomi said, wiping up the last of the mess. Then she went off to the kitchen. Or somewhere. Lou sat patiently for her waitress to return and offer her a second cup of tea, dessert, or at least thanks for the pep talk. But there was no sign of Naomi, and eventually Lou had to have the cashier make out a bill for her lunch.

After dinner Charlotte drove to the Whetstone branch of the Columbus Metropolitan Library near her house and looked up the pills she had seen in Stevie's desk in a copy of the *Physician's Desk Reference.* She found a picture and description of the distinctive pills without too much trouble.

They were one of several drugs called hypoglycemics prescribed for diabetic patients who were labile even though they used insulin. She sought help from a medical dictionary and found that diabetics who were labile were those who had blood sugar that fluctuated widely. So, the diamond-shaped pill helped some diabetics to regulate the wide swings in their blood sugar that they still had, despite taking insulin.

The fluctuations in blood sugar could explain not only why Stevie took the pills but also why her desk drawer contained so many candy wrappers and why she had demanded fruit in the commissary, Charlotte thought. Her condition might be quite serious. Diabetes could lead to blindness, among other things, Charlotte knew.

Then she read the symptoms that would prompt a physician to prescribe a hypoglycemic drug: light-headedness, dizziness, sweating, slurred speech, and eventually, extreme lethargy. Some of this sounded a lot like how Maria Pickard had described Stitcher at the picnic. Could he have been a diabetic, too? Or were these just symptoms common to a lot of illnesses? Charlotte wondered.

She went into the library lobby and used a pay phone to call her family doctor at home. After coming to the phone, the first thing he said was, "Well, Charlotte, I'm afraid you took me from my golf game," despite the fact that it was 8:45 in the evening and he was at home.

For twenty years he had used that line every time Charlotte called him at home, including once at 2:30 in the morning when Ty was little and she thought he was too sick to see the light of day. Charlotte liked Dr. Riner, but less because of his humor, he'd be sorry to learn, and more because of his forgiveness when she called him at all hours.

Tonight she apologized for bothering him at home and said she needed some help in understanding drugs called hypoglycemics. He seemed to think she needed the information for an article and she let him think that. It was at least partly true.

"Ask me anything," he said.

From what Dr. Riner told her, it was clear that a nondiabetic person would have had Stitcher's symptoms if he had taken—or been given—several of the pills she had found in Stevie's desk drawer. The pills would have lowered his blood sugar level to a dangerous level, and the symptoms would have gotten worse until the person's thinking became confused and he eventually became semi-comatose. But the tablets would not have killed him. Hearing that was a big disappointment to Charlotte.

But wait! Maybe that explained why Stitcher was found in his car with the motor running in the garage. Maybe the pills were used only to make him pliable enough to kill in a manner that wasn't easily detected as murder. She asked Dr. Riner whether hypoglycemic drugs would show up in an autopsy. Not in a usual drug screen, he said. But they would show up if the autopsy staff knew to look for them.

"Well, then, would an exceptionally low blood sugar level show up in an autopsy?" Charlotte asked him.

"Of course," he said, "unless the person had ingested some sugar as little as fifteen seconds before he or she died, in which case the blood sugar level would have righted itself."

"Within fifteen seconds?"

"That's right. Even if you have slipped into a coma because of low blood sugar, dissolving a mint in your mouth can be enough to bring you out of it if you are a nondiabetic person," Dr. Riner said. "The body is a wonderful machine, Charlotte."

Driving home, she tried to envision Stevie grinding up her pills and slipping them into Stitcher's food or drink at the picnic in order to make him so lethargic that she could kill him. If Jerry's murder seemed almost off-handed, then this scenario made Stitcher's murder seemed premeditated in the extreme. But what possible motive could Stevie have had in killing Stitcher? Stevie was ambitious, but enough to kill?

She came up with even fewer reasons why Stevie could have killed Jerry. Charlotte thought back to when she saw Stevie first after finding out Jerry had died. It was the morning his body was found. She remembered watching Stevie do that interview on tape with Ned Ellison. She recalled that Stevie seemed less poised than usual, but surely that could be expected under the circumstances. She also could be misremembering Stevie's manner. She wished that there was some way to check.

She was almost home when she figured out how she *could* check. She immediately drove across the bridge at West North Broadway, turned south on Olentangy River Road, and pulled into the parking lot at WCMH-TV. She entered the building and approached the security desk. After several telephone calls to a producer elsewhere in the building and Ned Ellison at home, she was permitted to watch unedited videotape of Stevie's entire interview the day Jerry's body was found. (She had persuaded Ellison by reminding him of how unceremoniously he had announced Stitcher's death to her.)

Alone in an editing room, with the tape running on the console in front of her, Charlotte carefully watched Stevie's interview. Yes, she did seem less confident than usual, but she still did a good job and looked great. There seemed to be something on the side of her skirt, though. Charlotte stopped and rewound the tape, enlarged the image, and slowed it down.

Now she could clearly see a mark on the right front of Stevie's skirt but still couldn't tell what it was. She gave up.

As she reached to set the controls to normal, she noticed the ink stains left by Stevie's pen bottom were still on her own fingers and thumb. If that pen bottom could stain fingers, it could also stain a skirt.

Into her mind flashed the memory of Stevie always carrying her pens in her right front pocket. Just today she had watched Stevie put her pen there. On the day Jerry's body had been found, maybe Stevie had put the pen bottom in her pocket without realizing that the top was missing and then the bottom had leaked onto her skirt. If that was the case, she had to have only recently lost the pen top or else she would not have been carrying that pen. Maybe she lost it the night before—when she pushed Jerry off the roof.

But why? Charlotte couldn't recall hearing either one even mention the other before Jerry died. In fact, in two months of working at the zoo, Charlotte had never known Stevie to ever be around the animals, except for the day she was at the petting zoo with the blind folks.

She mentally reviewed her whole experience with the pen top, from the day Barbara pried it out of Indy's foot pad to today—when Charlotte lied to Stevie about where she found it.

So much seemed to hinge on the pen top and where it was lost and when Stevie knew it was lost. But now that she thought about it, she realized she didn't actually *see* Barbara pry out the pen top. Barbara's body had shielded Indy's foot pad from her sight.

Barbara was smart enough to know that Charlotte would figure out that the only employees at the zoo who would use such a pen were administrator-types. What if Barbara had planted the pen top to frame Stevie for Jerry's murder?

Having speculated long past the point of enjoyment, Charlotte took one last long, slow look at Stevie's Rorschach test on her skirt and then left for home. It was after ten o'clock, she castigated herself. Surely she ought to be able to find some way to do her work between eight and five, like a normal person. But, then, most people weren't working to save their own lives.

Chapter **30**

Walt pounded on the bathroom door the next morning, shouting, "Come see the TV!"

Fifteen seconds later, Charlotte was out of the shower, in her terrycloth robe, and in front of the television in the bedroom.

There was a commercial on the screen.

"Well?" she asked Walt, who was by this time calmly tying his tie in front of the dresser mirror.

"Sorry. I thought you could make it in time," he said. "There's been an arrest in the Brobst murder case."

Relief flooded over Charlotte and she felt so weak that she sat down on the edge of the bed before asking, "Who?"

"I don't know. The anchor guy, whatshisname, said the police haven't announced it yet. Just said there will be a nine-thirty press conference at the Hall of Justice."

He took a second look at her and asked, "Are you okay?"

She smiled and said, "Much better already," and walked

into the bathroom before he had time to ask any more questions.

So Barnes had finally made his arrest. She looked forward to being able to do her job again without always having to look over her shoulder. But now that she felt safe, she had to admit to a twinge of disappointment that Barnes was having a press conference about it, which would give every newsperson in town equal access to her information. So much for individual initiative. Now every other newsperson would be looking up hypoglycemics. She looked forward, though, to learning Stevie's motive for killing Jerry.

Before she left the house, she called Lou and arranged to meet her for lunch after the press conference and a stop at the zoo. She promised she'd have a lot to tell her. Then she drove downtown and parked near the Hall of Justice, which she thought sounded like it belonged in the old USSR or Batman's Gotham City. After asking someone behind the information desk what room was scheduled for the press conference, she passed through a metal detector and rode the elevator to the sixth floor.

The scheduled room and the hallway outside were already crowded with reporters by the time she got there. She had just spotted Chris James from the *Dispatch* when a group of somber men filed in. There was Detective Barnes, an officer in uniform, a man in a suit with a briefcase (a lawyer, she guessed), and a slight figure in a ponytail and bright orange jail coveralls, handcuffed to another uniformed officer.

It was John Hogan! But what about the case she had so carefully constructed against Stevie?

Detective Barnes began speaking into the cluster of microphones, and the television cameras started taping. "I would like to announce that an arrest has been made in the murder of Jerry Brobst at the Columbus Zoo," Barnes said. "John Hogan," he nodded toward the figure in orange coveralls, "has confessed to the murder of Mr. Brobst."

At the word "confessed," several people gasped, including Charlotte.

Barnes said Hogan would be arraigned later that day and held for sentencing until a date in court could be scheduled.

"Mr. Hogan has asked to make a statement but will not take any questions. Afterward, I will be glad to answer your questions."

Hogan stepped in front of the microphones, cleared his throat, and began. "Naomi, I did it for you. I did it for us. I knew that you would—"

The door to the room was flung open and a petite young woman with a dark brown ponytail and bangs charged in, yelling "Stop, stop!" at the top of her voice. She was wearing what appeared to be a blue waitress uniform and white tennis shoes.

The cameras swung away from Hogan to the woman and followed her as she continued to move toward the microphones. "He didn't do it. He thought I was going to be arrested for killing Jerry, so he confessed. But he didn't do it."

By the time she was at the front of the room, she was saying, "It was me, officers. It was me who killed Jerry Brobst." She held out her hands, wrists together, for handcuffs. "Arrest me," she pleaded.

Clearly this was more drama than anybody had bargained for. Some very young reporters were probably going to get good air time on three newscasts today.

It certainly was not what the police had expected. Barnes spoke quickly into the microphones. "This press conference is terminated."

Shouts of protest rose from the reporters, including Charlotte. "At least tell us who she is!" called James.

"Is that Naomi?" someone cried.

Ah, the famous Naomi, Charlotte thought. So this was the young woman who had married Hogan and had an affair with Jerry. Well, she had certainly knocked things into a cocked hat this morning.

"They both couldn't have done it," shouted a reporter from a television station. "Which one are you going to let go?"

Barnes ignored him and he and the others hustled Hogan

and Naomi, the latter still without handcuffs but nonetheless firmly under official control, out of the room.

Charlotte left, reclaimed her car, and headed straight for the zoo. She dropped her purse and laptop off at her zoo office and then looked for Maria in her office but was told she was either at the gorilla compound or the petting zoo. She found her at the petting zoo, handing out a paper bag full of treats for the young animals. The lambs, goats, and calves gulped up the special pellets and looked around for more.

"That's all for today, my beauties," Maria said, as she leaned over to pat the heads that were gathered around her. "One of the perks of my job," she said to Charlotte. "It's like being the cookie baker for little kids."

She picked up a thermos. "I've got to take some garlic broth over to a sick gorilla." They started walking toward the gorilla compound.

Charlotte said, "Did you hear that John Hogan confessed to Jerry's murder?"

Maria looked surprised. "When? How did you hear?"

"He made a statement to the press downtown this morning, said he did it for Naomi—"

"Did it to punish Naomi, is more like it."

"Wait; there's more. He was saying he did it for Naomi and then a woman burst into the room and yelled out, 'He didn't do it; I did!' "

"Who was she?"

"I'd guess Naomi." Charlotte described the young woman and Maria said, "That's her. I don't know her very well, but every now and then I see her at the Riverview Restaurant. She's a waitress."

Suddenly several pieces of information in Charlotte's mind clicked together. Naomi Hogan must have been the waitress who had been missing the day after Jerry's body was found when she and Lou had gone to the Riverview for lunch. If Charlotte was remembering right, the manager complained that Naomi had been off a couple of days. Of course, the death of your lover might mean you'd miss a few

days' work, she thought. Especially if you killed him. Maybe
the police had their killer in Naomi, not John, Hogan. Wait
'til she told Lou.

Charlotte and Maria walked into the building that
housed the gorillas and Maria gave the thermos to a keeper.
They watched while she poured the liquid contents into a
plastic glass and handed it through the bars to one of the gorillas, who drank it right down.

Charlotte was charmed and wished she had a camera.
"They seem so human, don't they?" she said. "I've read that
poachers are still killing them in the wild, but I don't know
who could kill such a wonderful creature—one that seems so
close to being like us."

"Well, we don't seem to have any trouble killing one another, do we?" Maria said.

"I guess you're right."

As they stood there, Maria pointed out that all the gorilla
keepers were female. "That's on purpose, you know, because
the male gorillas seem to regard human males as competi-
tors. And now it looks like competition is what got Jerry
killed and is going to make a prison widow out of Naomi."

"Unless it was she who killed Jerry."

"Could have been. Maybe it was Jerry who broke up with
her, and she realized she was going to have to go back to John
Hogan."

"Talk about a life sentence!" Charlotte said. "But I've
wondered why you didn't tell me right off that Jerry and
Naomi were having an affair. When we first talked about who
could have wanted to kill him."

Maria looked surprised. "Because lots of women had affairs with Jerry," she said. "I didn't really think of that as a
reason to kill him."

She paused and then laughed, saying, "This is a zoo,
Charlotte. Things get born, live, and die here all the time.
That's the kind of business we're in. There's a pretty earthy
atmosphere around here. In case you haven't noticed, there's
a lot of sex going on in these enclosures."

Charlotte smiled, too. "I didn't realize that Jerry was so busy. I mean, Barbara Champion told me he was a womanizer, but I just dismissed it. Some feminists seem to think that sex is sex*ist*, and I just thought she was one of those."

"Yes, our Jerry was a busy man. He and I even had a fling for a while, but we parted friends."

Charlotte was surprised but tried not to show it.

"Who else?" she asked.

"What difference does it make?"

"I'm just curious. I liked Jerry, too, but he never really came on to me. Not that I would have done anything about it, of course. Maybe I'm just insulted that he wasn't interested."

"Oh, for heaven's sake," Maria said. "Let me think . . . there was Sal Terrence over in birds and Carol Case in the gift shop and Stevie and . . ."

Charlotte's jaw dropped. "Stevie and Jerry had an affair?" she asked, incredulous. "Jerry—who was so emotional and alive—had an affair with the cold, preppy Stevie?" She had trouble believing it was possible.

"Well, opposites attract, you know. I don't really know how far it went, but I did see them having dinner together a couple times. *Not* at the Riverview. They looked really involved."

"When?"

"Not long before he was killed, I guess. It was after John said he and Naomi were getting back together, because I remember thinking that Jerry had moved on to the next woman pretty fast."

"Well, I'll be damned," Charlotte said. It wasn't a sure thing, but it was a connection to the deaths of both Jerry and Stitcher. Two at the zoo.

She said good-bye to Maria and set off for her zoo office to get her belongings and then to go see Barnes.

"Where are you going?" Maria asked.

"To make sure the right person goes to jail," she called back.

Chapter

While Charlotte was gathering her belongings, Lou was sitting in Charlotte's Clintonville office. She had been waiting for some time. She and Charlotte had agreed to meet there before going to lunch. But when Lou had arrived, she had been greeted by a closed door and a large envelope taped to it with her name printed on it in large block letters.

When she had peeled off the generously applied tape and opened the envelope, she found the key to Charlotte's office and a note from her assistant, Claudia Pepperdine.

Dear Lou:

It's 9:50 and I have to leave to be at home while a plumber fixes a drain. Don't you think emergencies like this should be the responsibility of my landlord?

Just let yourself in if you get here before Charlotte. Please tell her that Deborah Mancini called from the Tulsa Zoo to say, "He acted alone." I swear, that was the whole message: "He acted alone." Is Charlotte working on something about the Kennedy assassination? Talk to you later.

Claudia

Lou laughed at Claudia's last question, knowing Deborah must have called about whether the Tulsa handyman had planted the snake at his own or Stitcher's instigation. She unlocked the door, put the key on Charlotte's desk so that she wouldn't forget to return it, and then settled into the comfortable armchair for guests with a magazine she found nearby.

She was deep into an article when the phone rang. Startled, she looked at her watch. She'd been there forty-five minutes. It was not like Charlotte to miss a lunch date. She was not the most punctual person in the world, but Lou had never known her to just not show up. She hadn't even called to say she'd be late.

Before Lou could pick up the phone, the answering machine switched on and all she did was listen. After the answering message, she heard, "Charlotte, this is Sigrid Olson. Please give me a call as soon as possible. I just found out that Jane Wilcox's father died from a fall. She probably didn't have anything to do with the fall, but it seems strange that Jerry Brobst also died from a fall, doesn't it? Uh—I don't think you ought to do any more checking on Miss Wilcox. I don't want you to be in a position where you might get hurt."

There was a click as Sigrid hung up.

Lou had listened to the press conference on the radio, but apparently Sigrid hadn't. She didn't know that the Hogans had both confessed to Brobst's murder. Or maybe she did know but was still worried about Charlotte.

Lou's imagination immediately shifted into high gear. Charlotte had planned to stop at the zoo. Charlotte was late. Cheetah Rita was almost always at the zoo. What if something had happened to Charlotte?

Damn. There was no phone in the shed that was Charlotte's zoo office. Who could Lou call who might know if anything had happened to her?

Maybe she should call Stevie Kimmel. She was probably at lunch, but, even so, that might be the best place to start. If any "accidents" had happened at the zoo, surely whoever answered the phone in the director's assistant's office would know about them.

Lou quickly looked up the number for the zoo in the telephone book. The secretary who answered the phone said that Ms. Kimmel was not in and had been away from her desk for almost two hours. She was expected back at any time, so would Lou like to leave a message?

"Have there been any accidents at the zoo today?" Lou asked.

"Accidents? Why, of course not. We run a safe park here." The secretary sounded miffed.

"Then have you seen the writer who's doing the magazine series on the zoo, Charlotte Sams? Or have you seen Cheetah Rita today?"

"No to both your questions. I didn't notice Cheetah Rita when I came into the office. Nobody knows where she is when she's not watching the cheetahs."

"Thank you," Lou said and hung up.

Now what? Cheetah Rita could be any place at the zoo. What if Lou had missed something in her chat with Cheetah Rita that should have tipped her off to a predisposition for violence? Those things were hard to discern. What if Sigrid wasn't the only one to have put Charlotte in a dangerous position with that strange woman?

Well. Enough speculation. She picked up the office key from the desk, put it back in the envelope, scrawled Claudia's name on the back, and pulled two strips of tape off the dispenser on the desk.

Once the door was locked and the envelope in place, Lou headed for her car and the zoo. Something was obviously wrong.

Chapter 32

As Lou arrived at the zoo, Charlotte sat terrorized in her little office that had seemed so safe the day before. She was backed into a corner, sitting on the rough and dirty wooden floor, her knees bent and her neck and shoulders slumped forward so that her arms were between her legs. Perspiration coursed down both sides of her face and she was having trouble breathing. She didn't know how much time she had left.

The initial blow had surprised her, having caught her off guard as she leaned over her desk to pick up her laptop. It had come from above and behind and landed along her right shoulder blade. It felt sharp, like a knife or claw. She guessed that her wrenching to the side and forward had increased the bleeding, because the back of her blouse was wet and it did not feel like sweat.

She had tried to fight back, but, of course, that had been impossible. Now she didn't know what to do.

· · ·

Lou parked illegally in the zoo lot in order to save time and was nearly running by the time she got past the ticket window. It was a long way to Charlotte's office, so she forced herself to slow down so she wouldn't have a heart attack on the way.

Sooner or later, Charlotte would have to make a break for it. Maybe it was worth a try to make her tormentor talk instead of just sitting there pointing that gun at her.

"Why are you doing this to me?" she asked.

"Shut up. It's your own fault."

"What did I ever do to you?"

"Questions. It's always the questions with you."

"Did you kill Jerry?"

"That was an accident."

"But he's still dead."

"It's just that he made me so furious. We often had sex on the roof of the pachyderm house. Took up a tarp or something to put down. Jerry loved it up there. That bird's-eye view made him feel like 'King of Zoos' or something. I think the marks we made in the dirt on the roof are what the police called 'signs of a struggle.' "

"What happened?"

"That waitress! He told me he was going back to Naomi."

It was quiet in the shed for a while. "I got so mad I pushed him. I really didn't mean to kill him, but he went over the edge."

"What about Stitcher?"

A laugh.

"What about him?"

"He was going to tell the police that he saw my car in the lot when he left the zoo that night. The night Jerry went over the edge. That was your fault. Because I couldn't threaten him any longer with going public about Tulsa."

So her story *had* been responsible for Stitcher's death, Charlotte realized. How sad that seemed, but also very far away.

"Why couldn't you just leave well enough alone? Why did you have to keep blundering into things that were better left alone?"

Charlotte stayed quiet.

"You've got more nerve than brains. I tried the car top and the tape, but you wouldn't pay attention."

"You were the one who cut my top? In broad daylight?"

"You were always running late and had to park at the back of the lot. Nobody could see me back there."

"The freezer, too? That was you?"

"Sure. I gave you every reason to stop poking around."

Charlotte had to do something. She put her hand up on the desktop and tried to pull herself up. But the gun smashed down hard on her fingers and she cried out.

"Sit down!"

Charlotte immediately obeyed and rubbed her throbbing fingers. When she could speak again, she asked, "Was it you who was blackmailing Stitcher?"

"No. Jerry was. But I knew about it. And since I needed a way to keep him from talking about me being at the zoo the night Jerry died, I used it."

Charlotte didn't know how long she could keep this up. She could tell her thinking was getting slower.

After a long time, she was able to form another question. "How did you get back for your car? After taking Stitcher home."

"Stitcher's canoe, of course. I always could handle a boat."

Things were getting increasingly confusing. Charlotte was having trouble remembering things exactly right. For instance, she couldn't remember who the police had arrested. Finally she recalled it was that groundskeeper. The one whose wife confessed.

Finally she managed to say, "Notebook page."

"Oh. Jerry stole the notebook late that afternoon, so he had it with him. He mixed up the pages. For laughs. And to get revenge for all the complaints she made about him. Get it? Her research results would all be out of order."

Charlotte remembered someone telling her that Jerry

acted like a bad school kid around Cheetah Rita.

"That crazy old creature. I thought I had taken all the pages with me when I left, but I must have missed one. Anyway, it came in handy when the police considered it to be evidence against her."

When she arrived at the base of the wooden steps that led to Charlotte's office, Lou was relieved to hear voices coming from there. Charlotte must have been able to arrange an interview at the last minute and didn't get a chance to call before she started.

But why was the door closed? There was no way she would interview someone in a closed shed in this heat.

Lou crept up the stairs, taking care to be quiet about it. At the top she saw an ankus leaning against the wall by the door. Thanks to Cheetah Rita's demonstration, she knew all about ankuses.

Now she picked this one up. An elephant keeper must be inside with Charlotte, she thought. Maybe the same one who had told her to reach inside the elephant enclosure just in time to be charged by an enraged bull elephant.

She could distinguish Charlotte's voice among those coming from inside and was alarmed to hear her slurring her words. Lou's first impulse was to flee and try to bring help, but Charlotte sounded so sick or hurt that she didn't want to leave her. She would have to go in and help her.

"The insulin. How long?" Charlotte noticed that Stevie wasn't even bothering to hold the gun on her now. It was on the desktop. There was no chance that Charlotte would be able to reach it. She couldn't even see it clearly unless she squinted.

"Before it kills you, you mean? It's hard to tell exactly. People react differently to insulin. I ought to know. I've been shooting up with it myself since I was seven."

"When did you know I knew?"

"That I killed Jerry? When you lied to me about where you found that pen top. I lost it on top of the roof and we both knew it. Jerry must have dragged it over the side with him."

Charlotte and, more importantly, Stevie, were completely unprepared when Lou burst open the door and hit Stevie on the head with the ankus. Even so, Stevie was able to reach for the gun, but Lou walloped her forearm and hit her on the head again. That did it. Lou ran to help Charlotte, who was lying quite still on the floor. She leaned over her friend and called her name.

Charlotte's eyelids fluttered and she said weakly, "Do you have a mint?"

"Honestly, Charlotte," Lou said, "I don't think this is a good time to be snacking."

Epilogue

Charlotte was rushed to Riverside Hospital by ambulance, muttering "Fifteen seconds, fifteen seconds," for reasons that no one else understood. However, the IV hooked up by the ambulance staff did the trick, and long before she reached the hospital, her head had cleared. She felt practically normal by the time Walt and Ty arrived to take her home. The body is indeed a wonderful machine.

At home she sat on the couch and tried to explain what had happened to her to anyone who would listen, which was mostly Walt, Ty, and Lou.

Lou's first question was about the elephant ankus. "Why was it outside the shed?" she asked.

"Stevie had brought it with her to plant inside my office—to try to implicate me in Jerry's murder. It was Jerry's and had his initials carved in the handle, and she'd had it since the night she killed him. But once she got to my office, she worried that she wouldn't be able to stab me with the syringe if she was carrying both the gun and the ankus. And she needed the gun, of course."

"Then whose ankus did Cheetah Rita have?" Lou asked.

"I have no idea. But who knows what stray zoo equipment she has? She probably has quite a collection."

"Well, I'm thankful Stevie left Jerry's ankus outside the shed. Otherwise, I wouldn't have had anything to hit her with. I'm also thankful for Cheetah Rita's earlier demonstration of how to wield one, although I think my technique might have been less than perfect."

"It did the trick, though."

Walt asked, "I don't know why Stevie made her move against you today. After all, the police had not one but two confessed killers of Jerry Brobst."

"I think that was the problem," Charlotte said. "She told me she listened to the press conference this morning and knew that Naomi had also confessed. She referred to the Hogans as those stupid people playing 'Gift of the Magi' at one point, I guess because their double confession reminded her of that O. Henry story."

"I remember that one," Tyler said.

"Anyway, I think she didn't think either of them would stand trial because they weren't very believable. And there was no way to tie either of them to Stitcher's death."

"How come you know all this stuff now?" Tyler asked.

"Because Stevie told me while we were waiting for the insulin to finish me off. I tried to keep her talking because it helped me focus my mind. To keep from drifting off. But it wasn't hard to keep her talking. Once she got started, it seemed as though she had to tell it all. To show me how clever she'd been, I guess."

"But it sounds like she didn't really murder Jerry," Walt said.

"It doesn't sound premeditated, does it?"

"She probably could have gotten off fairly lightly on a manslaughter or accidental death charge," Walt said. "Why didn't she just turn herself in?"

"Little Miss Perfect? Never. She was so sure that no one had seen it happen and so angry with Jerry that it only seemed right that he was gone."

"And she had to sacrifice only one person to cover up her part in it," Lou said. "Cheetah Rita."

"And eventually Stitcher," Charlotte said.

"She must be pretty cold-blooded if she deliberately let the police suspect Cheetah Rita," Tyler said.

"Well, Stevie thought Cheetah Rita was crazy, and she knew she dressed funny and was overly interested in cheetahs and didn't like people—the list goes on and on, doesn't it? Cheetah Rita didn't fit Stevie's definition of how people should act and dress and *be*. Today Stevie called her a 'throwaway person.' Stevie was perfectly willing to throw her to the police."

"I wonder if there's any hope for Stevie," Lou said.

"Surely she'll serve time for having killed Stitcher," Walt said. "But I don't know why she did it."

"He knew that Stevie had been at the zoo the night Jerry was killed," Charlotte explained, "because he saw her car in the parking lot when he left the zoo. Stevie told me he never had any trouble remembering that. So I guess his memory loss was all staged."

"Why didn't he just tell the police that Stevie's car was there?" Lou asked.

"Before he could, Stevie threatened to reveal the Tulsa allegations if he did. And since he really didn't have any proof that Stevie killed Jerry, he was willing to stay quiet."

"So when she knew your Tulsa story would hit the papers, Stevie knew she was going to lose her hold over Stitcher," Lou said.

"Exactly. I don't think she knew exactly when and how she would kill him, but she knew she had to. Then when Stitcher complained of the heat at the picnic, Stevie offered him some of her hypoglycemics as a good headache remedy, warning him not to eat anything or drink anything after taking them. When the pills made him feel worse, she offered to drive him home in his car. Even though the Stitchers lived just across the reservoir from the zoo, the trip took some time because she had to drive south to the nearest bridge and then back north to the Stitcher house on the other side."

"But didn't she have to get back to the zoo somehow to pick up *her* car?" Walt asked.

"Yes. But by that time, Stitcher had passed out in the car. She opened his garage door with the automatic opener in his car, drove in, and then pulled him over into the driver's seat. She left the car running when she closed the garage door."

Always looking out for the electronics, Tyler asked, "What did she do with the automatic opener?"

"I don't know. Maybe she threw it into the water when she used Stitcher's canoe to cross the reservoir from his backyard. It took her less than an hour, and she had that story about searching for a file for Stitcher all ready in case anyone asked about her whereabouts during the picnic."

"But then she had to get rid of the canoe," Lou pointed out.

"Which wouldn't have been difficult, with all the underbrush that's on the bank by the zoo."

"She was lucky Mrs. Stitcher wasn't home," Walt said. "And something else that seemed lucky was that Barnes was at the zoo today and could arrest Stevie right away."

"That wasn't exactly luck," Lou said. "It seems that Sigrid stayed nervous after having talked to Charlotte's answering machine. She didn't know, of course, that I had heard the message. So she called Barnes at police headquarters and asked him to go to the zoo and warn Charlotte."

"That was nice of him."

"Well, to tell you the truth, I think Sigrid had to twist his arm a lot before he agreed to make the trip."

"That sounds more like him," Charlotte said.

• • •

In the days that followed, the Hogans were released from custody, with strong admonitions not to clutter up the court system with false confessions. The police still weren't sure where John had gotten the idea that they were about to arrest his wife. Apparently the couple was going to try to keep their marriage together.

Barbara Champion continued in her work as head elephant keeper, praying that whomever the Zoo Association Board hired as the next zoo director would be trainable.

Maria Pickard was giving serious thought to moving away from animal nutrition to the field of computers and had begun carrying on several romances over the Internet.

Charlotte's zoo series was a big success and was even nominated for an award. Walt survived his busy summer workload and looked forward to taking his family on a short Labor Day weekend trip. He and Tyler began their annual revving up for the upcoming Ohio State football season.

Lou began making plans to participate in an Earthwatch dig in England, figuring Charlotte could stay out of trouble for at least a two-week stretch.

The police found the rest of Cheetah Rita's notebook in the trunk of Stevie's car. Familiar with her research as she was, Cheetah Rita was able to put the pages back in the correct order in no time at all.

Barnes told Charlotte that the older woman's obvious delight in getting back the data that she had spent two years collecting was heartwarming. This was the first news that Barnes had a heart, Charlotte told the detective. He actually smiled at her.

Grateful to have her notebook back, Cheetah Rita condescended to show Charlotte how she got into and out of the zoo—after Charlotte promised not to write about it, of course. So early one morning she followed Cheetah Rita from her small house along the Scioto as she trekked north along the east bank toward the southern tip of the zoo, briefcase in hand. She watched as the older woman clambered among the supports of the O'Shaughnessy Dam Bridge and

emerged inside the zoo near the polar bear exhibit. Cheetah
Rita retrieved her camp stool from behind some bushes and
went on her way, never looking back.

Cheetah Rita continued her study of the cheetahs. The
acting zoo director, temporarily moved up from his position
as coordinator of volunteers, decided that she should be considered one of the exhibits and provided the full protection
of the zoo.